THE
DUSK GATE CHRONICLES
BOOK SEVEN

BLADES
OF ACCESSION

BREEANA PUTTROFF

FIRST EDITION
ISBN 13: 9781940481203

~~~~~~~~~~~~

Cover Design: Mallory Rock
Editing: Jennifer Severino, Twitching Pen Editing
Beta Reading: Brett Jonas
Formatting & Layout: Mallory Rock

~~~~~~~~~~~

Thirteen Pages Press
P.O. BOX 350944
DENVER, CO 80035

Blades of Accession: The Dusk Gate Chronicles Book 7 is a work of fiction. Names, characters, places and incidents are products of the author's imagination, or the author has used them fictitiously.

A SURPRISE

ALL DAY, ZANDER HAD been waiting for the moment the bubble would burst. Ever since the kiss earlier — *that kiss* — he and Linnea had been together, pretending nothing had changed between them though he was pretty sure everything had.

The massive party celebrating the end of the war was the most incredible spectacle Zander had ever seen — even grander than the one so many moons ago for Prince Samuel's Naming Ceremony. Of course, it might have just been that he was enjoying this one more. He understood this world now and felt like a part of it. No amount of finery would have seemed like too much to honor Quinn's victory over Tolliver and Dovelnia.

He'd been chatting and laughing with Joshua Rose while Linnea went over to sit with her mother for a while to feed the babies, but now she was walking back toward him empty-handed. King Stephen and Queen Charlotte, along with most of Linnea's siblings, were soaking up every second they could with the tiny infant twins.

Something about the look on Linnea's face as she approached him made his stomach flip. He knew it wasn't his imagination because when Josh saw her, he clapped Zander's shoulder and said, "I'm going to go see what Daniel's up to."

He wanted to joke with her, to ask what he'd done this time and how much trouble he was in, but he knew it wasn't something simple and small. It was the first time all day she'd been away from him for long enough to actually have time to think. As he watched her with her parents, watched her brothers and sisters holding her babies caring for them, he knew she was probably wondering the same thing he was — what that kiss had meant.

He'd known that the bubble would burst. The edges of it had started to thin for him during the ceremony where he'd been given yet another medal for his service in the war. He'd been standing next to Marcus and glancing over at the babies in Linnea's arms, and all he could think about was how it shouldn't have been him.

Although he loved both Benjamin and Adeline already — missed them, even, when they were all the way across the room as they were now — they weren't his. When this party ended, he would go to his room, and Linnea would be alone with them all through the night.

She deserved so much more.

If he could, he would have given up everything to return Ben to her. But since he couldn't, he picked up two glasses of juice from the buffet table and walked over to meet her.

"Thirsty?" he asked.

She nodded. "Thank you." The tiny sip she took belied her answer, though. Of course, her family was doting on her, making sure her every need was met before she even knew she had it. At least she had them.

"You're welcome."

Her gray eyes didn't quite meet his, instead flicking between her glass and the dance floor. She was so beautiful — all eyelashes and long dark curls that he desperately wanted to put his fingers in, to brush the locks back from her shoulders, to watch her relax into his touch. But he was afraid he'd see her tense up instead, and so he kept his hands to himself.

"Are you…?" He didn't know how to finish the question, but it seemed to work anyway. She finally looked at him and nodded. He smiled. "Do you want to dance?"

The song was nearly over, but she nodded and handed him her glass.

As soon as he tried to set the glasses down on a nearby table so he could take her hands instead, the music stopped altogether, replaced by a tinkling sound that caused the entire ballroom to fall silent.

It wasn't hard to identify the source of the sound. Thomas stood in the middle of the dance floor, holding a crystal goblet and a silver fork.

Zander would have been mortified to have everyone's attention on him this way, but Thomas only grinned at everyone watching. No, grinning didn't quite describe his expression — he was beaming.

"Hello," he said, his voice ringing through the entire room.

"Is this what I think it is?" Zander whispered to Linnea.

"That depends on what you think it is."

He chuckled under his breath before realizing that she wasn't looking at him — and she wasn't smiling.

His heart dropped into his stomach with a dull *thud* and everything he'd been feeling about not being enough amplified. Linnea should not be standing here with him, watching her twin brother announce his engagement. It was too much. Too hard.

"I want to thank you all again," Thomas was saying, "on behalf of my brother, King William, and my incredible sister-in-law, Her Majesty Queen Quinn. It's an honor to be here to celebrate with all of you."

Thomas had the crowd. Even little Sarah, who was two, stopped jumping around the edges of the dance floor and her eyes locked on her big brother while she held on to the flowing gray skirt of Mia's dress.

"While you're all here, and especially while my *whole* family is here, I have another piece of good news I would like to share."

The pink in Mia's cheeks, and the way she held the fingers of one hand tightly in the other, her knuckles turning white, told Zander that he was right about what Thomas was doing.

Actually, the shiny new addition to the silver bracelet around Mia's wrist told him that Thomas had already *done* it — this was merely an announcement.

Everyone in the room cheered and clapped as Thomas invited Mia out into the middle of the dance floor with him. Zander couldn't hear anything except the people around him.

Mia's cheeks were still pink, but it was a different kind — her happiness was as contagious as her new fiancé's. Thomas put his hands around her waist and lifted her, twirling her around twice before planting an innocent kiss on her lips.

He was surprised that Mia didn't seem to mind the spectacle at all, and he turned to Linnea to say so — to tell her anything that might lighten this moment, make it more bearable. But she was gone.

When Thomas and Mia finally pulled apart, Linnea was the first one in the crowd that encircled them, pulling her twin into her arms and hugging him tightly.

From his position at the edge of the floor, Zander wondered if he was the only one who saw the drops of moisture in the corners of Linnea's eyes as Thomas let go of her. Only a second later, though, before he could even move, Quinn reached her and took hold of her hand. She led Linnea quickly but gently to the other side of the room and put baby Benjamin in Linnea's arms. Within seconds, she was surrounded by the rest of her family, distracting her, caring for her. She didn't need him. He probably only made things worse.

"Quite the happy day, isn't it?" The voice was right next to his ear, making him jump in surprise.

"It's a party, all right," Zander answered after taking a second to catch his breath. "How are you, Alvin?"

The old man grinned widely, his eyes — gray today — sparkling. "You know; nobody ever asks me that."

Zander chuckled. Somehow, he wasn't surprised by that. "Well, I'm asking now."

"There's not much of anything I don't like about today, Sir Zander. Even Lady Sophia appears to be behaving herself." He nodded toward a table in the corner of the room where Quinn's grandmother was actually almost smiling as she chatted with her daughter, Ellen.

"By behaving herself you mean she's not out there making comments about Quinn and King Stephen giving permission for Thomas to marry underage?"

Alvin laughed. "With some people you have to take what you can get. She's not over there plotting with anyone against the kingdom, either."

"Only because there's not anyone for her to plot *with*."

"Oh, there's always someone, I'm afraid. Today, however, is a joyous day. I think I even saw *you* enjoying yourself at dinner and on the dance floor."

"I was."

Over on the other side of the room, baby Adeline started to squirm in the seat someone had set her down in, and her little face scrunched and turned red. Maybe there was some way he could actually be useful tonight. "Excuse me, Alvin."

Before he was even halfway to Addie, though, Joshua got to her and scooped her into his arms, then carried her into the middle of the celebration.

"You are doing awfully well for being up so long past your bedtime," William said to the baby in his arms.

Samuel only smiled and gurgled in the same charming way he had been doing all evening, and William bent to kiss his head. "You are already better at this job than your father ever will be, little man."

"Oh, I don't think I would say that, Will," a voice said just behind him.

He turned around to see his own father standing there, wearing the crown and robe of the king of Eirentheos. His own ensemble closely matched his father's tonight, though William wore green and gold while Stephen wore purple and silver. "I didn't know anyone was near me."

Stephen smiled. "I'm sorry. I didn't mean to startle you. It's just that I would like to hold my adorable grandson," he said, reaching to take Samuel. "And I love him very much, but he's not yet the man and the capable king that you are, William."

"Thank you, Father. Although whatever we've accomplished here has been entirely Quinn's doing." He looked across the room to where his wife stood saying goodbye to some of the last guests. She was resplendent in her flowing green gown and cape, the emeralds in her crown catching the candlelight in a way that made them sparkle and shimmer just as her eyes did tonight.

His father chuckled. "I won't talk you out of that one. As it happens, I am even prouder of the husband and father you've become than I am of the way you help her defend and care for your people." He tossed the baby into the air, making him giggle wildly before catching him safely and blowing bubbles on his tummy. Then he turned back to William. "I know you weren't raised for this task the way Simon was, but that doesn't mean you don't have what you need to do it."

"All I need is them, I think," William said. "And the rest of you. Thank you, Father, for everything."

Stephen laid his hand on William's shoulder. "I wish I was the father I should have been for you. When I think of the things I kept from you, that you and Quinn had to overcome because of my choices... I'm still sorry for that."

"I know. But it's enough for me now, to understand that you made the best decisions you knew how at the time. I don't know that

I wouldn't have made the same ones." He looked over at Samuel. "I'm sure I'll make plenty of mistakes of my own, but at least I'll have your example of how to love him."

When Stephen held his arms open, William gladly went into them, hugging his father and son at the same time. Samuel tolerated it for a second but then squirmed and pushed, making both men chuckle.

"I think this one has had enough party and might be ready for some time with his mother," Stephen said, handing the baby back to him.

William nodded.

"However, once everyone's had a few minutes, *your* mother and I wanted to make you an offer. I overheard Quinn giving Mia the rest of the night and tomorrow off. We wanted you to know that there's plenty of space in the crib in our room if you and Quinn would like some time to yourselves."

There was a subtle undertone in his father's voice that made William wonder if there was something going on that he didn't know about, but it wasn't worth worrying about right then. Samuel was finally beginning to fuss, and his diaper felt heavier than it should.

"Thank you, Father. I imagine there's a good chance we'll take you up on that."

"Good." Stephen smiled. "It's not an offer we'll get to make very often."

He made his way across the room to Quinn, moving so he could sneak up behind her and whisper in her ear. "Hey beautiful."

She leaned her head back into his shoulder, letting her soft curls brush against his neck. "Hey," she said, looking relaxed, even though Samuel immediately climbed out of William's arms and into hers. "I think the party was a success." She smiled as she watched William's older sister carry her own sleeping son through the wide double doors that led from the ballroom to the great hall.

"I have to admit I was a little nervous beforehand," he said, chuckling. "Parties haven't always gone well for us."

She turned around, narrowing her eyes and jabbing her elbow into his ribs. "Don't jinx it. I need five minutes of peace."

He looked around the room. "Jonathan's already taken Sophia back to her new place. I think we're safe for tonight."

"I hope so. You know she didn't want to go, right? She sent Charles up to ask if she couldn't stay here for the evening because it's so late for traveling."

"What?" The blood just below the skin on his neck and chest began to heat uncomfortably. Neither he nor Quinn was certain they'd done the right thing allowing her grandmother to remain free after her betrayal and support of Tolliver.

"Yeah," she said under her breath, her eyes sweeping the room, reminding him what he already knew. They shouldn't discuss it here. The room was nearly empty now, except for a few servants cleaning up, and the guards who were tasked with watching their little family. Their voices would carry too easily in the large, echoing ballroom.

He cleared his throat. "Shall we head upstairs now, love? Before we have to ask someone to heat bathwater for us because our son's diaper didn't hold up?"

She nodded and he followed her and Samuel out of the room, keeping his hand on her waist because he just needed to be as close to them as he could.

As soon as they reached the landing by the hallway they'd all been using for temporary quarters, he knew something wasn't right. Their head housekeeper, Ruth, whom he *knew* had been dancing at the party earlier, was standing there in her work clothes with an odd expression on her face.

"Ruth, what's wrong?" Quinn got the words out before he did. The long moons of war and training had sharpened her observational skills — she'd already checked the positions of the guards following them, prepared to signal for help instantly if she needed to.

"Well, I wouldn't quite say anything is *wrong*, Your Majesties, but I'll need you to follow me."

That's it, Quinn decided, as she rushed to follow Ruth down the hallway. *No more parties for any reason, ever.* Even thinking about having one was apparently a good way to bring some new disaster upon them. William had already whisked Samuel from her arms so that she could have her hands free.

The baby let out a whine to show his displeasure but quieted quickly. Even at less than a cycle old, her son seemed to have figured out his role as the firstborn prince and heir to the throne.

Ruth navigated them through several hallways before Quinn realized where they were going — and that something else was strange.

"Has the damaged part of the castle been compromised somehow?" she asked.

That was where they were heading, she knew, though she'd only been to that wing of the castle once since their return, just to survey how bad things were. Much of the space — which had been their living quarters before the war — had been damaged by fire and battle.

She wondered if it was a bad sign that she was secretly hoping for a collapsed floor or something else physical that could at least eventually be fixed. And if this had anything to do with her grandmother…

"Come on Ruth," she said, as they approached the double doors that led to the damaged hallway, "just tell me how bad it is on a scale from one to ten at least."

The older woman stopped and turned around to face them. William's hand tightened around Quinn's waist, but the twinkle in Ruth's eyes spoke more of amusement than terror. "I told them surprising you might not work out quite as well as they hoped," she said

"Them *who*?" Quinn asked, although she already knew. Her body shuddered as the terrible tension of the past few moments escaped. If she hadn't been so preoccupied, so certain something was wrong, she'd have realized it earlier. The hallways back by the guest rooms where William's family were staying had been conspicuously empty. Everyone couldn't have been in bed already. "Where are they?"

"Humor them, please, Your Majesties," Ruth whispered.

William's hand felt relaxed and playful now, and he leaned in close to whisper in her ear, "This had better be good."

"Give me the baby," she whispered back. "It'll cut down on the risk of me murdering someone for scaring me like that."

But once Ruth opened the door to the hallway, Quinn couldn't have dredged up a negative thought if she'd tried.

The space on the other side looked *nothing* like it had a week ago. The shiny wood floor here was entirely new. In fact, everything was new. Even the tables positioned every few feet seemed to have just appeared there. Newly polished oil lamps cast warm circles of light on the vine-patterned carpet runner, all the way to the door at the end of the hall.

A familiar figure stood in the doorway.

"Thomas!" she shouted, practically running down the hallway toward him. "Shouldn't you be *inside* the room? Keeping this grand secret?"

"And miss the look on your face?" Thomas scoffed. "Never. I knew you'd figure it out before you made it this far, anyway."

Samuel was full of giggles as Thomas stepped back to allow them to enter the room — the sitting room of the master apartment.

After several minutes, she would be able to see the beautiful new construction — it had been entirely rebuilt from scratch, leaving no traces of the terrible things that had once happened here. But right now, all she could see were the faces of those who had made it happen.

William's family — *her* family — surrounded them. They were all here, Stephen and Charlotte, Max, Thomas and Linnea, William's younger brothers and sisters, including sweet Alice, who ran straight into William's arms. Even Zander was here, smiling in a way that she wouldn't have thought possible only a few moons ago.

"You're all amazing," she said, not caring at all that tears were dripping down her cheeks. "How did you manage to get all of this done in such a short time?"

"Well, don't open any of the *other* doors in the hallway," Thomas said. "That would ruin the whole illusion. And more than a few of the things in here are restored, not new. But we tried."

But there was nothing illusory about this. They'd even somehow managed to get the water running in the new bathroom. Quinn didn't mind the refurbished bathtub in the least when Charlotte scooped Samuel away from her to bathe him in it. William hadn't been kidding about the time limit on the diaper change.

Almost as quickly as everyone had seemed to appear, though, they disappeared back down the hallway. William's parents took Samuel with them, leaving only two of Quinn's most trusted guards posted near the apartment for the night. The only trace that anyone had been there at all was the fresh pot of piping-hot tea sitting on the on their little table.

William was — for once — more curious than she was. He wandered in and out of the various rooms before coming back to where she was leaning on the arm of a couch.

"It's bigger," he said. "They must have cut into one of the other rooms. The whole floor plan is different."

She smiled and nodded, taking his hand in hers. "I was fine in the trashed-out guest room, you know. Just happy they were *here*, and I could be close to them. They didn't have to work."

William lifted her hand to his lips and gently kissed her fingers. "I know. So do they, love."

She sighed, looking around for a moment, at the warm glow of the fire in the grate, at the rugs and curtains so precisely chosen by Charlotte to reflect a perfect blend of two worlds — the one Quinn had come from, and the one where she now belonged. "I love them."

He smiled and looked around, too. "As you can clearly see, the feeling is mutual."

"Yeah," she said, nodding and laying her head against his chest, right in the place where she could hear his heart beating, strong and steady… and hers.

"Are you tired?" he asked.

"When we first came upstairs, I was exhausted, but now…not so much. What about you?"

The way his mouth turned up in the corner and his gray eyes burned bright with emotion answered her before his words did. "I could stay awake a while longer and enjoy all of this…and you," he said, bringing his lips down to meet hers.

INTRUDER

AFTER THE BIG REVEAL of Quinn and William's new apartment, Zander watched Linnea walk away from him, heading down the hall with one infant in her arms. Her younger brother Joshua walked next to her, carrying the other. He wanted to follow her, to help change a baby, to kiss her goodnight, to…*something*, but he didn't know what or where to start. The two of them hadn't even talked since earlier downstairs at the party.

So he walked back toward his room alone. He knew someone was walking behind him, but the castle was so full of people right now, it didn't occur to him to pay attention. But just before he reached his room, a tap on his shoulder made him jump and whirl around, his hand moving automatically to the hilt of his sword.

"I'd say be careful with that thing, but honestly, I'm impressed with the instincts you've developed," Thomas said, nodding toward Zander's hand.

"Sorry." He dropped his hand and moved it instead toward the buckle that held his belt.

"I'm not bleeding. You're good." Thomas grinned.

Zander frowned. "Aren't you supposed to be celebrating with Mia now?"

"That's what I just spent the last several hours doing. Tomorrow, we'll sit down with her parents and mine to begin planning a wedding, but right now I think she's heading to bed. She *said* she was, anyway, and I hope she actually does after all the work she's done today."

"And what are *you* doing?" Zander asked, suddenly suspecting this was more than just a brief pre-bedtime stop in the hallway for Thomas.

"Right now? I'm acting the part of an older brother." Thomas opened the door to Zander's room and held his hand out, ushering both of them inside.

For a second, Zander wondered if they'd entered the right room — it looked unfamiliar. But then he realized someone must have come in and moved some of the piles of junk that had been stacked to one side. He sort of wondered who would do that during a party, but it wasn't his most pressing concern.

Whoever it was had cleared off a couch, which was nice.

Zander leaned against it as he watched Thomas close the door and turn to face him.

Thomas didn't waste even a minute getting to the point. "So, you and my little sister."

He rolled his eyes. "She's not exactly your *little* sister, Thomas."

"Oh, I wouldn't waste energy on technicalities with me." Thomas's chuckle was lighthearted, but underneath that, there was no question he was serious. "She's younger than me by just long enough for me to be able to say that she's been the most important person in the world to me since the moment she was born."

Zander swallowed. "And you don't like me with her."

"Are you *with* her?"

"I don't know. We kissed earlier, and we were having a nice time at the dance together, for the first part of the evening at least, but…"

now I think she's second-guessing all of it." It was probably a bad idea to spill his guts to Linnea's protective twin brother, but he couldn't stop himself. He needed to talk to someone, and everyone else in the castle was either just as protective of Linnea as Thomas was, or not someone Zander was at all close to.

"Did she *tell* you she second guesses it?"

"No. But she got all quiet and distant in the second half of the dance, and she wouldn't even really talk to me the whole rest of the evening."

"*She* wouldn't?"

"Well, she didn't."

"And so what did you do?" Thomas's voice wasn't angry at all. It was quiet and level, so Zander was reasonably sure that he wasn't going to get punched, at least not right now.

He shrugged. "So I just let her be."

"Mind-reading is a dangerous hobby, Zander. Almost nobody can do it accurately. Especially when hearts are involved."

"What am I supposed to do? Ask her if she regrets kissing me earlier today?"

"Yes."

"You don't think she's been through enough without adding that kind of stress on top of it? I don't actually know what you think of me, Thomas, but I'm not interested in pushing her into doing anything she doesn't want to do or that she's not ready for."

Thomas rested his back up against the footboard of the four-poster bed. "Just to clear the air, here, I like you. A lot. I think you and my sister have *both* been through more than any two people your age should ever have to go through. I respect the way you've handled yourself, and the way you've held off on pressuring Linnea, despite the fact that you started having feelings for her more moons ago than I can count."

"I thought you said mind-reading was a dangerous hobby."

"Some things are more obvious than others. Besides, twins are an exception to the rule."

Zander felt his face warm, but he didn't let it get in his way. "So if you're not upset that I kissed your sister, then what's with the big brother speech, Thomas?"

"Maybe because when it's me, you'll talk and say what's on your mind. When it's her, you're willing to mind-read and second-guess and let her walk away to bed without so much as telling her good night and what a lovely night you had."

"I don't know if she wants me to do that!"

"What do you want? Are *you* second-guessing this?"

Zander took a deep breath because now they were getting into territory he didn't know how to admit to. But when Thomas continued to look at him in an unassuming way, he found himself able to say it. "No, I'm not. When she finally kissed me earlier, well… That's how it felt. Like *finally* things were the way they're supposed to be. Except they're *not* supposed to be that way. She's supposed to have Ben, not me. I'm not supposed to be stepping in somewhere I don't belong, and I don't have any idea how she feels or what she wants."

Thomas closed his eyes for a moment before meeting his gaze again. "Believe me when I tell you I learned this one the hard way myself. But *that* part? The uncertainty? It's that hard for everyone, whether there are alternate universes and dead husbands in the background or not. But there's only one way to find out what *she* wants, and it isn't by whining about it to me."

He knew Thomas was right, but at the moment the advice felt overwhelming rather than helpful. Just because someone was right about something didn't mean it *mattered.* So instead of answering Thomas, he clapped him lightly on the shoulder. "Congratulations, by the way. I had no idea you were going to propose to Mia tonight."

For a moment, he thought it wasn't going to work, but then Thomas's eyes lit up. For several minutes, he was gone, on a long, excited spiel about wanting to do it when both his and Mia's parents were in Philotheum, and everyone was already dressed up and celebrating.

He didn't mind listening. Thomas and Mia deserved their night of unchecked wonder. By the time Thomas finally said goodnight and left, Zander's mood had improved considerably. *Maybe real happiness was still possible here*, he thought, flopping over the back of the couch and onto the cushions.

It wasn't a life he'd ever considered, not even in his wildest imaginings. Not that any kid his age from Earth had probably ever dreamed that becoming a guard and helping to win a war in a kingdom in an alternate universe was a real possibility. But here he was, probably stuck forever — and in…he couldn't yet bring himself to even *think* the word love, but he was definitely *in* something…with a widowed princess.

His life had officially become a fairy tale, although maybe not the happy-ending kind. He wondered when he'd get a unicorn.

The sharp, sweet smell of batter just beginning to caramelize on the hot outside edges of the waffle iron pulled at the edges of his consciousness, slowly rousing him from sleep. But it was the loud beep of the timer on the microwave that made him finally open his eyes, and the next smell made him throw off the covers.

Maple syrup.

He knew what that meant. Sunday morning and his dad was making breakfast while his mom slept in.

When he was younger, he'd looked forward to these mornings all week. His dad was always in a good mood, humming as he worked, eager to chat with Zander about whatever game they'd be watching in the afternoon. Bronco Sundays were the absolute best.

Although he would never have admitted it, in the same way, he wasn't so sure anything had changed now that he was older. Except that he'd discovered an appreciation for yet another smell in the kitchen — the one coming from the freshly brewed pot of coffee.

This morning, his father was already pouring two cups as Zander padded into the kitchen.

"Is one of those for me?" Zander asked.

"I figured it had been awhile since you had some," his father said, carefully sliding the mug across the counter.

That was when he knew he was dreaming. Asleep and dreaming of a world that he could only reach in his mind. But he didn't think he could have woken himself up, even if he'd tried. And he wasn't interested in trying, so he reached for the cup. It even felt warm, almost hot, as he wrapped his fingers around it and lifted it near his face. He didn't think he was supposed to be able to feel the steam, either, as it drifted up, but he could.

"It hasn't been that long since I've had coffee, but it definitely wasn't as good as this," he said, after he'd taken a sip that tasted better and realer than any dream had a right to. "Tobias brought some as a gift to Quinn after the war ended, but she gave it to me."

Despite the real smells and tastes, the dream itself was definitely unrealistic because his father gave him a half-smile and nodded as if anything Zander had said made sense to him.

For several moments, the kitchen was quiet except for the sounds of sipping and batter bubbling on the iron, but then his father cleared his throat and spoke.

"Is it my fault, Zander? That you left, I mean?"

His throat, so warmed by the coffee only a moment ago, now felt as if he'd taken a too-large gulp of ice water.

"No," he said immediately. While it was true he and his father hadn't been on the best of terms when he'd left, that fact hadn't had anything to do with his decision to follow Owen up the steps of the broken bridge that long-ago evening. Leaving his world had been more accident than anything.

"I'm sorry, Zander. I never meant to hurt you or make you feel like you didn't have any choice. I regret it now. There are many things I wish I'd done differently."

Now he knew he'd had this dream before, probably many times. The first time, and maybe even the twentieth, those words had cut to his core. He'd needed them so desperately then that just hearing his father say them was enough to shatter him. But this time, while he loved his father for being able to say them, they no longer had the power to get that deep inside. He didn't need them. He understood now, that even as an adult his father had never had all the answers or the power. He'd only been doing the best he could at the time. And Zander wasn't blameless, either. He'd been so young then, and his expectations had been those of a young, immature man who still needed to learn many things.

"I know, Dad. I'm not angry. It was a long time ago now, for me."

"Are you with Quinn?"

He had to take a long sip of his coffee to even consider the answer to that question. He was in the same place as Quinn, yes. They worked alongside each other, had just finished winning a war together; they even lived under the same roof. But he wasn't with her — not in the way he'd pictured them when they both were in Bristlecone. And he never would be. The Quinn his father was asking about, the girl he used to know, didn't even exist anymore.

He wasn't so sure the Zander his father was asking about existed anymore, either.

"She's here," he finally said. "I see her every day. But... she's not why."

His father flipped a still-steaming waffle off the iron and onto a plate, and then turned to face Zander. "Are you ever going to come home?"

He stared into the depths of the black liquid in the mug. "I don't know. I can't right now; I might never be able to."

"We're still here, Zander. Waiting. Loving you. Missing you. Hoping that one day we'll open the door and you'll just be standing there. Please remember that."

He needed a moment to figure out how to respond to that in the right way, and his cup was empty, so he turned to refill it.

Even before he turned back around, he knew his father was no longer there. The sounds and smells of breakfast had dissipated though the mug of coffee in front of him was still steaming. He grabbed it quickly before the counter disappeared, too, leaving him standing in his parents' family room instead.

"I knew it was a dream," he said to the man sitting on the couch.

"That coffee isn't going to do anything for you, except maybe wake you up because you need to pee."

He raised an eyebrow. "Either it's real or it's not. The way it tastes, I'll take my chances." He took a long sip to prove his point. "What am I doing here if I'm not even going to get to finish a conversation with my father?"

"Why are you asking me? It's your dream."

He glared at the old man for a moment, but only succeeded in wasting a few of the precious moments he had to spend here.

The family room looked exactly the same as the last time he'd been here — there weren't even any new movies on the shelf over the entertainment center. The same pictures hung on the walls. Sophia's preschool picture was still there, complete with her stuffed penguin, Felix. Ashley was next, grinning with one missing front tooth. And, of course, there was his own senior picture with him posed next to his beat-up black truck, a football tucked under his arm.

"Why don't they ever get new ones?" he asked, as much to himself as to Alvin.

"These are the new ones, still. It hasn't even been two months in their world. This is new, though." Alvin pointed to something red tucked between two movies on a shelf.

Frowning, Zander pulled it out. It was a folder, faux-leather-covered cardboard. In the center, gleaming gold-embossed letters spelled out Bristlecone High School.

He'd graduated, then. Apparently missing the last couple of weeks of school wasn't enough to ruin quite everything.

"They went, Zander," Alvin said quietly beside him. "They wanted to watch the rest of the seniors on the team graduate. That was when they realized that William has been missing, too."

There was no way William had finished all of his final semester's classes — he'd been gone since Spring Break. But knowing William, he'd probably long since had enough credits to graduate.

So Quinn would be the only one to not actually earn a diploma. That idea bothered him more than it should have, considering it would never make any difference to her.

Alvin opened the diploma and set it directly under Zander's senior picture. It was a good thing this was only a dream, or that move would have freaked his mother out in the morning.

He wondered what his parents would think of his most current portrait — him in the regalia of a full-blown Philothean knight. Sir Zander Cunningham, balancing his silver sword on its point.

Even that was outdated now; there would probably be a new painting commissioned soon, to display the honors he'd earned in the war.

"You never answered your father's question. Are you ever going to come back here?"

"I know it's a dream, Alvin, and I know it's you, but you could at least try to make sense when you speak."

"What if you could, Zander? What if you could go through a gate right now, and this could be real?"

He stared at the pictures on the wall again, letting his eyes drift to older ones, too. There were his younger sisters, all big eyes and even bigger smiles. There was a picture of all three of them together, Sophia's whole chubby little fist wrapped around his index finger.

Then he looked down at himself, at the clothes he was wearing, at the tunic of one of the most honored and respected men in the kingdom of Philotheum, at a faded streak of white on the leg of his black pants where baby Adeline had gotten spit-up on him just before the party.

"Would the gate work both ways?"

But Alvin wasn't there anymore. Neither was the wall of pictures. He was alone.

The room was pitch black when Zander woke, despite the fact that he'd fallen asleep on the couch without even closing the curtains. He was still fully dressed, too; he hadn't even managed to take off his shoes.

He stood and stretched, contemplating stumbling straight over to his comfortable bed and going right back to sleep, but after a moment he realized he wasn't at all tired.

He *was* cold; the fire in the grate had died down to just embers and a shiver ripped through him as he went to stoke it. When he got to the fireplace, though, he realized there was no more wood in the bin.

Odd, he thought, considering that someone had been cleaning up in here last night. Usually refilling the wood bin was the first task any servant working in a bedroom would complete. Then he rolled his eyes at himself and wondered just when he'd actually become so acclimated to — and even spoiled by — living in a castle. It wasn't normal for him to be thinking about having his room cleaned by servants.

He could get his own wood.

Slipping back into his cloak, the one piece of clothing he'd managed to shed, he left his room to head for the storage room where the extra wood for this wing was kept.

Or, at least that was where he told himself he was going. Whether it was his feet or his heart that chose not to cooperate, he didn't know, but he found himself in the hallway near Linnea's room instead.

He wasn't going to knock; he would never have disturbed her sleep before sunrise. But just as he walked past her door, an ear-splitting screech from inside let him know that she wasn't asleep, anyway. So, he knocked. And when nobody answered for several minutes, but the frantic noises inside continued, he let himself in. And then he froze.

Linnea was sitting in the center of the large four-poster bed, one crying infant in her arms, another next to her. He knew she hadn't heard him enter over the noise the babies were making, and now he knew she hadn't seen him, either. She probably couldn't see much of anything through the tears streaming down her cheeks.

He had no idea what to do. He wanted to help her; she obviously needed it, and he was sure he could do *something*, but the moment was so painfully private, he knew he shouldn't be here.

With guilt ripping through his insides over both choices, he slowly silently backed toward the door.

Of course Linnea chose that moment to look up and see him, of course she did. Her eyes went wider than he'd ever seen them before she quickly turned her face toward the wall, away from him and began wiping her cheeks furiously with the edge of a baby's blanket.

Not since he was a child had Zander so suddenly felt like bursting into tears of his own.

"I'm sorry," he stammered, "I knocked, but you didn't… I'm sorry." Every instinct he had was telling him to flee right now. To just get on the other side of the door as fast as humanly possible and disappear. To pretend this had never happened and never speak of it again.

And then the baby on the bed — it was Adeline — threw up. Not spit up. This was violent, projectile vomit that covered the whole side of the bed instantly. It was the sort of moment that made Zander understand exactly why someone in his world had invented birth control. Especially because she was now screaming louder than anything her size should be able to.

Sheer grace — or panic, more likely — was the only thing that kept him from leaving the room now and going to *get someone else*. The force of whichever it was sent him toward the bed instead of away from it, scooping up the baby who was now covered in goo.

"Why are you alone?" he asked in a voice that had far more bite than he'd meant to insert. Immediately, he felt terrible.

Her tears stopped in favor of glaring at him.

Despite the mess, he lifted Adeline to his shoulder and rubbed her back as he looked at Linnea. The screaming grew a little quieter, and the infant relaxed against his chest. "It's the middle of the night and you didn't want to bother anybody, right?"

She looked down at the baby in her arms without answering him. Benjamin was quieting as well. This was usually how it went; either both babies were fine, or both were screaming their heads off. It wasn't usually this easy to figure out who'd started it. Of course, he didn't know how long they'd been at it this time.

"Has she been throwing up like this all night?"

"No." Linnea's eyes were wide as she stared between her children. "She's just been crying for… I don't even know how long. She stopped when I fed her a minute ago, but she started again immediately… and then this one got into the act."

"Okay." He kissed Adeline's temple, noting that it felt cool and dry the way it was supposed to. That was a good sign. "She doesn't feel like she has a fever, but do you want me to go get Nathaniel to take a look at her?"

"What are you doing here, Zander?"

A million responses flitted through his mind, and he wasn't even sure of the answer himself, but this time he made a better choice about which words to allow out of his mouth. "I'm not sure, Nay. If you want me to leave, I understand, and I'll go. But, I'm awake, and I'm here, and I can help if you want me to."

"It's not your responsibility." Her eyes stayed trained on Benjamin, not on him.

He decided to ignore this. He didn't know if she was trying to pick a fight or if she was just hurting terribly. Probably it was both. Angry was easier than sad; he knew this too well. Whatever it was, though, he had nothing to gain by engaging it. So, before his words could make the situation worse, he carried Adeline into the washroom.

"Did you eat something you shouldn't have at the party?" he asked the baby as he pulled off her tiny pajamas. She was calm now, not even putting up her usual fuss at being washed and changed. But the look she gave him made him chuckle. "You're right," he said. "That was the most stupid question I could have asked a newborn. You are your mother's daughter."

Once Adeline was all clean, he grabbed the biggest stack of towels he could hold while carrying her and went back out to the bedroom.

Linnea was still sitting on the bed, snuggled with Benjamin, who was starting to doze off. She watched as Zander laid several of the towels over the mess.

"You don't have to do that," she said.

"Don't worry. I'm not cleaning it, just covering it up. Someone can deal with the rest in the morning."

This time, his words managed to draw a half-smile from her. He hadn't noticed that he was barely breathing until that simple gesture of hers brought an immediate gush of air back into his lungs, filling him with oxygen and instant relief. For a fleeting moment, anyway. Her next sentence made it hard to breathe again.

"I mean all of this, Zander. You can give her to me and go back to bed. I know you're not on duty tonight."

He almost listened to her. This was hard enough without her being annoyed with him, too. He moved Adeline down from his shoulder and toward Linnea. As he did so, she stirred and fussed — she'd almost been asleep.

The look of panic in Linnea's eyes was so brief he should have missed it. She hid it immediately, her eyes darting toward the other baby sleeping in her arms. But he saw.

Swallowing hard, he cuddled Addie closer and rubbed her back until she quieted again. Then he sat down in the rocking chair a few feet from the bed.

Recovered now, Linnea narrowed her eyes.

"I will leave," he said quietly. "Of course I won't stay in here if you want me to go. Just say the word, and I will pretend this never happened. But…" He ran his fingers through the soft down on Adeline's head. "I'm not here because I'm *on duty*."

She didn't answer him for a moment; she was still staring at her son and blinking furiously. Pangs in Zander's chest kept time with the frantic motion of her eyelids, but he stayed where he was, waiting to see if she would speak. The baby on his shoulder grew warm and heavy, giving out tiny soft sighs.

"Why are you even awake?" she finally asked, her voice steadier and clearer than he'd have expected.

This time, he was the one who kept his eyes trained on an infant instead of her. "How angry would you be if I said it had nothing to do with you? I woke up from a weird dream and I was cold and out of firewood. I was just getting more when I heard these two."

He couldn't tell whether she looked disappointed or relieved, and he wasn't sure which one he hoped it was, either.

There was a long pause. The only sounds in the room were the sleepy noises of the babies and the crackling of the fire — she must have tended to that herself at some point as well.

"Thank you," she finally said. This time her voice wasn't so clear. She leaned back into the pillows, settling in without disturbing the tiny boy in her arms.

"Linnea…" There were so many things he wanted to say, so many thoughts and feelings swirled in his head and his heart, but none of them would gather on his tongue. All he could manage in the end was, "You're welcome," but he suspected she heard some of the other feelings in those two words, just as he had in hers.

But it was late, and she had been up most of the night. He took a moment to look at Adeline, to see if she was completely out, and when he turned back to Linnea, her eyes were closed, too.

By the time he had managed to get both babies into the cradle without waking them, so that Linnea could stay asleep too, a swath of pale yellow light was showing under the curtains.

He yawned as he pulled the door to Linnea's room shut, guiding it slowly so that it wouldn't make a sound when it latched. Of course it would be morning by the time not really sleeping caught up with him. If he was lucky, he'd have time to catch an hour or of sleep before he was needed for something.

Halfway to his room, aided by a sudden freezing draft sweeping through the hallway, he remembered that there'd been a reason he left in the first place. *The firewood.*

A not-small part of him wanted to just forget about it, to hurry back to his bed and try to capture whatever rest he could, but he'd learned the hard way, several times now, just how difficult it was to fall asleep while a thin layer of ice formed on top of his water glass. So he sighed and headed in a different direction, this time determined not to stop anywhere except the wood storage.

Whether it was because he was so focused or she was so stealthy, he almost didn't see her.

All he could see were her eyes. Two tiny points of light focused right on him from the alcove where she stood, the light from the window illuminating her small frame. Despite her size, she wasn't a child. In the brief moment she stood there perfectly still, Zander could see that she was at least as old as Quinn, seventeen or so.

As soon as his eyes met hers, though, she blinked, extinguishing the bright amber glow of her pupils, and then she *ran*.

It was so unexpected that it took him a second to respond — a second was too long. By the time he realized that something wasn't right, that her running away was a sign that she didn't belong here and that he needed to detain her, she was gone.

THOUGHTS OF HOME

"YOU SEARCHED EVERYWHERE?" ALTHOUGH Quinn had appeared at the door only moments after Zander knocked, she was still rubbing the sleep from her eyes.

"The entire floor and all the stairwells leading from it. Kian and Ethan are continuing to search and we've got more guards expanding the search to the rest of the castle now. Everyone's awake now, which is probably not a bonus."

"No," she scoffed. "But oh well. You're sure it wasn't one of the maids? There are new ones, and we haven't been back long. It could just be someone you don't know."

He was sure, but he shrugged. "It's possible. I don't know why a maid would run, though, and I'm pretty sure I'd still want to search for one who did. And we've trained all your personal guards on the servants who've been cleared to work on this floor."

Quinn's gaze dropped to the floor. "Of course you have. I'm sorry, I wasn't thinking."

"Don't apologize. It's my job to know that. You have enough on your plate." Although the long moons of war had transformed her from an unsure girl into an astute leader, he knew that this transition back to the castle was an altogether new challenge.

They'd spent the war in a rural estate that belonged to Quinn's uncle. It had been tight quarters and a lot of work, but it wasn't the same as getting dressed up every day and hosting fancy dinners and running a castle full of servants.

Her eyes crinkled at the edges as she studied him, taking in his clothing. "You're sure you *saw* someone? It doesn't look like you've slept. You haven't changed."

Although he felt his face warm at the fact that she was right, he snorted at her insinuation. "Sleep or not, I'm not imagining things, Quinn. There was a girl. I could draw you a picture if you want me to. I don't know where she went, but…"

To his surprise, she chuckled.

He narrowed his eyes. "You weren't serious."

"Not about you imagining it, no." She was laughing now. "I know you didn't. But the look on your face…"

Sighing, he leaned against the back of one of the newly reupholstered overstuffed chairs. "You're really just asking why I didn't sleep."

"That too. I've always had a problem with curiosity." She pursed her lips for a moment, studying him. "Something to do with Linnea?"

He coughed. Was it that obvious? How? *"What?"*

"There's spit-up on your back."

Heat seeped from the base of his neck to the spot just behind his ears, but he did his best to ignore it. "Of course there is." He shrugged out of his cloak, stepping closer to the fireplace as he did so. Sure enough, the back of his cloak was covered. "Adeline decided she wanted to be a middle-of-the-night volcano."

He waited for her to ask, for her *curiosity* to strike. Now she'd have *questions*, would want answers about what he'd been doing in Linnea's room in the middle of the night, about what he was doing with Linnea, period. He couldn't blame her; he wanted answers to those questions himself. So he braced himself for the worst, scrambling to come up with answers that he didn't even really have.

But she just grabbed the cloak out of his hands and crossed the room to toss it into a basket of dirty linens. Then she went to the coat rack by the door and pulled down a different cloak in a plain dark green with white fur trim around the hood. It was just enough different from the type the guards wore to be much more noticeable than a little spit-up.

"That's William's," he said, not reaching for it.

One auburn eyebrow arched itself upward on Quinn's forehead. "It's a cloak. It will fit. The castle is too cold to be without one, and William won't mind. He probably won't even notice."

He knew this was true, but it wasn't what made him uncomfortable. "You can't give me special favors, Quinn. A guard can't walk out of here wearing the king's clothing."

She tilted her head. "Because it would just be so weird and unexpected if I treated you like a friend instead of a servant?"

He opened his mouth but then closed it again. It wasn't "proper", or so he'd heard at least several dozen times from the whispers among older castle guards and members of Quinn's own family — though usually when she wasn't around.

"I'm the queen. I get to make the rules now. I'll give a cloak to whomever I want to. Besides, I didn't think you really wanted to stay with the whole guard thing."

"Stephen told you that already?" His hand dropped to the hilt of his sword without him meaning it to. It was such a habit now, instinct, even. He wasn't sure he wanted to give it up any more than he was certain he wanted to keep it.

He'd had a discussion about this with Stephen, not long ago. He hadn't said, definitively, that he no longer wanted to be a guard, though it really wasn't something he could imagine doing forever.

"Sort of. He said something in passing that made me think that was what he meant. I probably only caught it because I already figured that."

"I…"

"You don't have to explain it, or give me a definite decision right now. You're good at it, Zander. Better than good. I don't know what I would have done for the last ten moons without you. Regardless of what you decide, you're still going to have to put up with being my advisor forever, you know. But you have other options besides the guard. And the sword is yours." She nodded toward his hand. "You might think I give you special favors because we're friends — and maybe I do — but you've earned your titles. Nobody would ever say otherwise."

"Besides," he said, grinning now, "you're the queen, and you get to make the rules now."

"See, that's why I need you. You catch on quickly."

They both laughed then, the kind of genuine laugh that felt right, reminding him that he and Quinn had really somehow managed to bring their friendship back full circle. The war ending had brought significant changes and adjustments for both of them, but it was a good thing. With any luck at all, the coming days would bring much more of this kind of laughter and less of the strife they'd been dealing with for so long.

But when they stopped, the look she gave him made his insides feel heavy again. "How are you doing, anyway?"

"I'm fine." He knew he said it too quickly.

"Yeah? That's why you're not sleeping and you're getting yourself covered in baby vomit in the middle of the night?"

"Who sleeps when there are newborns?"

Her new apartment was spotless, but she picked up a throw blanket from the back of the couch and started refolding it. "I had a dream about home last night," she said quietly.

This brought him up short, unprepared. That was the last thing he'd expected her to say. He'd been bracing for a discussion about

Linnea, not this. And he couldn't help noticing the way she'd referred to the world they'd both come from as *home*. She never did that anymore; she'd given that up a long time ago. All he could do was stare.

"It happens pretty regularly, it always has," she said, laying the blanket over the back of the couch again, messier than it had been when she'd started. "But the dreams tend to be more frequent around big events or changes in my life here…or just when I'm missing my family the most."

That there had been big changes here lately was an understatement, though the wistful tone in her voice made him think it wasn't those changes that had prompted the dream this time. "What was your… who did you… what was your dream about?"

"Owen. It's almost always him, although every once in a while, I see someone else. Owen and I have long conversations, though. Sometimes I wonder if they're real. He said to tell you congratulations on your new medal."

His hand flew to his chest, where the shiny new honor was pinned to his tunic, along with the numerous other rewards he'd earned for his services to Quinn. He was supposed to be proud of these achievements, and sometimes he managed to be, but mostly they were reminders of events he'd rather forget.

As much as those medals meant here in this world, though, Owen didn't know anything about them. Zander had earned all of them after Owen had left, and there was no way to communicate between the worlds for real. At least, he didn't think there was. After retrieving his jaw from the floor, he looked at her. "You don't think it actually is real, do you? Like you actually had that conversation with Owen?"

She shrugged. "It's not real in the same way that me standing here talking to you is real, no. I think it's possible that Owen is dreaming the same thing at the same time as I am, but I don't even know if that's true."

"He knew you and William were in trouble here because of a dream he had," Zander said, remembering how he'd wound up in this world in the first place.

"I know. But even then, there were other dreams that I'd had about Owen while I was here, and I told him about them, and he didn't remember them or anything. Sometimes I think it's just that in my heart I know what he would say."

"Yeah, maybe." He bit the inside of his cheek, trying to remember the details of the conversation he'd had with his father last night. "Or maybe it's what you *wish* he would say."

"Maybe," she said, unaffected. "I'm not sure there's a difference. Not one that matters." Now she was rearranging the pillows on the couch. "I'm not sure that makes them not real, though. Maybe it's just a different kind of real."

He watched her for a long moment as she moved every pillow on the couch at least twice. The blanket was still crooked, so he picked it up to refold it himself. As he did so, his own words spilled out. "I dreamed about home last night, too."

She didn't react; she just continued using her fingers to untangle the green fringe along the edge of one of the pillows. "Who did you talk to?"

"My father." The rest of the words poured out, unbidden, the whole dream, even details he hadn't remembered until he started telling her about them. When he was finally finished, he sat down on one end of the couch, pressing his back against the pillows, mostly to stop himself from fidgeting with them the way she was doing.

Quinn nodded. "That dream would keep me up looking for something to do the rest of the night, too."

"I wasn't… with Linnea… you know…"

"I'm not looking for gossip," she said. "Well, I am, but only because I'm nosy and I'm sure one or both of you will spill the beans some day when you two actually know what you're thinking or feeling. You're both adults now, you don't owe me an explanation — even if I do ask for one."

"All right," he said, chuckling again.

"If I did stick my nose in *at all*, it would be to say don't make any decisions about that right now one way or the other."

She was surprising him all over the place today. "Why? What do you mean?"

"You've both been through a lot lately, and now everything is changing again... I just think maybe you both need time before you're ready to...anything, really."

"But you're not interfering."

"No. Let's go back to your dream."

He blinked. He hadn't expected her to change the subject back so quickly. It relieved him — a little — that she was dropping it, but under that, there was a small sense of disappointed. As much as he *didn't* want to talk about it with Quinn...he did want to hear what she thought. But he wasn't going to steer the conversation back there, so he went with her topic instead. "It's like you said, even if it was real, it's not *that* kind of real."

She was quiet again for a moment; her hands were still now, no longer frantically searching for a way to keep busy. "What would you do if we found another gate?"

The simple act of her asking the question made his stomach twist in two directions at once. Panic or hope — he wasn't sure which it was. He didn't know if he even wanted to think about it.

"Probably be on the front lines to try to get it closed. It's too dangerous. You know that. I know that. It's a bad, bad idea."

She pursed her lips, staring at him. He could see the complicated swirl of his own thoughts reflected in her eyes. He'd given the easy answer, the one he *should* give, the one he knew was right. But it wasn't complete.

The truth, the whole truth, and nothing but the truth. He understood now that there were three distinct things on that list. They both knew what he wasn't saying, what he couldn't say because he didn't know the answer at all. *The whole truth.*

"What would *you* do?" he asked.

"I know what the right thing to do is, Zander. You're right. I would have no choice but to make sure it gets closed, to make sure it doesn't present a threat to this world from the other one, or even vice versa I suppose."

"You realize that causing wars here in this world between kingdoms is an even bigger risk than the other world is, right?"

She nodded. "I'm new at this whole being-a-queen thing, but I've figured that one out. If the wrong person found out about a gate..."

Terror mixed with something else swirled in his stomach again. The idea of someone else discovering a gate was too awful to comprehend, but he couldn't quite ignore the swell of hope at the thought there might really be another gate somewhere. He couldn't entertain it, though. "Anyway, it's not even worth thinking about. What are the chances that there actually is another gate that's open and we could use?"

"You're right," she said. "It's...we've got other things to worry about." She walked toward the fire, busying herself with swinging the kettle-hook over the flames.

The whole truth wasn't any easier for her right now, apparently.

"You don't, actually," he said. "The war is over, it's peaceful. William's family is here; everyone is celebrating. Maybe you should take some time to actually enjoy it."

She narrowed her eyes. "You should know better by now than to say things like that."

"What? That it's peaceful?"

"Yes! That. That's like saying, 'It's not a big deal that I didn't do my trigonometry homework because there's not going to be a quiz.'"

He laughed. "I know for sure that you're not going to be taking any trigonometry quizzes, Quinn."

"No, but we'll regret it. I don't know how, but we will."

For at least a little while, Quinn was wrong — about them regretting Zander's words, anyway. The following days were peaceful. A thorough search of the castle for the girl or anything else suspicious yielded nothing, and everyone was able to enjoy the last week of Stephen and Charlotte's stay.

Long days of work followed by evening meals in the new common room filled with laughter, conversation, and games became the norm again, and this time Zander felt like a real part of all of it.

She was right about other things. He didn't dream about Bristlecone every night, but it happened too often for him to be surprised when it did. He could even anticipate a dream if he spent too many daytime hours thinking about his little sisters or his parents — or yearning for microwaves and central heating. Sometimes he was certain that the dreams were his brain's way of replacing television.

On the evening he decided to spend trying to teach William's siblings how to play football, his entire night was filled with visions of games at Bristlecone High and long talks with his old friend, Adam. He woke wondering if it was true that Adam had broken up with his girlfriend.

And Quinn was right about Linnea, too. Now wasn't the time to make any decisions, especially while her family was here. Unless he wanted to keep stalking her in the midnight hours, there wasn't much time for them to talk alone. And he was pretty sure some of her family were taking turns staying with her in her room most nights after that disastrous one, anyway.

A few days before everyone was set to return to Eirentheos, he overheard a conversation that made him want to avoid Linnea altogether.

"There's plenty of room in my carriage," Max was saying to Rebecca. "What's two more babies? They're small. I'm sure Emma and Alex would love to help as well."

The overloud pounding of blood against his eardrums shouldn't have been possible. Considering that his heart was shattered in a million pieces, it shouldn't have been able to beat at all.

But it did. The rushing rhythm kept raging, obliterating every other noise as he hurried to turn another corner and get as far away from there as he could. Mercifully, it cut off the rest of their words, too.

There was a part of him, of course there was, that wanted to run straight to Linnea's room, to beg her not to go with them, to ask her to stay, to promise to help her and to be everything she needed once her family was gone.

He couldn't, though. It wasn't right. He couldn't ask her to stay here, in a damaged castle, several days' travel away from her parents and most of her brothers and sisters when she had the option to be with them. They could do so much more for her than he could; they could take care of her, Benjamin, and Adeline.

So he stayed away. He busied himself helping with the reconstruction of the living areas of the castle, and keeping Ember, his horse, exercised out in the cold winter arena. In the evenings, at dinner, he chatted with Linnea along with everyone else, but he kept it friendly and casual, not wanting to cause her to doubt her decisions at all. He did steal as much time as he could with the babies, breathing in their sweet scents, memorizing every detail of the tiny faces that would change so much before he saw them again. Hopefully she'd at least bring them back for Thomas's wedding in a few moons.

This was worse than leaving his family had been — this process of knowing beforehand and agonizing over the upcoming farewells was so much worse than just having it happen one day with no warning. Now he was almost grateful for the way Quinn had once broken things off between them. That had been brutal, but it had also been quick, and then she'd been gone.

On the night before they were slated to leave, he didn't dream of Bristlecone. He didn't dream at all. No matter how he tossed and turned, how many times he paced the floor, or rekindled the fire, sleep refused to come.

At some point between midnight and dawn, he again found himself in the hallway outside Linnea's room, but this time everything was quiet. No baby screamed, or even fussed to give him an excuse to open the door.

"Is everything all right, Sir Zander?" The voice made him jump several feet into the air, but the guard it belonged to pretended not to notice.

"Yes, Sir Kian, thank you. I was just…" His brain failed the simple task of coming up with an excuse.

"Making a final check of the hallways before you head to bed?" Only the tiniest glint of amusement in Kian's eyes belied his straightforward tone.

"Sure, let's go with that."

"Trouble sleeping?"

He nodded. He'd known Kian for a while now; the guard wasn't much older than him, although his experience at the job dwarfed Zander's. They'd spent the entire war together, holed up in Tobias's estate, and returning in victory. Sometime over the past moons, the other guards had gone from treating Zander with suspicion and humor at his lack of skills to respecting him, even at the times he'd needed their help.

But he didn't *know* any of them all that well. He would have trusted Kian with his life — but not with his emotions. He hadn't crossed that threshold with anyone outside of the royal family yet.

"That's common around here. Come with me."

Zander frowned, but followed Kian down two hallways to the wing where the majority of the guards lived. Not for the first time, he wondered what the rest of them thought of his housing nearer to the family. Marcus Westbrook was the only other unrelated person whose rooms were in the family wing — and he'd long been promoted from guard to advisor. Besides, he was the grandfather of Linnea's twins, so, really, he was family, too.

But if Kian thought anything about it at all, he didn't show it as he stopped in the middle of a long hallway and opened a door, ushering Zander inside.

The room was just as nice as the one Zander was staying in, cleaner, because it wasn't filled with piles of boxes and crates from the rebuilding. And yet, Kian had more *stuff*, things that clearly belonged to him. A pair of knives hung over the bed as a decoration, and a tapestry with designs and symbols Zander didn't recognize took up half of another wall. The bottom corner of it looked like it had been damaged, probably in the destruction of the castle, but Kian had strategically placed a wooden chair in front of it to help hide that part.

Something else caught Zander's eye. A piece of paper, stuffed into the edge of a wooden frame. It was a drawing of a young woman. It wasn't a work of art, but he could tell that the girl was pretty, and the clean, sharp edges of the paper told him that the drawing was new.

Kian followed his gaze and grinned. "It's a good time to be a returning war hero."

"That's… she's your…?"

"Maybe," Kian said, shrugging. "I barely know her yet, but we'll see what happens. Here." He pulled open one of the doors on a tall armoire.

Zander's furniture contained mostly clothing — he didn't have much else here — but Kian withdrew a heavy pewter flask from his. He unscrewed the cap and poured some sort of amber liquid into it, then held it out to Zander.

"What is this?" He sniffed at it. The fumes burned his nose and made his eyes water.

"It will help you sleep."

Zander's eyes narrowed. "Forever?"

Kian laughed, loud and deep. "Don't worry. I'm not trying to poison you. I've used it often enough myself. I'd drink some right now, to prove it, but I'm on duty and, it works. It's just enough."

"Where did you get it?"

"You really are new to Philotheum, aren't you?"

A shiver ran down Zander's spine. This was the discussion he couldn't have; it was one of the biggest reasons he hadn't pursued many friendships here. His past wasn't something he could talk about with anyone. "Yes," he said bluntly, hoping Kian wouldn't press the issue.

He didn't. In fact, he changed the subject completely. "What are you doing tomorrow night?"

Attempting not to wallow in a puddle of misery because Linnea will be gone. *"I'm not on duty, so… nothing?"*

"You should come out with us."

"Out with who? Where?" He didn't know why the invitation felt so strange. Back in Bristlecone, he'd never been one to turn down an invitation. He'd been what he supposed was popular at school, friends with everyone. Actually, in Bristlecone, he would have been the one doing the inviting. Here it was so different; he didn't know how to navigate the social scene here, even though he should have. He wondered if this was how life had felt to William in the other world.

"If you come, I'll show you. But you might want to drink this, so you can actually get some sleep tonight, first."

Zander was rather certain that he wasn't going to be up to 'going out' tomorrow night — was that where Kian had met his nameless girl? — but he didn't want to deal with the refusal tonight. Kian and whoever else was included in 'we' would probably forget all about him by the time tomorrow evening rolled around, anyway.

He gave the cap another suspicious sniff.

"You don't have to," Kian said, holding out his hand for it.

He didn't *want* to, but he *really* didn't want to hand the drink back to Kian, so he lifted it to his mouth, and tipped its contents down his throat.

Considering the acrid, burning smell, the liquid was unexpectedly smooth. It slid down his throat, leaving a warm, relaxed sensation in its wake, all the way to his stomach. He blinked, already feeling a little sleepy.

"Now go to bed," Kian said. "You can thank me in the morning."

Kian was right. By the time morning came, Zander wanted to rush right to him and thank him — and to demand his own bottle of whatever that potion was.

He didn't even remember walking back to his rooms and climbing into bed. The rest of the night had disappeared in peaceful black dreamless sleep, and he woke more rested than he'd felt in a long time. He was actually awake and alert and relaxed all at the same time. It was blissful. Peaceful and quiet. *Too quiet.*

The calm peace melted in a sudden wave of panic. The bright patch of sunlight on the cushion of the window seat meant that he should be hearing the pattering sounds of children running up and down the hallway. Their shouts and giggling should have woken him long before this. There should be conversations and rustling — but there was nothing. Everything was silent.

Less than a second later, he was up. He didn't even notice the chill temperature of the room as he ran to the window, throwing open the heavy curtains and desperately searching the landscape. Every inch of him hoped he wouldn't see what he was looking for.

But it was there.

Far out on the road already, moving quickly along the outside edges of the city, almost out of sight already, it was there: the long line of carriages carrying King Stephen and his family back to Eirentheos.

The sun was dipping below the other edge of the horizon, and the guards' stables were full of horses and empty of people by the time Zander returned to the castle. He and Ember were both exhausted and sweaty, despite the bright chill of the evening air.

He was grateful for this; the time it would take him to cool down the horse in the indoor yard and then groom him would keep him out of the castle until it was plenty late enough to just eat and retreat to his room. More of Kian's sleeping draught would be nice, but probably not worth having to talk to him to get it.

On the third loop around the track with Storm, the horse slowed down and neighed, forcing Zander to look up for the first time since they'd stated walking. A few feet ahead of them, right in the middle of their path, was an enormous bird, blinking up at him with her glittering black eyes.

"You'd better move, Larya," he mumbled. "You'll get run over."

The bird did move — though he doubted it was because she actually believed the horse would run her over — but she landed again almost immediately, this time resting her talons right on Zander's shoulder.

"Come on, bird," he said, attempting to wave her down with his hand. "It's not like I haven't fed you enough treats today." Indeed, Larya had appeared from some perch in the trees every time he'd stopped today.

She moved, but only to light a few feet in front of him, bobbing her head expectantly.

"I don't know why I'd expect you to start behaving now." He sighed and dug some more dried meat out of his pocket, tossing it to the ground in front of her.

The look she gave him was distinctly disapproving — she preferred to eat from his hand — but she wasn't one to turn down a treat, ever. She snatched it up in her beak, but then, instead of eating it then and there, she flew off. When she didn't land again a few seconds later to continue harassing him, he frowned and stopped to look for her. He didn't see her. She had to be somewhere overhead, in the rafters of the arena but she was apparently hiding. *Odd.*

"I think it's me, not you." At one time, an unexpected voice like this would have made Zander jump out of his skin, but tonight it just moved his sword from its sheath to a protective position in front of his chest. He lowered it a few seconds later when he spotted the intruder.

"What are you doing out here, Kian?" His voice came out a little more harshly than he meant it to — but only a little.

"Looking for you."

He closed his eyes. Of course everyone would be looking for him after he hadn't even shown up this morning to tell Linnea goodbye. "I suppose they sent you to find me?"

Kian looked sincere as he shook his head, though. "Who?" he asked with a confused frown. "I came out because the guards at the gate said you'd come back, and I thought I'd find you here."

He shivered and shoved his hands in his pockets, trying to decide whether what he felt was relief that he hadn't caused an uproar, or dejection that he hadn't been missed at all.

Kian sounded so sincere that Zander knew he was telling the truth. He shivered and shoved his hands in his pockets, trying to decide whether what he felt was relief that he hadn't caused an uproar, or dejection that he hadn't been missed at all. Kian didn't need to know any of that, though. "I thought you were going out somewhere tonight?" He was certainly dressed for it. Zander now noticed that Kian had the strap of a leather bag slung over his other shoulder.

"You mean *we* were going into town tonight? I've been waiting for you."

"Yeah…about that…" He stared at the ground, unable to meet Kian's eyes. "I haven't even bathed today, and I've been out riding…"

Suddenly something hit him, hard, forcefully across his whole body. For a second he couldn't breathe, couldn't catch his breath under the weight of whatever it was. And then, just as quickly, he realized that it hadn't hurt. But he was wet. Soaked and dripping onto the dirt floor beneath him. Make that mud. And he was *freezing*.

"What the hell?!" he finally spluttered, once he was able to catch his breath.

"Now you're clean. Go get dressed." Kian grinned and set the now-empty bucket down.

"You just dumped a bucket of water on a knight! That's like, treason or something."

"So kill me, *Sir* Zander. Or go tell on me to the queen."

But the anger was fading as fast as it had come. Probably because he was too cold to hang on to the heat of fury. "You could have at least brought me a towel."

"There's one in there." The leather bag was already flying at him as Kian spoke, but Zander's reflexes were fast these days and he managed to catch the strap before it flew past him. "Clothes, too. Get dressed."

There was no room in his head for the voices that wanted to argue, to yell at Kian for throwing water on him, to tell him that he *wasn't* going anywhere with him tonight, especially not now. At least not until he reached the heat of the stove in the tack room.

The anger came back as he dropped his soaking clothes onto the floor in front of the enormous black stove and then made his way over to the large wash tub. He jerked the handle of the pump unnecessarily hard, though the rough iron didn't mind. Deciding he might as well get clean while he was already wet, he grabbed the bar of soap.

His skin was a lot less accepting of his harsh feelings, so after a few moments, his face and arms were red and raw, but he was calm enough to think.

It was true that he didn't particularly want to go "into town" tonight with Kian and whoever else was going. He really wasn't in a mood to meet Kian's new girlfriend (or whatever they called that here). But as horrible as going out sounded, he'd now had time to consider what it would be like to head back into the castle. That idea was a million times worse.

Fifteen minutes later, he was standing in front of Kian again, this time freshly scrubbed and wearing clothes he'd never seen before. Although dressing up wasn't uncommon for him these days, "going out clothes" — crisply pressed black pants and a silky blue shirt that somehow twisted and buttoned at the side felt different.

Kian already had the horses saddled and ready to go. "So are you going to come, or go inside and tell everyone what an ass I am for dumping water on you? Before you decide, the bucket was clean."

Inexplicably, this made Zander smile, and the rest of his anger and annoyance with Kian disappeared into it. Maybe he'd halfway managed to make a friend here. "So where are we going?"

 THE WOODHOUSE

IT OCCURRED TO ZANDER, as they rode past the gates of the castle and down into the streets of the city of Philotheum, that he knew literally nothing about where they were going or what sort of people they would meet.

Of course, he'd been out of the castle. He'd been all over both this kingdom and Eirentheos, visited houses, ridden through the woods, fought in battles. But all of it had been with some sort of purpose, with some precipitating event behind it. He'd had things to do.

He had never just gone to town to see the sights or do shopping or anything. Linnea and Thomas and Mia often left the castle for fun, or at least they had before the war. He knew there were markets and shops and things to buy and see and do. They'd even invited him a few times, but he'd never accepted. Back then, he hadn't been comfortable enough with them, and besides, his guard training had been intense enough to leave him worn out during the few moments he had free.

Now that he had the time, he still hadn't gone. It wasn't because he couldn't afford it. His position as a guard paid well and each advancement had brought even more rewards.

When he'd put his riding cloak on in the tack room, he'd discovered that Kian had slipped an overfull velvet pouch full of coins into the inside pocket. It didn't even bother him to know that the other guard had been able to so quickly find his money. He'd never found any use for it here. Everything he needed was provided for in the castle, and he spent almost all his time there. When he did leave, as he had today, he tended to spend as little time in the city as possible. He'd ride quickly through the outskirts and the surrounding villages until was safely away in the woods and the countryside.

Tonight, Kian led him down the main road and right into the center of the city. Within minutes, they were in the enormous, open city square. Zander recognized it — sort of — though tonight there were no crowds, cheering or hostile, just people in warm clothes scurrying between the buildings. Warm yellow light poured onto the cobblestone whenever people entered or exited what appeared to be inns and pubs and shops.

Most of them paid little attention to the two men on horseback, but as they passed by the large stone fountain in the center of the square, two young teenage boys stood up and saluted them.

His mouth went dry and he suddenly felt too warm in the chill evening. He didn't know how to respond to this. A threat he could have handled, but being saluted felt fifteen kinds of wrong. He glanced desperately at Kian.

The other guard gave a quick smile and salute back and then kept riding as if nothing at all strange was happening.

Zander tried to do the same though but then they were already well past the two boys and he just felt even more awkward and stupid. Fortunately, Kian either really didn't notice, or was kind enough to pretend.

He sighed in relief and kept riding, hoping he'd do better if there were a next time, but mostly hoping there was no next time at all.

"Hey, Zander!" The call and shrill whistle that accompanied it made Zander nearly jump out of his skin before heat flooded through him again, this time setting his whole body aflame.

Kian had stopped, about ten yards behind him now, and was dismounting in front of a low stone building.

This is why I don't leave the castle, *he thought, as he turned Ember around and went back.* Nothing good happens; I just make an idiot out of myself.

"You okay?" Kian asked, taking Ember's reins as Zander dismounted.

"Fine."

He could tell that Kian didn't believe him, probably because Kian had an IQ greater than ten, but he was also a castle guard and a Friend of Philip who knew enough about hardships and secrets that he didn't press Zander. He just held his hand out toward the streams of people going in and out of the door under a hanging wooden sign that read, "Al's Woodhouse."

Zander led the way inside.

Whatever a "woodhouse" was, it was also a bar. Zander realized he should have expected this — he'd just been so busy trying to get out of going altogether that he hadn't devoted any thoughts to the details of "going out."

He'd never gone to an actual bar at home though this place was more like something out of a movie than anything that might be real in Bristlecone.

Many patrons recognized them immediately as guards, even though the only things identifying them were the small embroidered-gold emblems at the neck of their capes. People moved aside as they entered, some bowing their heads respectfully, others casting wary glances.

The men, anyway. Some of the women seemed to move closer. One woman, who couldn't have been more than a year or two older than Zander, nearly made him jump again when she rubbed her hand against his shoulder. "What can I get for you gentlemen?"

"Uhhh…" Zander looked around aimlessly for a second, glancing at the cups and bottles on the tables and in the hands around him. "Can I get a glass of water, please?"

The look on the woman's face told him he'd already made a fool of himself, but all she said was, "All right."

"Water for me, too," Kian's voice said from beside him. "And two nobs of whiskey and two beers." He held out his and deposited a silver coin on the tray she was carrying.

So there was beer here. This was useful information, he supposed. And whiskey, too. Apparently, some things really were universal. He raised an eyebrow at Kian.

"You're not on duty, Cunningham. You can relax for one evening. Drink it or don't, but I figured I owed you at least one round."

Kian walked off in the direction of a couple of other guards Zander knew. Loud laughter and back clapping erupted when he reached them. The men weren't alone in their group, either. Several of the guards stood with girls beside them, and a dark-skinned young woman greeted Kian with an enthusiastic hug. She was much prettier in person than in the drawing, he noted.

They were all smiling, happy, having fun.

And he was just standing here by himself staring at them.

When had this become his life? He'd never been the guy standing at the edge of the party in Bristlecone — he was always one of the ones *over there*, in the middle of everything, surrounded by friends.

As great as Quinn, William, and Thomas all were, his life here wasn't the same as theirs. He didn't even mean enough to Linnea to make her stay here. Watching the scene in front of him, he felt as though he'd given up everything — his entire *world* to protect their family — and for what? So he could stand here like an idiot with his mouth agape watching everyone else have fun?

By the time the server returned with the tray full of drinks, he'd made up his mind. "Set the rest over there," he said, pointing to the table nearest Kian with one hand, while he picked up the small glass of whiskey with the other.

"You want one more before we head back?" Kian asked, swirling a small glass of amber liquid as he approached.

Zander's head swayed slightly, keeping time with the drink. "I don't think so. I'd rather be able to ride my horse home without falling off."

Kian laughed so hard the whiskey in the glass sloshed up the sides. "You haven't had that much."

"Did you *see* me on the dance floor?"

"I did. I think the blonde girl was impressed."

Warmth flooded his cheeks despite the chill air on the back patio of Al's Woodhouse. "I think I'll leave the girl-hunting to you for now, Kian. Marisa seems cool."

"She's cold?" Kian's head moved quickly from side to side, searching.

Zander couldn't help laughing. "She left already," he said, taking the glass from Kian's hand and turning it over, letting the liquid splatter between the planks of wood under their feet. "I think we've both had enough."

"Admit it, you actually had fun tonight."

He steadied himself on the back of a chair. "Is it that obvious I'm terrible at it?"

Kian shrugged. "I figure it's just because you're from Eirentheos. That's what everyone from there is like, isn't it?"

He laughed again; the statement seemed somehow both true and ridiculous at the same time. Certainly nobody had ever invited him to a bar in the little time he'd spent in Eirentheos. "Have you ever been there?"

"No. But Ben was from there, too, and it took us forever to talk him into coming out with us. Longer than you, even."

Stone cold sobriety hit Zander like a freight train. "You brought Ben here?"

"Well, we tried to. But he was less fun with you. He wouldn't even dance."

Of course Ben wouldn't have, Zander knew. The only time he'd lived in Philotheum was while he was engaged to Linnea, waiting to be reunited with her for their wedding. So many moons they'd been separated, and too few they'd been together.

He suddenly felt sick to his stomach, and the whiskey had nothing to do with it. Not that much, anyway. "It's late. We should be getting back."

The crowd inside had only thinned a little as he and Kian made their way back through the pub. Most of the other patrons, including the other castle guards, weren't ready to end their evening yet. However, the room had cleared just enough to give him a view of the tables he hadn't seen earlier. Including one in the far back corner.

He wouldn't have even been sure it was her; the hallway in the castle had been so dark that morning. Even though her features had burned into his mind, he wouldn't have been able to be sure. But she saw him at almost the same instant, and she fled.

One moment she was sitting there, safely enclosed in a wooden booth at a candlelit table, and the next, she was gone, somehow lost in the crowd.

He searched; all of the guards he could notify without causing a disruption searched too. Kian led several guards out to circle the building, and the surrounding areas. Fifteen minutes later, they all returned empty — just like the other morning. It was almost as if she was magic.

This time, however, she did leave a trace.

Zander found it, a folded piece of paper, ripped from a notebook, peeking out between the cushions of the bench where she'd been sitting. It was trash, scratched out and discarded notes, but as soon as he opened it, he knew she hadn't meant to leave it behind.

At least, it wasn't anything he wanted anyone to see. The writing on those lines made his heart almost stop, and he folded the paper back up quickly, shoving it in his cloak pocket and standing up. "Nothing here," he said, hoping the other guard wouldn't notice the way his voice shook.

The castle was dark and quiet by the time Kian and Zander returned.

"Do you think we should wake Her Majesty and notify her about what you saw?"

"It was the same girl, Kian. I know it was."

"Which is why I'm asking you. Is this something the queen should be aware of before morning?"

Zander sighed. "I'd prefer not to disturb her this evening if we don't have to. I'll ask the on-duty captain to have an extra sweep done before I head to bed. It's Dorian tonight, isn't it?"

"I can take care of that, if you'd prefer."

"Thank you."

He didn't know if this was the right decision. Keeping secrets about *any* sort of issue that could impact their security here wasn't exactly wise. Considering what he'd found in that booth… this wasn't just "any" small issue, either. But he didn't want to wake Quinn and William in the middle of the night. Especially when there was little they could do about it anyway. The girl was gone. Also, though he didn't want to admit it, he wasn't ready to share this information. He wasn't ready to think about what it meant.

So, ignoring what he probably *should* do right now, he left Kian to handle the details of the extra security sweep, pressed his hand protectively over the pocket where the piece of paper was, and headed up to his room.

He was wary and on high alert as he walked, so the shadowy figure in the hallway didn't startle him, but still, for a moment, his heart stopped beating when she stepped out in front of him, blocking his path.

"Where have you been?" she hissed.

All he could do was blink and stare. The image in front of him didn't make any sense. This wasn't supposed to be possible. He currently didn't even know the answer to her simple question.

Confusion and concern mixed with the blatant anger in her expression. "Is something wrong?"

"No, I… just…" Something in his brain finally clicked. "What are you doing here?"

"I *live* here. What is going on? Have you been *drinking?*"

"No, I… well, yes, but I'm not…"

"What is going on? What do you have there?"

He didn't know what she was talking about, didn't even understand what she was doing until she'd moved his hand from the spot where he'd been holding it, cradled over his pocket the whole time they were standing here. No part of his body seemed to be functioning correctly; he just kept staring at her as she reached into the pocket of his cloak and pulled out the piece of paper.

The little crinkle he was so familiar with appeared in her forehead as her gray eyes scanned the paper. The closest he came to a coherent thought was to wonder how well she could see it in the dim light from the oil lamp burning several feet away from them. And then those eyes went very, very wide. "Oh, I see," she said.

She did? Any chance she might be able to clue him in? Because he didn't see anything.

He would spend the rest of the night wondering if things might have gone better if he'd said those words out loud, but he didn't. He was still too stunned and confused to speak.

The fact that he *had* been drinking couldn't have helped any, either. His temples were beginning to pound in time with his pulse.

She shoved the paper back into his hands, turned, and disappeared back into her room.

Only then did he wonder where the babies were.

THE GIRL

"YOU THINK THE GIRL left this on the table?" William asked. "And you're sure it was the same girl you saw in the castle that night?"

Zander shrugged. "I know the girl was sitting at the table where I found this. It was the same girl. I don't know how I'm sure, but I am. Besides, if it is a different girl, that's even more concerning."

Quinn picked up the paper for the fifteenth time, her eyes poring over every inch of it, as if she'd discover something new on this reading. "I'm not sure it can get more concerning."

"No. Do you think it's real? That this girl — or whoever wrote this — actually knows something?"

"It's possible," William said. "Hang on a minute." He stood from the table and disappeared into one of the other rooms in the massive apartment.

Zander frowned at Quinn, but she didn't look confused; he suspected she knew what William was going to search for. There was nothing else to discuss about the paper right then. Or at least, that's what he told himself to justify changing the subject.

"When did Linnea decide to stay?"

The instant confusion on her face confirmed the fear that had kept him up the rest of the night pacing the floor of his room. "What do you mean? Was she planning on going somewhere?"

He was an idiot. An idiot with the kind of headache that was going to have him seeing double for the rest of the day. He shook his head gingerly, careful not to aggravate the pounding again. "Apparently not."

"What's going on, Zander? You look terrible. We couldn't find you yesterday — Linnea wanted to introduce everyone to the new wet nurse Charlotte and Rebecca hired for her. I think she might have been hoping to get a few minutes alone with you, actually. But you weren't anywhere. Now you tell me you were out drinking with the guards last night, and you come back with *this*?" She waved the paper again. "Is there anything else I should know?"

"Am I not allowed to go out and do what the other guards do on my nights off?"

Her mouth dropped open, but at that second, he couldn't bring himself to care. "Of course you are, that's not what I meant. You know that."

"Do I? That's what it sounded like you meant. That everyone else gets to have whatever social life they'd like to have here, but I'm expected to — what? Just hang around the castle to be introduced to other new servants and attend to everyone's needs and whims?"

Now she was the one staring at him, unblinking, clearly at a loss for how to respond. It didn't matter right now, though. He was angry and confused and a mysterious swirl of other emotions that were beyond his ability to handle right then.

"If you don't actually need me for anything right now, may I be dismissed? I'm still off duty until tomorrow morning."

She closed her eyes and took a deep breath. "Of course, Zander. Go and enjoy yourself, please."

Even before the door to the apartment banged closed just a little too loudly, Quinn knew she wasn't alone in the room.

"What did I miss?" William asked.

"Your guess is as good as mine. He's obviously upset about something."

"Well, this is probably enough all by itself," he said, setting a notebook on the table next to the paper Zander had left there.

"I think your sister might have something to do with it as well."

He ran his hand down her arm as he sat down in the chair next to hers. "I'm not getting involved in that, and you shouldn't, either."

"They're both hurting."

"I know. But do you think that if they just began to court it would fix all that?"

She closed her eyes. "As much as I wish it would, no."

"Don't even start wishing that would, love. If you wish it, you'll end up trying to influence it, and then you'll be doing the same thing my parents did with us."

"You're right." She sighed. "And that almost ended badly for all of us."

"Well… I like to think I'd have won you over regardless," he said, smiling in a way that made her insides warm and tingly.

"I think you might have managed it." She smiled back and reached to take his hand in hers. "But you're right about not interfering. Those two are more stubborn than we are, and we could make it so much worse."

"And I don't know if being together is what would make them truly happy, either," William said. "Especially when I look at this." He slid the notebook he'd brought out closer to her and set the paper Zander had left on top of it.

"Could this be real?" Quinn asked, studying the paper yet again.

"Of course it could. It might not be. In what little research I've been able to do since getting here to Philotheum, it's actually common for people to believe in portals between worlds. Most of them don't have any idea what the portals are like, and some people have some strange ideas about what "another world" means, but there are many people who believe it's possible."

"Yeah, well, this is a little bit more than just believing another world might exist," she said, tapping the paper.

"You're right. I don't think we can take that chance. We have to treat it like it's real."

"And a real threat. Who is this girl?"

William held up his hands. "And why would she be breaking into the castle?"

The heavy weight of dread that Quinn had been feeling all morning sank deeper into her stomach. "Do you think she knows?"

"I think we have a massive problem on our hands if she does. Even if she only managed to spread rumors about us…"

She couldn't just keep sitting here; she stood and started pacing around the sitting room. "We have to find her."

Zander had barely closed his bedroom door behind him when there was a knock on it. "What now?" he muttered. Was it really too much to ask to have an hour or two to himself in a dark room? The headache was making him feel like he hadn't slept in three nights, instead of just one.

He pulled open the door a little more roughly than he should have. Too late, it occurred to him that it might be Linnea on the other side and that his anger would only make things a hundred times worse. He was still annoyed — but relieved — when it turned out to be Kian.

"Is there something you need?"

"I just thought that I should check on you," Kian said, inviting himself inside and closing the door behind him.

"I'm fine. I don't need a mother." Neither of these statements felt like the whole truth right now, but he would stick by them if it meant being *left alone*.

"Maybe not, but I thought you might benefit from these." Kian held out a small, dark purple, glass vial. Something inside rattled when he shook it.

"What is it with you and your weird potions? William and Nathaniel are doctors, you know. I can get real medicine from them if I actually need it."

Kian frowned. "I thought His Majesty and Her Majesty's uncle were healers. What is a doctor?"

Damn it. He wasn't in the mood for this, at all. "It's a term we use in Eirentheos," he lied, ineffectively. On top of insulting Kian, he'd just officially insulted William, an offense worthy of discipline among the ranks of the guards.

He was shocked when Kian didn't press the issue. "You really look like you could use them," he said instead, popping out the cork on the vial and tipping it into his hand. "They're what Sir Nathaniel uses — I just keep a supply of them for occasions like this when it's probably best not to ask him for them." He grabbed Zander's hand and tipped the bottle upside down, shaking out three familiar white tablets.

Ibuprofen. They were the kind Nathaniel and William had learned to make themselves out of strange concoctions in a basement laboratory. They smelled funny and tasted awful for the few seconds they were on your tongue, but… Suddenly Zander wasn't quite so annoyed with Kian.

Or at least he wouldn't have been if Kian had left instead of standing there long after he'd choked down the foul pills.

"Do you need something?" he finally asked.

"I just returned from visiting the Woodhouse again."

Zander raised an eyebrow and took another sip of his water, hoping to wash the rest of the taste away.

"It's a different place during the day than it is at night. I thought I might have some luck asking around about your girl."

"My girl?"

"Turns out, she's been there a few times, and other places around the city, as well, although I only made it to one other tavern, and nobody really knew anything there. Al doesn't think she's from the city."

"There's really an Al at Al's Woodhouse?"

Apparently, it took more than a few snide comments to faze Kian. "It's a rather close crowd at Al's — people there looked out for each other during the war. They know strangers when they see them."

"Huh. I guess I assumed some of the weird looks we were getting last night were because we were castle guards."

"Not at Al's. Don't just show up at any tavern in the city if you don't want trouble. But whatever you saw last night was all about you. The elusive Sir Zander Cunningham. Personal advisor to the queen. Hero."

"Did you get some kind of bonus points for getting me there or something?"

"You think two nobs of good whiskey like that only cost one silver crown?"

It should probably annoy him that the other guards viewed him as a piece in a game, but right now there were other things on his mind. "So what else did you find out about the girl?"

"Al thinks her name is Leah. She's shown up a few times since the end of the war. Before that, he remembers seeing her once or twice, but the visits were spread far apart. If she has a family, they're not from the city. The only thing he knows about her is that she's quite interested in gate mythology."

Zander almost choked on his water. "In what?"

"You know…people who believe there are gates to other worlds and they try to find them?"

"People do what?" It was hard to breathe, and his headache was getting worse, not better.

Kian frowned, studying him for several seconds. "Are you okay?"

"Except for the lack of sleep and the headache, I'm fine." He was lucky polygraph machines didn't exist in this world. Not that he was fooling Kian, anyway. This conversation had to end, now. "Thanks for trying to find out what you could about her. Knowing her name is a start, even if you didn't learn anything else useful."

"You're welcome. I assume you'll inform Her Majesty."

It was a loaded question. Kian was very interested in how he would respond, but Zander couldn't tell *why*, didn't know what he was looking for. He felt like he was walking straight into a trap while looking right at it, but there was no way to avoid it. "Of course," he said, maintaining eye contact. "And you'll let me know if you find out anything else about this girl?"

"Right away."

His whole body felt shaky and wrong as he waited for enough time to pass between Kian leaving the room and going out into the hallway himself. Strategizing for a battle was beginning to seem easier than this. Then again, maybe that's what this was.

Whatever Kian thought, however annoyed he'd been at Quinn this morning, as soon as enough time had passed, Zander made a beeline for the master apartment.

The only mistake he made was not watching where he was going.

"Zander! What the —?"

Linnea *looked* petite, but the weight of her hand on his upper arm brought him to an instant halt, spinning him to face her.

"Sorry," he said. "I wasn't paying attention. I'm kind of in a hurry."

"What else is new?" Fire blazed in her eyes, making them look almost black. "Are we ever going to talk about what happened this morning?" The catch in her voice on the last word was so small he almost missed it. She covered it immediately, clearing her throat while continuing to stare him down. But that tiny falter changed everything, melting all his anger and annoyance.

"Linnea… I'm sorry."

"Where were you yesterday?"

"Nowhere. I just rode Ember around for most of the day, and then I was going to go to bed, but Kian found me and…I don't know how he managed it, but he talked me into going into town with some of the guards."

"You couldn't have at least *said* something? Told me where you were going?"

"I didn't think you were here."

Her mouth fell open.

Crap. He hadn't meant to admit that to her, ever.

"Where did you think I was?"

What little breakfast he'd eaten an hour ago threatened to make a reappearance. He tried to answer, but his voice wouldn't cooperate.

It only took a few seconds, anyway. Linnea was painfully astute. "You thought I was going back to Eirentheos with my parents."

"I…" Still no other words would come out.

"You didn't ask *me*. Here I am, still not even speaking to Max — I told him he'd be lucky if talked to him at Thomas's wedding because he dared to *suggest* it… He at least *asked* me, Zander! He anticipated that I'd probably say no, but he asked. But you… You just assume that's what I want? You think I'd decide something like that and not even tell you? Not even say goodbye?"

He knew he'd messed this up, probably worse than he'd messed up anything in his life before this. Even staying on this side of the gate when he knew it was closing didn't compare to this. At least then, he'd been doing something good, trying to help save someone's life. All he was doing now was hurting her. Her furious blinking confirmed just how much damage he'd done, but all he could do was stare in helpless horror.

She was about to leave. She was going to walk away, perhaps forever, and there was nothing he could do to stop her.

Before she managed it, though, they were interrupted by the too-fast sound of footsteps on the hard wood floor. Both of them turned to watch William run the last few feet.

"Where's the fire, Will?" Linnea asked, sounding for all the world like everything was normal and they hadn't just been having the worst conversation of Zander's life.

"There's something I need to show Zander," he said. "You can come, too, of course."

"Nothing like being *everyone's* afterthought," Linnea muttered under her breath. Zander could tell that William didn't hear her. Despite her words, she followed her brother back down the hall and into Zander's room.

Once they were in, William closed and locked the door behind them and walked all the way to the other side of the room before laying out a cracked leather notebook and the paper Zander had given him this morning. Then he cleared his throat. "After you showed those notes to us, I realized that you had never seen this," he said, opening the notebook.

Linnea sucked in a breath, but when Zander looked at her, he could tell that she had seen this before, whatever it was.

"Tobias gave this notebook to me when we were staying at his house. It's something I should have remembered before now, because it is something we should investigate, but it took you finding this paper for me to really think about it." He flipped carefully through the yellow pages until he found what he was searching for, and then laid it open in front of Zander and Linnea.

"What is that? A picture of a river?" Zander asked.

"Not just a river." William traced part of the drawing with his index finger, stopping just where the water curved around a bend next to a large tree. "We believe that this, right here, is the place where you entered this world. The drawing doesn't show the bridge, so it may be older than the structure."

"Wait. That's the gate?" Zander had to clasp his fingers together to keep from grabbing the notebook to flip through the rest of the pages himself. "Is this a book that tells how to use it? Or where other gates are?" Trepidation coursed through every inch of him, but that feeling wasn't nearly as disconcerting as the other emotion dancing around the edges — hope.

"We don't know exactly," William said. "There's only one other page in the book that might have anything to do with the gates, but it doesn't really tell us anything."

"Probably because at least half of it is missing." Linnea reached for the book.

"What do you mean, missing?" But by the time he had the words out, he understood — and his stomach was flipping in ways it wasn't designed to.

Linnea had the ancient book open to another page. This one showed a drawing of a different river, but she was right. Half of it was missing. Originally, the drawing had spanned two pages, but now there was only one page and a ragged edge where others had been ripped out. "We don't have any idea where the missing pages of this book are," she said. "For all we know, they've been destroyed."

"No, they haven't," Zander said. Two pairs of gray eyes snapped up to meet his. "I've seen that river, the other half of that drawing."

"How? Where?" William sounded as shocked as he felt.

"Right here, in this room. Just the other day. I was going through this cabinet over here..." He walked over to the large window seat and knelt to open the cabinet underneath. When he reached his hand in, though, there was nothing there. After a brief second of panic, he remembered. "That's right. I took them out. I was going to show the pages to you when I had the chance. I thought they were interesting, but not *that* interesting. I didn't think they were a map to a gate."

Linnea and William both followed him as he crossed the room, to where the junk had been piled on — and then cleared from — the couch. "It probably got moved," he said. "Someone was in here cleaning up the other night."

"What are we looking for?" William asked. "Papers?"

"Yes, a stack of papers."

Linnea frowned. "There aren't papers around here anywhere."

Maybe because he didn't want to understand, he joined the two of them in searching under every chair and table for several minutes before he allowed the truth to dawn on him.

No amount of ibuprofen in any world would be enough to cover *this* headache.

"It's gone. It was here, the night of the party the night that…" He glanced at Linnea, the image of her crying in her bed with the babies burning into his mind. *The night I saw that girl in the hallway.*"

William collapsed into a chair. "In light of you discovering *this* in her possession," he said, picking up the paper he'd found at the pub last night, "I think it's safe to assume this is what she was after — and she must have gotten it."

Zander nodded, looking over the paper again. He held it up to the page in the notebook, comparing the writing on the two. "Some of these numbers match," he said, pointing. He'd seen the numbers on the paper repeatedly last night and this morning, but they hadn't seemed to make sense.

"Who *is* this girl?" Linnea asked, sounding irritated. *At least it's not all directed at me,* Zander thought. Or hoped, anyway.

"Someone who might have all the information she needs to find another gate," William said. "If she knows what she's looking at."

"I'll bet she does," Zander said. "I was actually on my way to talk to you and Quinn. Kian Mondragon found out that her name is

Leah. She's a stranger in this area, but she's been asking around for stories of people who believe in gates. I didn't know that was a thing here, but apparently, it is."

"Believing in them is one thing," William said. "A lot of people do. But having the directions to find one…"

"Do you think another one really exists? That if we had the directions, we could go there and use it?" That small hint of excitement should not have been creeping into his voice, Zander knew. But he couldn't quite squash all of it.

"We need to find this girl," William said. "That's the only way we're going to get answers. Right now we don't even know if there is another gate."

Zander bent over the book, studying the page again. "But this looks like it's a good possibility."

"I need to go check on the babies," Linnea said, and the next instant she was gone; the door closed behind her just a little too hard.

William's eyes darted between the door and Zander. "Did you want to…?"

"What? Follow her and make things even worse?"

"Is that what you think will happen?"

He picked up the folded paper the girl had left again, though he wasn't really looking at it. "Who's with the babies, anyway? Quinn said something about hiring someone?"

"Um… Yes. My mother and Rebecca spent a couple of days before they left interviewing wet nurses. They found a nice young woman; she's a few cycles older than Linnea. Her name is Elisa."

"Wet nurse… is that what it sounds like?"

"Someone who can help with the babies enough to actually allow Linnea to sleep sometimes or even go out for the day. It wasn't easy to get her to agree or to trust someone, even knowing that the person would be working under close supervision."

"I'll bet." Zander was feeling guiltier by the moment for the way he'd avoided Linnea the last couple of weeks, though he still didn't know whether his presence would have been welcome.

"But then they found Elisa. She has one child, a baby girl five moons old — and she was widowed during the war."

Zander swallowed hard; he didn't know what else to say.

"I'm sure you'll have a chance to meet her soon. Perhaps later today."

"Oh, I don't think Linnea's going to be introducing me to anyone *today*."

For several minutes, they were both silent, poring over the page and the notebook. Zander still wasn't sure how to interpret the notes on the page, but it was clearly about travel between the worlds, including several lines about the time differences. "This doesn't seem right," he finally said. "One day in the other world is equal to ten here."

"*About* ten," William said, without looking up. "It can be off at different times in the cycle — you can't correlate it exactly. There are times in the cycle the gate we know about in Eirentheos opens every nine or eleven days. Or, it used to, anyway." He slid the paper away from Zander. "If I'm reading this correctly, I think the gate it's discussing opens on a different schedule — maybe only once a moon."

"What does that mean on the other side?"

"Could mean lots of things. Could mean there's a gate there that only opens every two or three days. Could mean it's a gate that leads somewhere else entirely."

"Like… not Earth?"

"Maybe."

The bubble of hope that had been inflating the edges of his anxiety over this discovery suddenly popped, tightening everything in his chest and throat. "You think there are more than two worlds?"

"I don't know. I think it's outside anyone's comprehension that there are two, but since there *are* two, I don't think three is a stretch."

"Why not a hundred?"

"Or a thousand," William said, sighing. "I don't know what any of this means, besides *danger*. We need to find this girl."

"Any ideas about how we do that? I've tried searching for her twice now, but she just disappears. Maybe there's a gate somewhere on the castle grounds, and that's where she's going."

William folded his hands and rested his chin on them. "Why would she risk sneaking into the castle to get those pages if she already knew where a gate was?"

"I was joking."

"Are you all right, Zander?"

The question seemed to come out of nowhere. He was unprepared for it, which was probably why he answered it honestly. "Not really. I have a headache, and I haven't slept, and there's this paper and this notebook and this girl, and Linnea… Sorry. I'll be fine once I've had a nap, I think."

"You think a nap is going to help you with my sister?"

"Maybe I at least won't think about it while I'm asleep." Apparently, his filter was completely broken at this point.

William stood and paced around the table, looking like he couldn't decide what to say. Zander couldn't blame him. He didn't know, either.

"Look," William finally said, "I swore I would stay out of this — and I *am*, mostly. But I think maybe I should give this to you." He reached into his pocket and pulled out something too small for Zander to see.

He frowned, but before he could say anything, William held his hand over the table and dropped something tiny and gold. It clattered and spun for a second before settling. A coin.

"I don't need money, Will. And Linnea is not the kind of girl who can be bought for anything — even if I was the kind of guy to try."

William didn't laugh. "Off his game" didn't begin to describe Zander's day today. "It's not money," William said, pushing the coin across the table toward him. The metal-on-wood noise made him grit his teeth, so he scooped it up quickly and held it in his palm.

"What is it then?"

"It's just a coin. It's got a picture of a thorn on one side and a dandelion seed on the other. It's not really worth anything, but it has meaning to some people."

He studied each side of the coin, wondering why William would show it to him in the context of this conversation. "What does it mean to Linnea?"

William sat down again in the seat next to him. "In my family, the thorn represents the adversity one must go through sometimes to get to the beauty in a relationship — the 'rose'. The dandelion seed represents what happens when you avoid the difficulties, when you neglect to pull the weeds while they're still small and manageable. Eventually, they take over everything."

"Interesting." He rubbed his thumb over the etching of the dandelion seed. "My mom always said she loved dandelions. She didn't call them weeds; she said they were flowers that could survive anything you throw at them. No matter what, they always manage, not just to survive, but to cheer up a place with their color." Once the words were out of his mouth, his cheeks grew a little warm. "I guess that was sort of the opposite of your point."

William shrugged. "Symbols can have different meanings to different people. It's more about how you use the symbol than anything." He paused, his eyes boring into Zander's in a way that made him shift in his chair. "But if you're going to side with the dandelion…shouldn't you be thriving in your circumstances and doing what you can to cheer up the place with your color?"

If "color" was referring to his neck, then he was definitely lighting up the room with a vivid hue at the moment, but if William noticed, he ignored it. "Anyway, thanks," Zander said, pushing the coin back across the table. "I get it — sort of, anyway."

"You're just not sure you're going to listen to any of it, right?"

"Listen to what? The advice you're not supposed to be giving me about the situation you shouldn't be involved in?"

"Yeah, that," William said, snorting. He picked up the little coin and studied it for a second, then held it out toward Zander. "You should keep this. Pretend we never had this conversation, but…keep this."

He held up a hand and shook his head. "That's much too important to you and Quinn for me to keep."

"We have more."

Zander raised an eyebrow.

"Quinn and I are both prone to distraction and we lose little things. We keep our 'important' set of coins in a small box, but the ones we keep in our pockets… let's just say we have a stash of those." He set the coin down on the table in front of Zander.

"You two are weirder than I thought." He stood as he picked the tiny gold piece back up and placed it in William's hand. "And I think we've got more pressing concerns to worry about at the moment."

William didn't argue or change the subject this time as he looked back down at the piece of paper.

NATHANIEL

THEY NEEDED TO FIND the girl. That was really all there was to it. The kingdom would be in danger and their questions would go unanswered until they found her. Or until they found the gate, he supposed. But if she had those papers now, then they weren't going to find the gate without her, either.

It became an obsession. Over the next days, the quest to find the girl, this *Leah,* began to occupy all of his waking hours, and even some of the ones he probably should have been sleeping through.

He found himself at Al's Woodhouse on more than a couple of nights, although he only socialized in an attempt to subtly draw information out of people. Most nights, he would end up alone at a table along the back wall, using Choice cards to play his own version of Solitaire. Here, he could listen.

After nearly two weeks of absolutely nothing, he was beginning to feel hopeless. No matter how many conversations he participated in or eavesdropped in, the name Leah never came up.

He did learn that Kian had been correct. There were people who believed *something* about gates and other worlds. Or, perhaps more accurately, people once had. Although his stomach had lurched the first couple of times he heard someone mention "gates" or "another world", he quickly realized that it wasn't something most people took seriously. People didn't *believe* in gates here anymore than people in his world *believed* in horoscopes or Greek gods. But still, the terminology and stories were common enough knowledge that they came up in conversation. He didn't believe in star signs, but still he knew that he was a "Taurus."

There were people doing it at the table next to him that night — Zander was listening to one young man teasing another that the girl by the bar was "not from his world" when his concentration was shattered by someone sitting down in the seat across from him.

The cards he'd been shuffling flew everywhere.

"I'm sorry. I didn't mean to startle you. I thought you saw me." It was Nathaniel, whom he hadn't seen in weeks.

"It's fine, you didn't," he mumbled, rescuing a card that was teetering on the edge of his glass. "I'm a little surprised to see you here…but you're welcome to join me," he finished quickly.

Nathaniel ducked under the table and emerged a few seconds later with three cards in his hand. As he was helping Zander gather the rest, a waitress set a drink on the table in front of him, and Nathaniel handed her a gold coin. Then he looked at Zander sheepishly. "I suppose I should have waited for you to invite me. Did you really want to be alone?"

Zander raised an eyebrow. "I'd almost never *rather* be sitting alone at a bar late at night."

"And yet…"

"It's not like there are many people I can invite to come sit here and eavesdrop with me."

Nathaniel didn't bat an eye at his admission of eavesdropping, even though he hadn't told anyone that was what he was doing here. "Particularly when you're not showing up to meals or spending much time in the castle around people who might understand."

He swallowed. "You're not always around either."

"It wasn't a criticism, Zander. Just an observation — commiseration, even, from someone else who often ignores his relationships with others in favor of pursuing his projects."

Zander began shuffling the cards in front of him again, trying to decide how he felt about this. "It seems to have worked out all right for you."

They were both quiet as Nathaniel took a long sip of his drink. Then, he reached over and took the deck of cards from Zander, cut it, and then began dealing cards to both of them. "I suppose that depends upon how you look at it," he finally said. "I have visited many places and accomplished a lot of things. But it has cost me, Zander. Nobody wants to marry a man so caught up in his own interests that he's always away."

He almost dropped the cards again, though this time he managed to cover his surprise with a cough. "But… you are getting married."

A sinking feeling in his stomach grew into a gaping hole as Nathaniel blinked back at him.

"Because you're not around enough?" he asked once the answer became painfully obvious.

"Among other reasons, I imagine. She's a kind woman; she didn't enumerate her list of my faults, although I've no doubt it's lengthy. She deserves more."

The once-once cozy wooden booth suddenly felt cold. "When did this happen?"

"Honestly? Decades ago, when I decided to be a world-jumping healer. It was quite unfair of me to pretend that I could ever be the sort of man who stays in one place and has a family."

Zander quickly scanned the room around them, hoping fervently that nobody had overheard the world-hopper bit. Days of eavesdropping had made him vigilant about anyone overhearing him in return. Nathaniel seemed unconcerned, but Zander tried to keep the discussion on the other topic. "Were you really pretending?"

"For a while? To myself as much as to her, but yes. Quinn had just become queen, there was to be no more traveling to..." This time he made a meaningful face, and Zander relaxed a little. At least he was being discreet now. "I thought I could do it. Enjoy my role as a prince, stay near the castle most of the time, become a husband and a father. William has managed it beautifully — flourished with it. I just don't think I'm built that way."

"And she didn't understand that?"

Nathaniel frowned. "Why should she? That isn't what she thought she was agreeing to. I was the unfair one in the situation."

"You're a good man. You deserve to have someone."

The look Nathaniel gave him across the table was one he'd remember for the rest of his life. It was like an arrow aimed into the center of his very being. "Nobody *deserves* to 'have' another person, Zander. A relationship isn't some kind of prize you win for saying the right things or buying flowers or even being a good person. She doesn't owe me something just because I was nice to her when I bothered to be around."

Zander stared at his cards, attempting to process Nathaniel's words. "Do you think there are some people who are just never meant to get married?"

"I didn't say that." Nathaniel turned over the top card on the draw pile. "I think if someday I were to meet someone who wants the same things I do, whose life was more journey than destination, like mine is, it might be different."

The whole conversation was making Zander's head spin with questions and thoughts he'd never before considered, but he wasn't sure how to put any of his thoughts to words, especially not words he was ready to share with Nathaniel. So he concentrated instead on whether he wanted to steal the card on the top of the pile.

"Anyway," Nathaniel said, after Zander had decided to discard instead. "That's not what either of us came here for tonight." He picked up the card Zander had just laid down and then spread his entire hand out on the table, winning the hand.

Zander groaned and began scooping the cards up for another round, but Nathaniel held his hand out over the cards. "Any chance you'd take a walk with me instead?"

Outside, the full moon made the sky nearly as bright as morning, though still Zander could see more stars than he'd ever imagined existed — which was saying something. Before coming to this world, he'd believed that light pollution wasn't a serious issue for Bristlecone.

"So, are you making any progress finding out about the girl or the gate?"

He shook his head. "No, nothing." He took a few minutes to tell Nathaniel about the few things he had overheard, and his realization that "gate" stories were a lot like astrology in the world he'd come from.

Nathaniel laughed. "I never really thought of it that way." Then, mid-chuckle, he suddenly stopped, and his eyes grew wide. "You know there are really people who believe in that stuff in your world, Zander."

"Does that matter? None of it is true."

Nathaniel held up one finger, then pressed it to his mouth, his forehead scrunching as he thought. "Maybe it doesn't matter…over there."

A shiver ran down Zander's spine. "But over here…it is true."

"Exactly. And who are the people over there who know the most about it?"

The bright circle of the moon almost felt like a literal lightbulb over their heads. For a second, anyway. "One problem."

"What's that?"

"The people I'm talking about *here* don't actually believe it. They're just talking."

"Maybe so. But that isn't the problem you've been assuming it is — with all of your hushed whispers and wishing we'd take the conversation outside."

The lightbulb was back. "You think we could just ask people to point us to the nearest…whatever the equivalent to astrologist is."

"Something like that. We could probably do exactly that if both of us weren't so well-known, but I think if we got away from the city, traveled to smaller areas to listen to people and their stories…"

"Are you suggesting I do that?"

"Actually…" Nathaniel rubbed at the back of his neck. "Yes. I am. And I was wondering if I could join you."

Nathaniel didn't waste time. They spent the rest of that night talking, a day packing and preparing for the journey, and the morning after that, Zander found himself up before the sun, standing in the hallway dressed in traveling clothes and wearing a single sturdy leather pack.

Linnea's door was closed. They'd barely talked over the last couple of weeks, and he hadn't even had the chance to tell her he was leaving. He wasn't sure she even wanted to really talk to him, not after the way he'd acted about her leaving.

Then he thought about the coin William had left with him, even after his protests. Perhaps he should try?

He made it as far as her door, hand in the air to knock. But it was *so quiet* in there. No babies crying, no movement. She wouldn't appreciate all of them being woken up so that he could…what was he going to say, anyway? Now Nathaniel's choice played in his head. Those babies in there weren't his — they were Ben's. He'd had no business taking an interest in Ben's wife in the first place. And now he was leaving to go running off all over the kingdom, leaving her here alone. He wasn't good for her. He needed to take a step back and let them be.

He put his hand down.

Quinn knocked on the door as quietly as she could, hoping she wouldn't accidentally wake a sleeping baby. But when Linnea answered, she could see that it wouldn't have been a concern. The twins were both laying on blankets on top of the bed, gurgling and kicking their feet.

She smiled and carried Samuel over, setting him down on the bed, too, though a couple feet away from his cousins.

"That won't last," Linnea said, laughing as Samuel immediately pushed himself into crawling position and made his way toward the nearest baby, which happened to be Adeline.

"Be careful, Samuel," Quinn said. "Gentle with the babies."

Linnea snickered. "He's a baby himself. He doesn't know what that means."

But he seemed to. Although he headed toward Adeline at a full barrel, as soon as he reached her, he stopped and sat, then stretched his hand toward her ever so carefully, resting his tiny palm just where her downy hair met her forehead.

"Oooh!" he cooed.

"That's right, Sam," Linnea said. "She's soft, isn't she?"

"Oooh!" he said again.

After a couple of minutes, Samuel tired of the stationary newborns, and Quinn lifted him down to the floor where he promptly headed for the basket of toys Linnea kept for him.

"Have these two let you sleep at all?"

Linnea nodded. "It's been a lot easier since we hired Elisa. I'm not sure what I was thinking, though, having two babies."

Quinn wanted to laugh, but she couldn't. She knew Linnea loved Benjamin and Adeline more than anything, and that she wouldn't have traded them for anything in any world — but two infants all on her own was more than Linnea had ever been prepared to handle.

Quinn didn't think she could have done it. Maybe not even with William. Not now. Just as she thought this, Benjamin's gurgles turned into fussing noises, so she hurried to scoop him up off the bed. He still didn't quiet, so she kissed his miniature nose and stood up to walk with him a bit. "So," she said, "Zander and Nathaniel left yesterday morning."

"Mmm-hmm." Adeline was still happy, but Linnea seemed to suddenly need to check her diaper.

"Are we going to talk about that?"

"What is there to talk about?" The diaper didn't look wet or soiled to Quinn, but Linnea was undressing Adeline, pulling off the diaper and digging in a nearby basket for another one. Apparently the diapers on the top of the stack weren't the right ones. "They're off riding around the kingdom or something. It doesn't have anything to do with me."

Quinn looked at baby Benjamin and rolled her eyes. He closed his in return. "I thought you two were…getting along rather well before."

"Zander and I get along just fine, Quinn. We're not fighting or anything. He's off doing his thing; I'm here doing mine. I'm not sure what you're getting at."

The baby in her arms hadn't opened his eyes again. Quinn almost had to smile at the fact that it was *this* tone in his mother's voice that comforted and lulled him to sleep. She carried him across the room to the large wooden cradle where both infants slept, snuggled together usually. Then she turned her attention back to her sister. "There's no way you would let me get away with what you're trying to get away with Linnea. I'm not going anywhere until you actually talk to me."

She waited for the comeback. Linnea was always able to snap back immediately with the perfect response. But this time, it didn't happen. She was quiet as she finally selected the right diaper, and then a new knitted-wool cover and re-dressed her daughter. Then she sat down in the rocking chair next to the bed and began to feed her. "There's nothing to say, Quinn. He's incredible; I won't deny that. I'd say that I don't know why you chose William over him, but…well, I get that. You're you. Even so, Zander was a good choice."

"So he's a good man. What's the problem, then?"

Linnea's eyes drifted down to the baby in her arms and then over to the cradle, lingering for a moment before she turned them back to Quinn.

"What? You think he doesn't like Adeline and Benjamin?"

"Of course I don't think that. He's wonderful with them, too. But right now, he's out doing what an unattached man his age *should* be doing. Traveling the kingdom, having adventures…"

And then there was the part Linnea wasn't saying. "And looking for a gate."

"Yeah. And looking for a gate. A gate that would lead to his actual world, Quinn. The place he came from. Where his actual family is. Where there aren't wars and strange diseases and responsibilities that he never asked for."

Quinn had to sit down. It hadn't been real to her, this idea that there might actually be another gate somewhere back to her world. It was too much, really, to think about. Too much hope for something that was probably impossible. "They're probably not even going to find a gate, you know."

"That doesn't matter. That's not what it's about. He didn't choose this — not any of this. He didn't choose for Ben to get him stuck in this world and then *die*. He didn't choose to have babies at eighteen. I mean, that's not very old even in this world — but for *him*?"

"You're right, Nay. If he was in the other world, he would never even be considering babies at this age, or marriage or any of it. That's absolutely true. I wouldn't either, though. And look at me."

"Even if you were with William over there?"

"No. Definitely not. That's the thing, though. I'm not in that world. I'm in this one. And so is Zander. Why are you deciding for him what he does and doesn't want? Shouldn't he be the one to decide that?"

Linnea made a sweeping gesture toward the window. "Isn't that what he's doing?"

Quinn closed her eyes, trying to reiterate her promise to herself not to get involved in their relationship. She shouldn't have brought it up. She was only causing trouble. And yet, she couldn't help herself. Linnea was so... Quinn hadn't ever seen her like this. Usually, her sister was so self-assured and confident. Before all of this, Linnea would never have had a problem going after anything she wanted. And Quinn had seen it. Zander was on that list.

"Linnea... What is this actually about? Why are you just letting him run off like that and not saying anything?"

"I didn't make him leave."

"No, you didn't. But you didn't ask him to stay, either. And it's not like he left forever. It isn't as if he's never coming back."

"You don't know that."

"Nay... What is this really about?" This time, her voice was quiet as she asked, and she sat down on the side of the bed, facing Linnea, only a few inches away from her. "What's going on?"

Linnea was quiet for a long time. Her bottom lip shook a bit as she rocked and fed her daughter. But Quinn was patient. She just sat there and waited, until the baby fell asleep. Until the tiny little hand fell away from her mother and she was out.

Quinn stood and picked up the baby, wrapping her up in a soft white blanket and then laying her down in the crib next to her brother.

Samuel was still content, chewing on the ear of a stuffed bunny over by the toy basket.

She sat down across from Linnea again, this time making eye contact and refusing to break it until she finally spoke.

"Am I a terrible person, Quinn?"

A wave of shock rippled through Quinn's chest. "What? Why would you even ask that?"

Linnea leaned forward in the rocking chair until her elbows were touching her knees and her chin was propped on her hands.

She glanced over at the cradle. "I only just married Ben. We were barely even together, ever. We weren't together when we were courting, and then how long were we actually married? Five minutes? Long enough for me to get pregnant is all. And now, I just had his babies, and I'm kissing another man. What kind of wife am I?"

Linnea wasn't crying, although Quinn didn't understand how, because hot tears threatened at the corners of *her* eyes, and there was nothing in the way of them starting to fall. She reached instinctively for the embroidered handkerchief in her pocket.

She had to swallow hard several times before she cleared her throat and could speak, and when she did, her voice shook, because she was positive that any answer she could give was going to be the wrong one.

"I think that's the thing, Linnea. You're not a wife at all."

Now Linnea's cheeks sunk in as she bit the insides of her cheeks.

"In my world, the wedding vows say 'until death do us part'... and you did." Images of William flashed in front of her eyes, and the impact of what it would mean if something happened to him made her whole body feel heavy. But she and William had talked about this before. When they were in the middle of a war, they'd had to. And there had been twice now, once for him and once for her, where they'd had to actually consider the possibility.

It was only because she'd had these conversations with her own husband that she had any idea what to say to Linnea now — although how it would go... She was taking her chances. "You know that my real father died when I was very young... my mom, sometimes we used to talk about that. She went through what you're feeling, I think, when she met Jeff and then decided to marry him.

"She said something once that I don't think I can ever forget. She said that all marriages come to an end. Bad ones, of course, end by choice, but even good marriages are meant to end. And if you're lucky enough, if you do marriage the right way, then it ends how yours did. It's just part of being human. So you weren't a bad wife, Linnea. You did everything right. You won the marriage game. That's something to be proud of, not tear yourself apart over."

Tears flowed freely down both of their faces now. Quinn's handkerchief lay abandoned in her lap.

"It wasn't supposed to be like this," Linnea said. "It wasn't supposed to be when he was nineteen. It wasn't supposed to be before our children ever even got to meet him."

Quinn nodded. "You're right. That's not how anyone imagines it. That's not the sunshine-and-roses version of marriage. But that doesn't make you a terrible person, Nay. It just makes you the victim of a tragedy, and there's not a wrong way to deal with it. Do you think Ben wanted you to be alone forever?"

She lowered her eyes and picked at a piece of string on her pants. "Did you know that before he died, Ben asked Zander to take care of me?"

"Yes."

"I'm not sure he meant for me to kiss Zander, though."

"I think he meant for you to be happy, Linnea. For you to have the life he wanted to give you but couldn't. I don't think he would care whether you kiss Zander or not. I think he just wanted you to be happy. If kissing Zander doesn't make you happy, then don't do it. But you're not honoring Ben by avoiding something that does make you happy. Not at all. Did it make you happy to kiss Zander?"

Linnea sighed and stared at her hands, but eventually she nodded. "At least it did at the time."

"And then what? I don't think this is all about Ben."

Linnea sighed and stood, pacing back and forth between the rocking chair and the window, bending down to hand Samuel another toy, rubbing his soft black hair. Then she wandered near the cradle again.

"Did you know I told Ben that I didn't want to have children right away?"

Quinn gulped and shook her head.

"I mean, I wanted them. I wanted to be a mother, I always have. But...first I wanted Ben. We barely had any time together when we were courting — he was here in Philotheum, and I was in Eirentheos. I'd only ever even been out of the kingdom for your wedding. I wanted...a little while, you know? To have adventures, maybe, like everyone else got to. I was excited about getting married and moving to Philotheum, about seeing and doing new things for a little while."

She couldn't blame her at all. Linnea had grown up watching William and even Thomas take trips to the other world and all over Eirentheos while she'd remained at home most of the time. And even when Quinn had entered their lives, dragging them all into kidnappings and intrigue and wars, Linnea had still been on the sidelines for most of it. For the good parts, anyway. "What did Ben think?"

"He agreed. He wanted what would make me happy. We talked about it a lot. He said that even if we did have a child before I was ready, he would make sure that didn't stop me from getting to see and do new things. He promised we'd have adventures anyway. But we definitely didn't plan for...this. Not right away."

Quinn looked over at her son, who was playing happily on the floor, and she thought about how this morning, like most mornings, it had been William who'd cared for their son. He'd gotten up with Samuel and the sunrise, brought the baby to her to feed, but then she'd gone back to sleep and William had taken him out and around the castle. Most mornings, she knew they went down to the stables to say hello to the horses, but she didn't know what they'd done today for sure. She'd slept and then met with Marcus and Charles. She hadn't even seen William and Samuel again until nearly lunch time.

And now she got it. The thing that Linnea was feeling, but would never say out loud. The thing Linnea would likely not admit to even if Quinn could figure out how to put it into words.

"You know you're not alone, Linnea. And neither are Benjamin and Adeline. All three of you are surrounded here by people who love you. You don't have to do this as if you're alone. You don't have to give up on the idea of having adventures and seeing things just because these little blessings decided to pop into our family without a formal invitation."

"They're not anyone's responsibility besides mine, Quinn."

"Don't be ridiculous, Linnea Jane. Of course they are. You have two brothers right here in the castle who would do anything for any of you, and you have me. We're your family. And besides…we do have a really fantastic baby nurse and now a wet nurse, too. I'm not going to tell you what to do. Whatever you decide with Zander or doing the things you want to do… don't let guilt make your choices for you." She grabbed Linnea's shoulder and turned her so they were facing each other, then gave her the biggest hug she could.

"You are still here. I still can't believe I got lucky enough to have you for a sister. And you haven't done anything wrong, just because your life looks different than you expected it to. Ben's death didn't stop your life, and having these beautiful children certainly didn't. I don't know if Zander's the right guy. But you're the right girl. Start doing what you want to do again. The rest… Well, the rest will do what it's supposed to do."

VISITORS

LET'S TRAVEL AROUND TO the villages, I said. It'll be fun I said, Zander thought as he carried another stack of blankets outside into the cold night. He dumped the whole pile into a giant iron cauldron suspended over a fire, trying not to think about witches and potions as he did so.

The ghostly white shapes of blankets and sheets drying on the lines and fences around the small yard didn't help.

As he turned to go back up the steps, something else hanging from one of the lines caught his eye. A tiny naked rag doll hanging up next to its clothes. He couldn't help it; he stopped and went over to see if the thing had managed to dry in the cool weather. It had, so he carefully pulled the doll and the tiny pants and shirt down from the line. Its hair had seen better days, and one of its stitched eyes had come loose. Both black eyes had bled dark blue dye all down the doll's face while it was being boiled.

He sighed as he carried it inside and over to the bed of the child to whom it belonged.

She was silent as she took the doll from him, her brown eyes traveling over every inch of the thing before she set it down gently on the quilt in front of her and began slipping its arms through the tiny shirt. "He's all clean now?"

"Yes. He got all washed and dried outside. We could fix his eyes."

She blinked and ran a finger over the streaks and the frayed thread. "I can sew it. He won't make my family sick?"

Zander swallowed back the lump in his throat. He probably shouldn't have brought the doll back in here. "He might need washed again once you're all the way better. I just thought you might like to have the company tonight."

"Maybe my mother will bring me some buttons once she can come back in here. I thought he should have button eyes anyway."

He tried to smile, but the corners of his lips wouldn't go up all the way. "I'm sure she will. Actually, I bet I could even track down some buttons for you." *He had plenty of extra shirts.* "Now, did you finish your soup?" He nodded toward the wooden bowl on the nightstand.

"I'm just not that hungry." As if to prove her point, the little girl dissolved into a fit of coughing that lasted several minutes. It took Nathaniel coming over with a breathing treatment made from some kind of boiled herbs to get her to finally stop. Once she did, she fell asleep almost immediately, exhausted. Zander didn't like the pale blue coloring of her hands and lips.

"Do you have any idea what this is?" he asked Nathaniel once they were back outside with the laundry, out of earshot.

"I do have an idea, although I hope I'm wrong. I need to take some blood and send it back to William, to see if he can analyze it. All I know is that we'd better hope there aren't any women in the village who go into labor and come here."

They were in a small village called Yellowtree, in a region of the kingdom that had been a stronghold of support for Quinn during the war. Lured here by news that the village's resident healer, who was also the midwife, had a sick daughter, Zander and Nathaniel had been greeted at the village entrance as heroes.

Sir Zander and Prince Nathaniel, come to bring the queen's greetings and thanks to the men in the village who'd fought for her. A war hero and a healer famous for curing impossible illnesses, come to help a poorly little girl.

"It's really that contagious, then?"

"If it is what I think it is, yes."

"And you think us wearing masks is enough?" Zander asked, picking up the large wooden stick to stir the boiling laundry. "For you and I, I mean?" Overall, they were doing far more than wearing masks. Maria, the little girl, had been moved into the front room of the house, and then they'd sealed it off. Nobody was allowed in or out except Nathaniel and Zander, who only went through the front door and out into the yard. Everything in the house that could be had been thrown into the cauldron, and boiled until no germs could possibly have survived.

"If it's what I think it is, then you and I won't catch it. We're at a rather…unique advantage."

Zander frowned, about to ask more questions, but then he saw why Nathaniel was speaking so cryptically. The midwife had just come around the edge of the house and was watching them.

"Can't I please go in to see her?" she said. "She has to be lonely and…"

"She's asleep now, Johanna," Nathaniel said gently. "And she's all right for now. But I'm not going to tell you that you can't see her. It's just that if you do…"

"I can't go back to the other side to cook and to see my son. And I can't go and deliver any babies if I need to."

"Right."

"I don't understand this. How could I get someone else sick?"

Nathaniel had explained germs to her several times already. It had never occurred to Zander how absurd it sounded to someone who hadn't grown up with the knowledge. Johanna had understood dirt. Midwives were quite good about keeping things clean here in this world. But not because they believed there were tiny living things that could move between objects and between humans and make them sick.

Patiently, though, Nathaniel explained it again. "I have a special tool back at the castle I can use to actually see the germs," he said. "If you would like, sometime, I'd love to have you there to look at it and see for yourself. Once Maria is better."

"She'll get better?"

This time the lump in Zander's throat felt like it stretched all the way up his face, making his eyes and nose burn.

"I will do everything I can."

"There aren't any women in the village close to delivery. I can just declare myself closed. There's a healer in Yew who can handle emergencies. I just need to be with her."

"You know that you could get sick, too?"

"So could the pair of you, from the sounds of it, and yet here you are, risking yourselves for my little girl. I just need to be with her."

"As I said, I certainly won't stop you. You'll likely both sleep a bit easier tonight. We can get you a bed set up with the clean sheets and get you a mask as well. It's not a guarantee, but it will help."

"Why are you so willing to take the risk, if it's so dangerous? You know a little boy died last moon in Yew and it was probably this sickness."

Zander's mouth fell open, but Nathaniel didn't look surprised. "Yes, I've spoken to the healer there. He said that little boy had classic grey throat."

Johanna's chin shook as she nodded.

"Now, Maria doesn't have that symptom yet, so we can hope that's not it. And I have some treatments no other healer does, even if it is. However, back in the other kingdom, Sir Zander and I both have had doses of a special medicine that keeps you from ever getting grey throat."

Johanna gasped, which was lucky, because it covered up the surprised noise that Zander made. He didn't know what Nathaniel was talking about. He'd certainly never had any such thing in Eirentheos. Although he did note Nathaniel's careful use of language. He hadn't *said* Eirentheos.

"Such a medicine exists? Can you send for it for my little girl?"

"Unfortunately, no." The sadness in Nathaniel's voice was so profound it would have been impossible not to trust him. "I…lost my supply and haven't been able to get what I need to make more. Also, the particular medicine only works before one ever becomes ill. If I had some right now, I would administer it to you and your husband and your other children. But it wouldn't help Maria, not now."

Now Zander understood. Grey throat must have some other name in his world, and he would have been vaccinated against it as a child.

More than ever, they needed to find a gate.

"What if we never find the gate?" Nathaniel asked as he unfolded a blanket and set it down next to the fire. Zander looked up from tending the small flame to stare at him. "That could still happen. Even if this thing with Leah pans out and we find the place where she's been hiding — she could have been wrong, all along. There might not be a gate where she thinks there is one. Even if there once was, it might not still be a portal back to your world."

Zander frowned, poking at the fire with a long stick. "Did you think I don't realize that?"

"Realizing something and being prepared for it aren't always the same thing. A potential gate is a threat, sure. But only in theory. We're not being attacked. And yet, from the moment you became aware that it was a real possibility, you've been relentless. I'm still not sure why you agreed to camp out in the wilderness with me and follow me into strange towns when you could be enjoying life back at the castle. And even before I suggested this trip, you were spending all your time looking for the slightest possibility of a clue. It just makes me wonder what your hopes are."

Zander began digging in the food bag for something to begin preparing, now that they had a fire. They had just restocked their supplies in Yellowtree — their food at least. They were considerably lighter on medical supplies than they had been at the beginning of their journey, though.

At first, Zander had felt tricked, like his search for Leah and a gate was only an excuse for Nathaniel to have his help for his own pet projects. After their time in Yellowtree, though he'd come to understand just how much Nathaniel wished to be able to restock in the other world. There was a small part of him that wondered if Nathaniel was *too* attached to being able to travel between Earth and Deusterros, if he'd ever really be able to let it go and keep a gate closed.

Then again, knowing there was a simple way to prevent illnesses like Maria's just on the other side was a temptation too great for anyone.

"Well, if we don't find a gate, then we're not going to get the medicine we need to help those children." Since the time they'd first arrived in Yellowtree, two more children had come down with similar symptoms. Maria's little brother, and a neighbor child she'd been playing with before she got sick.

It was definitely contagious, and they definitely needed help.

"We won't find a gate in time to help them, Zander. I can only hope that they recover, that the treatments I gave them to try will be effective. But it's spreading, and if it spreads much further or more quickly…"

Zander didn't need to hear the end of that sentence to know just what a difference finding a gate would make. This journey had only served to heighten the challenges they faced here in Philotheum without one.

And Nathaniel hadn't been wrong about talking to people, either. A late night conversation with Johanna had yielded a disclosure that she'd met Leah — the strange girl who seemed to travel from town to town "compiling legends" about a gate that would lead to another world.

From there, they'd been able to establish a trail through several other villages Leah had visited, and now, they were only a day's travel from a place that seemed the likeliest suspect — near a village where there was evidence that Leah might actually have a home.

But Nathaniel was right. Now that they were this close, there was no guarantee how it would go. Finding her home was just as likely to be the ultimate dead end as anything.

If it was all a myth, they were done. Nathaniel would go back to trying to build clinics in some of the villages, and Zander would... Well, he wasn't sure what he would do.

There were many choices in their food bag now, but nothing sounded appealing. Or maybe the conversation was dulling his appetite. "I don't know if I'm hoping anything," he said. "I've tried not to. All I've been thinking about the whole time is that we need to find that gate so that nothing bad happens. I haven't thought much about anything else."

This was mostly true. Especially the part about trying not to. If there really was a gate... He didn't actually know what it would mean.

"Would you go back?" Nathaniel asked. His voice was quiet and calm, as it always was. Nathaniel had always been easy to talk to, even back in Bristlecone when Zander hadn't known him well. Back then, he hadn't understood why, but now, after spending all this time alone with him, he'd figured it out. Nathaniel was so quiet, unassuming. He never really pushed, and he always just accepted whatever answer you gave to him. This conversation here was perhaps the most Nathaniel had ever pried into his thoughts, and Zander found words pouring out, almost of their own accord.

He shrugged. "I don't think I could resist at least going through.... that's my home. My family is there. How could I not go through and...?"

Nathaniel reached and took the bag from him, taking over the task of laying out root vegetables and a knife, which he used to begin peeling an onion. "And what?"

"That's the real question, isn't it?" Zander now dug through the bag for a second knife, grateful to have something that would keep his hands busy without much thought. "What would I do if there was a gate I could actually go through — if I could actually go home?"

"Would you call your parents?"

He gulped. This should have been a simple question. Of course he would want to call his parents; he wanted nothing more than to hear their voices again. And undoubtedly they would be desperate to hear his. After the way he'd just disappeared on them with no warning...he couldn't imagine anything worse than never hearing from him again. But it was so much more complicated than that. Nathaniel's question seemed like a simple and easy one, but really it was one that cut to the heart of the very issue. What would happen if he called them?

He was still thinking, considering his answer when something huge and feathery flew right past his face, making him jump back and sneeze at the same time. "Larya! Jeez!" he shouted, before realizing that the bird landing a few feet away from him wasn't Larya.

He stared at the bird for several seconds, trying to comprehend. William and Quinn both had been sending regular communications to him and Nathaniel. Even Thomas's bird had made a few appearances as they'd traveled. But this bird wasn't any of theirs.

"Zylia!" Nathaniel's voice was as surprised as Zander's. "What are you doing here?"

Zylia. Linnea's bird. What in the...? The bird strutted forward, fluffing her tail feathers back out as if Zander had been the one making kamikaze dives at her face. She stopped right in front of him, pecking at the ground, obviously demanding a treat.

Zander sighed, reaching into the pocket where he always kept something for Larya, looking skyward as he did so, hoping his feisty pet wouldn't hop down from a nearby tree and object. "Here," he said, holding a piece of meat between his fingers so that she'd have to come stand next to him to get it; he wanted to look in the canister on her leg. He hadn't exchanged any messages with Linnea the entire journey. He was more than a little surprised to be hearing from her now.

But when he unscrewed the silver lid on the little canister, it was empty. There wasn't even a little pencil inside like normal.

He frowned at Nathaniel. "There's nothing here."

"Are you sure?" Nathaniel walked over and knelt down by the bird, sticking his finger into the canister for himself.

"You didn't believe me? Really?" Zander was amused when the bird imposed her own consequence for Nathaniel's disbelief. She pecked at his hand until he, too, coughed up a treat for her. She was lucky they'd just stocked up on everything.

"Do you think she came out here all on her own?" Nathaniel asked.

"Just to check up on us or what? That would be weird. Are there any other birds around?" He stood and began walking around the campsite, searching the darkening sky and the outlines of trees that were quickly turning into silhouettes in the dusk. But there was nothing. Zylia seemed to be alone — and she didn't seem to care, either. She was strutting around near the fire pit, turning up dirt to make a seat for herself.

Weird bird.

Zander was heading back toward the fire himself when he heard it. A noise that he shouldn't have been able to hear at all out here, so far away from any villages or homes.

The distinct sound of hooves against gravel and grass. Enough noise that there had to be at least two horses.

Instantly, his dagger was out of the sheath on his leg and in his hand. He didn't even have to look to know that Nathaniel was now beside him, brandishing his sword. Zander crept silently backward, keeping his face turned toward the noise of the coming intruders until he reached his belongings and picked up his own sword. He tucked the dagger back into its place so he'd have two weapons at the ready, just in case.

His heart pounded, pulsing a powerful rush of blood and adrenaline throughout his body. It had been awhile since he'd seen any kind of battle, but all of his training had paid off; readiness now came naturally to him. "Two or three?" Nathaniel whispered.

Zander listened as he twirled the handle of the sword easily in his palm. "Two, I think." He wouldn't know for sure unless the riders spoke. He thought they were maybe still too far for him to hear if they did, though.

He took a deep breath, looking up at the emerging stars, trying to calculate their exact position, and he let out a low whistle, this time summoning Larya to come perch in the trees close to him, in case he needed her at a moment's notice.

Zylia, sensing the sudden tension, he supposed, finally moved and took to the sky, too, though he didn't see where she went.

And then voices did break through the evening air, changing everything.

"Nathaniel?" a familiar voice called out. "Zander?"

"Thomas?" he called back.

"Yes, it's me."

"Who's with you?"

"Marcus…and Linnea."

His first thought was *that explains the bird,* but it was quickly followed by a freezing sensation that flowed from his head to his toes, leaving everything numb in its path. The glance he threw toward Nathaniel felt desperate, but Nathaniel only shrugged.

A second later, three horses came into the clearing. Thomas was first, then Linnea was followed by Marcus. She didn't make eye contact with Zander, although she had a big smile for Nathaniel.

"What are you doing here?" Nathaniel asked as he reached up to help her dismount Snow. She was by herself; there were no babies.

Zander couldn't help himself. He hurried over to Snow and busied himself tending to the horse so he would be close enough to overhear the conversation.

"We brought you something." Linnea sounded flushed and happy from the exercise, although Zander thought he could hear a nervous little rise in pitch at the end of some of her words. It might have been his imagination, though.

Half a second later, she was standing next to him, reaching for the clasp on one of the saddle bags.

He cleared his throat. "Hello."

"Hey," she said, still not looking at him as she put her hand in the bag, searched around for a moment, and then pulled out a leather-covered portfolio. She carried it over to Nathaniel, leaving Zander no choice but to follow.

What is this?" Nathaniel asked, carrying it over near the fire where he could get a better look at it in the light.

"It's... Well, we're not exactly sure what to call it," Thomas said, following Nathaniel. "Linnea and I found it in a stack of papers we first discovered a long time ago — the first time we ever visited the castle."

"It's a giant storage room in a back hallway." Linnea joined them and began sorting the papers inside the folder — clearly searching for something in particular. "We'd forgotten about it. When I remembered the other day, we weren't sure the room would even be there anymore, let alone anything inside of it. Not after all the damage."

Thomas nodded. "But that room looked untouched. Almost like nobody even found it during the war."

"Okay, but why did you come all the way out here to bring it to us?" Zander asked.

"Because..." Linnea looked up at him now, with an expression on her face that suggested exactly nothing; he might as well have been a stranger. "It tells us where there's a gate."

The air around them went still. All sounds ceased. Time itself stopped as he stared at Linnea's unblinking eyes. Or at least that was what it felt like.

"What do you mean?" After an eternity — or a few seconds — Nathaniel's voice broke the silence.

Zander was still stuck back on a single word: us.

"Right here," Thomas said, pulling one of the papers out of the stack. "This is just like those pages in the notebook, except it's even more detailed. If this is right, that's the exact location of a gate."

"And all the rest of these papers talk about when it opens and how to find it and what the schedule is like on the other side. William thinks this gate opens every three days in the other world."

At this news, Zander's tongue finally managed to work again. "Is it the same 'other world' — my world?"

There was only the tiniest flick in Linnea's eyelashes when he said those words — my world — but he saw it so clearly it might as well have been on a movie theater screen.

He didn't know how to handle having her here. At all.

Nathaniel was studying the papers intently now. "It looks like it's the same world," he said. "Probably. Maybe." He shrugged. "There's really only one way we're going to find out."

"Is it near where we were already heading?" Zander asked. "Were we close?"

Nathaniel nodded. "Really close...only I don't think we'd have ever found *this*. Not unless we found Leah's house and she had a map hanging on the wall. This changes everything."

Thomas nodded. "That's why we brought it."

"What are we going to do with this?" became the refrain among all of them, as they sat around the campfire that night, enjoying a treat of stew Thomas had brought in a large tin from the castle. Heated up, it was nearly as good as if they'd been sitting together in the common room. All night long, the discussion raged, and then continued the next morning, even before the sunrise.

Linnea participated in the discussion as much as anyone, although she was careful to sit on the opposite side of the circle from Zander, and she rarely responded directly to his comments.

Or maybe he was the one doing that to her. He wasn't sure. All he knew was that it was difficult to discuss the gate at all with her sitting right there.

The real question was whether Leah really knew where the gate was, or how to use it — if it worked. And of course, regardless of any of that, what they needed to do was make sure the thing was closed.

There were many times during their discussions where Zander just sat, silently listening. He didn't quite know how to feel or what to think. The idea that there might be a gate back to his world, so close to where they were right now was overwhelming.

The biggest question he asked had a terrifying answer as well. "If the gate does open, when would it happen?"

"According to this," Thomas said, running his finger down a page that was getting so worn from their research that Zander wished it was laminated. "Three nights from now. It looks to open around every twenty-seven days at this time of the cycle, if any of this information can be trusted."

"Or two weeks from now," Linnea said dryly. "Apparently not all of the translations are so simple."

But the possibility that a gate might open in just three days changed everything. Suddenly, Zander knew what he had to do. "I want to do it," he said. "If it works, I want to go through it. I want to see what's on the other side."

He didn't know where the certainty came from. The whole time they'd been on this journey, no matter how much they'd discussed a gate as a real possibility, he hadn't been able to make up his mind. He knew what it meant, knew what could happen. Even though the chances were very high that if the gate worked one way, it would work coming back...he wasn't so certain that he'd be able to come back if he left.

His declaration changed Linnea, too. As they packed up the camp, in preparation for traveling forward she actually came to him. He was tearing down the tent he and Nathaniel had been sharing when she walked over and started helping him pull the stakes from the ground.

"You're sure about this?" she asked quietly.

He looked around. Everyone else was busy with their own tasks, far away from the two of them. They were as alone as they could be right now. "Yes," he answered. "And no. But mostly yes. I just feel like it's something I have to do."

"Will you ever come back?"

The truth was on the tip of his tongue, that he didn't know, and he had every intention of saying that, of giving the honest answer. Or what he'd thought was the honest answer — because what actually came out was, "Do you want me to?"

Her whole face went white, even her pink lips grew pale where she pressed them together. And he almost missed it, because the gesture was so small, but she nodded.

But her words didn't quite match her nod. "Does it matter if I want you to or not?"

It shouldn't have. He couldn't make this decision because of her. He shouldn't put that weight on her shoulders, making her bear the burden of what he ended up doing. That wasn't fair. But his heart didn't want to cooperate with being fair. "Maybe."

She bent down to pull one of the stakes out of the ground and busied herself for a moment straightening the whole little stack of metal stakes so they were all pointing the same way. "If I asked you not to go through the gate, to come back to the castle with me — what would you do?"

He'd thought his heart had shattered into a million pieces once before, but he'd been wrong then, because that was nothing compared to this. His body felt hot and cold at the same time, and he couldn't even move his hands to continue working on the tent. He tried not to know the answer to that question. He didn't know if he was trying to convince her or himself as he mumbled something about still having to *find* the gate, that they needed to find Leah, that the gate needed to be closed, but his real answer came out anyway. "I would stay, Linnea. I would stay if you wanted me to."

There was no decision, no gap between when he said those words and when her lips went from being pressed to each other to pressed against his. *A kiss* wasn't even the proper description for what happened between them then. For a long moment, he couldn't tell where he ended and she began. He wrapped his arms around her and held her tight. Breathing her in was like getting oxygen after having been deprived of it for moons. This was everything. He never wanted this moment to end.

But it did, of course. She finally pulled away from him, dragging his shattered heart as she went, and then breaking it even more when she said, "Then you have to go."

"I don't understand. I just told you that I would stay if you wanted me to."

The sides of her mouth wobbled as she nodded. "I know. And that's why you have to go."

It felt like he couldn't breathe again, like everything around him was swirling too fast for air to reach him. "That doesn't make any sense."

She dug into the back pocket of her riding pants and then held her hand out, opening it so he could see the small object she'd retrieved.

A golden coin.

It was just like the one he'd refused to take from William, but then had found again later, sitting on his night table. The one he didn't want to admit was currently safe in a small pocket of one of Ember's saddlebags.

He put his hand over hers, trapping the coin between their palms. "Isn't this supposed to be about going through difficult things together, rather than drifting apart?"

She bit her lip as she studied him, and then eased her hand from his so she could hold up the coin. "Maybe that's what it's supposed to be. Maybe that's even what it is for most people. When the thorn is something that happens between you and it's something you can actually remove and get back to roses. But us… we're not roses, Zander. This isn't a flower we planted on purpose and now we should be feeding and watering it so it keeps growing. This thing between you and I is something that popped up where it shouldn't have. One day, it was just there; a little bloom in hostile ground. A weed that I know we've both tried to pull, because we both know it shouldn't be there…"

"And yet, it just keeps growing, doesn't it?" He took the coin from her, rubbing his thumb over the engraving of the dandelion seed. "Everywhere you turn, there it is, sprouting up in impossible places. Maybe it's not a weed."

"It will be if it destroys something, Zander." She was staring at the coin now, not at him. "If we let it grow where it shouldn't, if we let it snuff out some part of your life that you need, that's what it will be. It can't get in the way of you getting answers about the gate, and it really can't be the reason you lose your home."

He didn't have an answer. She was right about all of it. He could only stare at her soft, perfect face and nod.

She stretched up on her toes and kissed his cheek. "Travel safe."

"I thought you and Marcus and Thomas were coming along with us at least until we find the gate."

"We are."

THE GATE

"I KNOW WE HAVEN'T talked about it, Zander," Nathaniel said as they rode. "But I think we're going to have to choose, here. We either have to find Leah *or* go through the gate. We can't do both."

Zander nodded. "How far away is the gate?"

"Assuming these maps are correct, if we stop at nightfall and pick up again first thing in the morning, then we'll arrive there midmorning tomorrow. A day and a half before we expect the gate to open."

"And how far is that from where we projected Leah's home to possibly be?" He knew roughly the answers to these questions, but he'd been so distracted by Linnea last night and this morning, and then by his decision to go through the gate, he hadn't really been focusing on much else.

"Half a day. We could still try to explore and find her, but we might cut it close. Marcus and Thomas have expressed some interest in searching as well, even if we're gone."

He nodded. "Does it really matter if we do find her? If we find the gate, and we manage to get it closed somehow, then we won't need to find her. It will solve that problem."

"That's true."

He was satisfied with himself, with that answer. It was a relief to have at least one of their pressing problems solved. Even if Leah did know where the gate was, if they could stop her from using it, then it didn't matter. She could go back to just being some strange girl. Maybe, he thought in his optimism, it had all been meant to be somehow. Leah had shown up in his life just to give them a reason to search for a gate, just to lead them to the information that would help them find one. He wasn't normally superstitious like that, but then again, he'd been practically forced into this world by a strange person in the first place. "How does Alvin travel between the worlds, anyway?"

Nathaniel scoffed. "That's not a question I have an answer to, Zander. You'd have to ask him."

"You think he'd give me a straight answer if I did?"

"Nope."

And then a thought occurred to him that turned his blissful satisfaction into nauseating terror. "We're going to show up in the other world with nothing, Nathaniel. I don't have any money or anything. I couldn't call my parents if I wanted to."

"I have that taken care of, Zander. I've been doing this for a long time. So long as we wind up in the world we're expecting to on the other side, I'll be able to work it out. It's only been a couple of months on that end, you know."

This was it. The moment Zander had so long ago resigned himself would never happen. Or at least the moment before he'd get a definitive answer about whether it was possible to ever see the world he'd come from again. He felt like he was in a science fiction movie, about to step over a precipice that might lead him anywhere.

He wasn't ready. But he was going to do it anyway.

This gate, like the others, was by a river. Unlike the others, though, there was no bridge, nothing to indicate there was anything here besides water flowing lazily along its bed, deep in the woods.

Nothing anyway besides a single tree, right at the edge of the water that was different than all the other trees. It was older, taller. Its wood was a deep reddish color that Zander had sometimes seen in his world, but never here. An evergreen in a deciduous forest.

And right now, as the daylight began to fade into dusk, he picked up a pebble, just as he had dozens of times since this afternoon, and he threw it into the small space between the base of the tree and where the water began.

This time, unlike the other times, the pebble didn't splash into the river, and it didn't *clunk* scattering other rocks along the riverbank.

It didn't land at all.

"All right," Nathaniel said. "Let's do this."

He bent to pick up the backpack that held all the supplies he'd be able to carry with him, and he turned to wave a final goodbye to Thomas, Marcus, and Linnea.

"We'll return in twenty-seven days," Thomas said. They'd discussed this dozens of times now, but it felt right to hear him say it again, to have a plan, even when there were no guarantees. "If we're wrong about the timing, if you end up here alone, the birds should be able to get us a message. It's not so far to a village from here."

It was half a day's walk, not exactly close if they didn't have the horses, but it wasn't anything he and Nathaniel couldn't survive if they had to.

There were no prolonged goodbyes. None of them could have handled it. There was just some nodding, and then Zander hiked the bag onto his shoulder, closed his eyes, and stepped forward through the invisible gap.

For a fraction of a second, he thought they'd been wrong. Nothing had happened. Everything sounded the same. The crunch of pine needles, the sound of flowing water, the fading light of dusk.

And then, just as he realized it was much too warm, that there was no longer a cold bite to the air against his exposed skin, something large and heavy slammed into him, sending him headfirst into the water.

For a long, confused couple of minutes, he didn't know what had happened. First, he thought he was drowning; he couldn't breathe, and his whole head was under the water with something heavy pinning him down. But then the heavy thing moved, and he realized it wasn't a thing at all — it was someone. Nathaniel. Then Nathaniel's hands pulled his face out of the water just in time for them both to hear another loud splash of something else landing in the water near them, sending another torrent of water that left Zander unable to breathe for another minute.

By the time he had stopped coughing and spluttering for long enough to understand his surroundings, both Nathaniel and Linnea were standing in the water, staring after a figure whose boots made loud gushing sounds as she ran away from them.

"Leah?" he coughed in surprise, trying to drag himself to his feet to go after her, but his waterlogged bag was too heavy and made him lose his balance in the slippery current, and he fell again, this time banging his head on a rock in the creek.

He would never remember anything about the next few moments. There were some dreamlike images of being helped to his feet and semi-dragged to the bank. There was the sensation of his bag and coat being pulled from his body, and of a cool cloth being applied to the side of his head where he'd hit the rock, but the first words he remembered were, "That's going to leave a bruise."

"Will he be okay?" Linnea's voice was worried.

"Yes, I'm fine," he said, scrunching his whole face in the effort to stay sitting upright. "We have to catch her!" He tried to get to his feet, but failed. Mostly because Nathaniel's hand was on his shoulder, pushing him back down.

"She's gone," Nathaniel said. "She disappeared into the woods up that way. We don't have a chance of finding her now. And you're not ready to run."

Neither of them were well-armed, either. Although Zander's dagger was buried in the bottom of his backpack, they'd decided that bursting into some suburb somewhere carrying a sword was a disaster waiting to happen.

He nodded, relieved when the motion didn't make him dizzy again. He raised his hand to the bump on his head, accidentally knocking Linnea's hand out of the way in the process. That was when he realized. "Linnea! Why are you here? You have to go back!"

Linnea didn't answer him; she just picked up a rock and threw it into the space where the gate was — or where it had been, a moment ago. It clanked loudly against another rock before it splashed into the river.

"What? No! Why? Why would you do that? You can't be here for..." He didn't know how to finish the sentence. Shock and terror had taken over, and it was all he could do to keep breathing right now.

"I didn't." Linnea said. "Not that I hadn't thought about it — jumping on the only chance I'm likely to ever have to come to this world, but... I couldn't. Not on purpose." Her eyes began widening now into the same kind of panic Zander was feeling, although hers had to be even worse. Her babies were over there.

"What do you mean? What happened?"

"I was standing there..." her breath was beginning to come in gulps now, too. Rivulets of water dripped from her hair down into her shirt. "I watched you go, and then Nathaniel followed you a minute later — I had just finished hugging him..." She sat down on the ground and wrapped her arms around her knees. "And almost as soon as he'd gone through..." Her whole body gave a violent shake.

"Are you okay?" Zander dropped the cloth from his forehead and reached for her hand. It was ice cold, even in the heat of the evening.

"Yeah... I just...." Her teeth began chattering too hard for her to finish the obviously untrue assertion.

The pack Nathaniel had been wearing on his back had survived better than Zander's. He set it on the ground next to Linnea and dug through it until he found a small blanket. Zander helped Linnea out of her dripping cloak and then Nathaniel wrapped the blanket tightly around her, rubbing her arms to try to warm her up.

After a few moments, the shaking stopped and she seemed a little less freaked out. She took a deep breath. "As soon as Nathaniel was through the gate, she was just standing there — that girl — Leah? I don't know how she got there. Marcus and Thomas were only a few feet away. She had to have passed right by them..." Her forehead creased in deep lines. Zander recognized the emotion — she was trying to figure out what had happened before she'd even finished remembering it in her own mind.

"Just say what happened. Tell us what you remember," he coaxed.

"She tried to follow you, Nathaniel. At least that's what it looked like. She just ran right for the gate after you went through it. But it... it was like it wasn't there. She walked through where it was supposed to be and she just came out on the other side. I remember thinking that it had closed awfully fast, but..."

"It's hard to remember things when they happen too quickly to process," Nathaniel said gently, rubbing at her back and arms, still trying to warm her.

She was getting agitated again, though, and she pushed herself off the ground and began pacing, still holding the blanket tightly around herself.

"So the gate was closed already?" Zander asked, frowning.

"I thought it was. Marcus and Thomas must have thought so, too, because they started going for her, to get her. But I was closer, and she just grabbed me."

"Grabbed you?" The hair on the back of Zander's neck bristled against his wet shirt. "Grabbed you how?"

"Just… she grabbed my arms and started pushing me toward the gate. It wasn't very far. I tried to get my arms free, to push her off of me, to get away from her, but then I slipped and we both fell into the water, and then… I don't know. She was on me for a minute, she almost fell on me, but then she let go and just started running. I was going to… I don't know what I was going to do. Chase her? And that was when I saw Nathaniel pulling you out of the water."

"And that was it? Did she say anything to you?"

"She said something, but… I don't know, Zander, I don't remember!"

"Okay," Nathaniel broke in. "Let's just… we're all confused and upset and I doubt we'll ever figure out exactly what happened. Let's just figure out where we are and what we need to do next. We need to get everyone dry and make sure we're somewhere safe. Everyone take a deep breath."

The only thing a "deep breath" did for Zander was make him feel lightheaded, but he knew Nathaniel was right, so he tried. His mind was going too fast to just *stop*, though. "I guess we should have gone with finding Leah first."

"We can play the *should have* game all the way back to the first time Samuel and I ever used a gate, Zander. It doesn't accomplish anything. Just calm down."

Linnea laughed out loud, sending a little shock through Zander's middle. "You think telling someone to calm down ever works?"

Maybe *calm down* didn't work, but Linnea's outburst did, and Zander actually smiled. The scene in front of him grew a little less blurry around the edges, and for the first time he was able to keep a single complete thought in his head. "Where *are* we?"

As near as Linnea could tell, they hadn't gone *anywhere*. Everything looked almost the same as it had on the other side.

The only visible difference was that Marcus, Thomas, and the horses had all disappeared. Along, of course, with all of her supplies, leaving her stranded here in the wet clothes she was wearing, but she didn't want to think about that right now.

After a few moments, she noticed the other difference. Her clothing was already beginning to dry in the warmth of the evening. She'd stopped shivering and was now on the verge of being comfortable — besides the wet socks and undergarments. She could have done without that.

Otherwise, they were just in the woods at sunset, a creek gurgling songs below them, the nighttime insects beginning to sing their songs. Okay, well, maybe some of those noises were different than in her world. Every few minutes there was a loud, clicking chirruping sound she couldn't identify.

And now that it was getting darker, something about the sky was wrong. She couldn't quite figure out what...maybe there were fewer stars than there should have been? Or that, despite the lack of any moon, she could see her surroundings entirely too well. And there were other noises now — faraway and distant, but definitely nothing she should have been hearing from deep within a forest.

They were still sitting there — or, pacing, which the three of them seemed to be taking turns doing. Zander had stripped as best he could without undressing completely, and after a few minutes of prodding, Linnea had followed his lead. It was a relief when she finally decided to get out of the horribly damp socks. Already a blister was forming near her heel. That wasn't a good plan when they'd be traveling in a strange world.

Nathaniel was shaking out her cloak and laying it over a rock to dry when suddenly a new light appeared on the horizon, making them all freeze.

Linnea grabbed Zander's arm, dragging him to her. "What is that?"

He shook his head as if he didn't know, but answered anyway. "It looks like there's a building over there. Someone just turned on a light."

"It's that bright?" Linnea had to hold a hand over her face to even look at it for a moment. But after a moment, her eyes adjusted and she could see it, too. The light was a perfect square, pouring out the window of some kind of small building. As they watched, the light disappeared, as if a candle had been snuffed out. But now she could see other, smaller lights on the sides of the building, where there must be windows leading to other rooms. She was familiar with electric light — they had it at the castle in Eirentheos. Most of the capital city in her home kingdom was lit that way now. Maybe because it had been awhile now since she'd been there, but she didn't remember electric light ever being so bright.

"We need to go," Nathaniel said. "If we're that close to one building, there are others around. We can't just stay here all night. We can follow the river. That usually leads to somewhere."

"Or at least keeps us from traveling in circles," Zander agreed, reaching for his boots. Before he pulled them on, though, he looked at Nathaniel. "I don't suppose you have two more pairs of dry socks?"

For a long time, as they walked along the river, Linnea wasn't sure she believed Nathaniel that it was going to lead anywhere. She was afraid they were just going to be wandering all night in the wilderness, in a strange place. "Is this your world?" she asked Zander.

His eyes widened as he shrugged. "How would I know? There are forests and rivers in your world, too. We could be anywhere."

They had traveled for less than five minutes since that conversation when the near-silence was broken by the most terrifying sound Linnea had ever heard. It started as a dim, faraway noise, but it was growing louder, telling her that it was moving closer to them. It was a shrill, screeching, noise that kept repeating itself. Bile rose in her throat. No human or animal could make a noise like that.

Zander, who'd been just ahead of her on the path, whirled around to face her, a look of concern on his face. "I think that might be my answer," he said. "That's a siren."

She wasn't precisely proud of the language she used as she asked him what a siren was — though she wasn't ashamed of it, either. Judging by the sound, it had to be something horrific, coming to kill them all.

Before he could answer, the whole woods lit up in a dramatic display of flashing red and blue. Linnea dropped to the ground and curled into a ball, trying to escape whatever was flying right at them.

A second later, Zander was beside her, crouched down, his hands on hers. "Hey, it's okay," he said. "They're not going to hurt you. They're not even going to come this way. There's not a road."

And sure enough, just as quickly as everything had lit up, it went dark again, the flashing lights disappeared, and the noise receded into the distance with them.

"What they? What was that?" she asked, struggling to her feet again.

Zander assisted her. "Sirens. They're...they put them on emergency vehicles so that other cars will get out of the way. They help people."

"Help them how?" They'd been in this world less than two hours, and already she was confused and overwhelmed. She wondered how William had ever managed it. "Come on, I'll explain it as we walk. It's getting late."

When Zander explained about police and ambulances and fire trucks, she wanted to crawl under a rock. Of course she'd heard about these. She didn't know why she was having so much trouble understanding things right now.

Far from frightening them, the sirens seemed to have cheered both Nathaniel and Zander up. Now they knew where to go. Less than ten minutes later, they emerged from the woods onto the strangest road Linnea had ever seen. It was solid and hard, like stone, but not quite, and black with white and yellow lines.

Now they definitely weren't in her world.

More bright lights appeared while Linnea was still studying those lines, only this time they were solid white and approaching far too fast. She wasn't in the way, but Zander still pulled her back far from the road as those lights went speeding past and the bright white was replaced with a softer glowing red.

"A car?" she asked, desperate to prove she wasn't stupid. She'd listened to all of the stories her uncle and brothers had brought back from this world. She had a remote idea of what at least some of the things were.

"Yes."

"So that's what Quinn almost hit William with?"

"Yes," said Nathaniel.

"I never heard that story," Zander said, chuckling. "You'll have to fill me in."

But Linnea was still stuck back on, "Quinn can do that — what we just saw? Work one of those, that fast?"

"So can I." Zander's voice sounded like maybe he was trying to impress her, though she didn't know if it did.

Nathaniel cleared his throat. "They come in quite handy. That's one of the first things we need to do — try to obtain one. Traveling will be so much easier. Hopefully we're not too far from somewhere we can rent one."

"I don't even know what country we're in," Zander said. "So, good luck with that."

"That car had New York license plates."

Linnea tried to ignore their conversation for a few minutes. It wasn't that she wasn't interested in everything, it was just that so many of their words made so little sense that it felt like they weren't speaking the same language. After a lot of talking, a few more cars zooming by, and coming up along a tall metal sign on the side of the road, she understood that both Nathaniel and Zander were now sure they were some place called New York. But she didn't know what that meant. "How far are we from Bristlecone, then?" she asked when there was finally a silence between the men.

"Far." Zander answered. "Even if we did have a car, it would take us about four days to get there. Less if we didn't ever stop to sleep, but still, it's a long way."

Her mouth fell open. "But the gate opens again in three days."

Her presence here would make everything more difficult, then. Zander and Nathaniel could have been gone from the other world for as long as they needed to — Zander, maybe even forever. But there was no way she could stay here for longer than one opening. Her babies... No, she couldn't go there. Thomas would go immediately back to the castle and tell everyone what had happened, and of course Benjamin and Adeline would be well-cared-for in her absence, but...even the few nights she'd planned to be away from them had been harder than expected.

She'd been doing so well at keeping her mind off of that, but now it was too much. She didn't know how long they walked as she obsessed over the fact that she was stuck in an entirely different *world* than her children; all she knew was that when the dark road gave way to more lights than she'd ever seen in her life, Zander had to put his hand out to keep her from stumbling forward again.

"What is this place?" There were literally lights everywhere, coming from above and the side, and from several cars which were stopped underneath what looked like a giant outdoor ceiling of lights.

"It's called a gas station. Cars need fuel to run, and people come here to get more when their cars run out."

This was inexplicably funny to her, and she started giggling uncontrollably. "So they're like horses. They need fed, too."

She wasn't sure that Zander understood her words between her giggles, because the look he gave her was very concerned. "Kind of like horses need fed, I suppose. And *people*." He directed a pointed glance at Nathaniel.

"I'm going to go inside for a few minutes," Nathaniel said. "I think you two should wait out here while I see if my credit card still works."

"But we don't have a car — we don't need fuel for it," Linnea was still trying to choke out words. "Or is this where you get one of those, too?" This thought sobered her. She was not at all certain about getting inside something that could go so fast on those black roads.

"They sell other things at gas stations, usually. Snacks and drinks. It's been hours since we ate, and I think we all need to get something in our systems."

She couldn't argue with him. Although she hadn't noticed it until he'd said something, she was famished. Her stomach rumbled and now she realized that might explain the giddiness and lightheadedness she was feeling.

There was a weird blue metal bench outside the gas station, and Zander led her over to it so they could both sit down. This need, too, she hadn't noticed until she paid attention. Now she wasn't sure how she'd managed to walk so far on such shaky and exhausted legs.

Zander looked as terrible as she now felt. His clothes had dried, but his hair was mussed and tangled from his time underwater, and the bruise on the side of his forehead was blooming ugly hot shades of red and purple.

"Are you okay?" she asked him.

He raised an eyebrow so far it ran into the bruise and made him wince. "Since when do you and I play the stupid question game?"

These words twisted her insides into unexpected shapes. She'd spent so much time over the past several weeks pushing herself away from Zander, telling herself that their relationship wasn't right, reciting all of the reasons why being interested in him romantically was a terrible idea, that she'd completely forgotten the truest thing about her. He was her *friend*. The one who got her jokes. The one who wasn't afraid to call out her stupid questions and admit to his own. The one who always felt as out of place in their new lives as she did.

And *oh*, she'd missed him.

All of those arguments, all of those reasons, even the ones that were entirely true melted away right there on that gas station bench as she leaned up against him, and he put his arm around her without a word.

"HOME"

ZANDER HAD EXPECTED THAT a trip through the gate would be strange and probably even difficult, but still, nothing had prepared him for *this*. It wasn't just the additional shock of Leah dragging Linnea through the gate with her, either.

Although it was true that having Linnea here, watching her reactions to seeing this world for the first time was a lens that brought everything into sharper focus, this world was overwhelming to him already, too. The cars, the lights, the sirens, this gas station — everything was too bright, too shiny, too *much*. And this was mild, he knew. He was having a hard time believing that they were actually in New York, because so far, everything had been trees and a two-lane state highway. This wasn't what he'd pictured when he thought of New York. At all.

He was okay with just sitting here for a while, trying to wrap his head around everything, feeling Linnea safely up against him. Only a few cars pulled into the station while they sat there. One, a white fifteen-passenger van, pulled up to the pump closest to them and began expelling young men and women. All of them had to be about

Zander's age, if not a cycle — a *year* — or two older. And all of them were dressed in togas.

What in the… He began to seriously rethink their certainty that they'd arrived in his world. Although — he did recognize the brand name of the driver's black-and-white flip-flops.

Several of them walked right past Zander and Linnea without even noticing they were sitting there. They were all chattering happily about something and oblivious to their surroundings. But once most of them were inside the store, he realized the driver with the expensive flip-flops was staring at them while he filled the tank.

By the time he realized and dropped his gaze, it was too late.

"Hey mates!" The guy called in what sounded like a thick Australian accent — if television shows were to be trusted. And if they were in the right world at all.

Zander gave a tentative wave.

Flip-flop guy looked them up and down. "Haven't seen youse around before. Youse work at Timbergrass?"

He was at a complete loss. He wasn't even sure they spoke the same language here. Linnea's body had gone tense beside him. "Just say yes," she whispered.

She was probably right; a no might invite more questions. "Yeah. How'd you guess?"

"Had to be something with those outfits. Is it Color War over there already?"

He and Nathaniel had tried to dress as inconspicuously as possible, but of course the rough linen and the handmade denim pants wouldn't pass the scrutiny of someone in name-brand flip-flops. And Linnea… The only hope they had was deflection — and a desperate hope that they weren't actually in a new universe with a strange obsession with ancient Roman fashion. "What's with the togas?"

"They're having a Toga Night at The Beach! Should be heaps of fun. Youse should come if it's your night off."

"Uh… thanks, but we really can't."

Fortunately, before Flip-flops could finish a long spiel about the rules of Toga Night (participants were only allowed three garments besides the toga — including shoes), several of his friends came pouring back out of the store. All of them were loaded down with bottles of soda, and bags of chips and sunflower seeds. One girl was carrying a box of laundry detergent.

"Wonder if that strange hat counts as that one's third garment," Linnea said, nodding toward another guy who was wearing a Yankees baseball cap and, also, expensive flip-flops. Maybe there was a uniform.

He snorted. "I really, *really* don't want to know."

Nathaniel finally emerged from the store just as the last van door closed behind the toga crew. Zander stood to help him with the two large bags.

"I'm not so sure we're actually in my world," he confided as he carried one of the bags over to the bench. He told Nathaniel about what they'd just seen.

"I saw them inside," Nathaniel said. "Sounds like they're counselors. Work at a camp around here somewhere — when they're not having Toga Night at the local bar."

"O-kay."

"They invited us," Linnea said, laughing. "Too bad I left my bedsheets at home."

"Judging by the way Flip-flops was looking at you, I think they'd let you in anyway."

"I'm rather certain I have enough trouble without adding a young man in a bedsheet to the list. The party sounded kind of fun, though."

She was almost serious, which made Zander realize that there had been a time when he'd have thought so, too.

"Anyway," Nathaniel said, looking back and forth between the two of them. "I bought some snacks and supplies, and got a map.

This *is* your world Zander. Or a very close replica, if we're entertaining unlikely theories. The only way to know for absolutely sure tonight would be to make a phone call or two." He reached into the bag and withdrew a box. Zander gasped when he realized what it was — a prepaid cell phone.

"I… don't know if I'm ready for that right now."

Nathaniel nodded. "I'm sure. You can wait and decide what you want to do once we've found a place to stay for the night. We're not in a big place — no luck on a rental car."

"If this is really New York — can't we call a taxi or something?"

Nathaniel was exceptionally good at not laughing at people, but right now he was having trouble hiding that he wanted to. "New York is a big state, Zander. Most of it is nothing like New York City. Just like Bristlecone has little in common with Denver."

Of course. That was stupid. He'd probably have felt better if Nathaniel had just laughed.

"Anyway, this isn't a big town, at all. But we're not totally out of luck. It's big enough that there are a few stores and restaurants, and a hotel up the road. The cashier said it's about a five-minute drive into town, so we should be able to walk it before everything closes. You'll want to be careful with those."

"These?" Zander held up the bag of chips he'd been about to tear into. He was starving.

"Yes. They didn't have much selection in there. No hot food or anything, just chips and candy and such. I bought a couple of different things, hoping something will be okay until we can find some actual food somewhere."

"Why? Are these expired or something?" He glanced at the dates before realizing that he had *no* idea what day today was.

"No. They're safe."

Nathaniel wasn't making any more sense than flip-flop guy. Zander ripped open the bag and shoved a chip in his mouth.

It took every ounce of willpower he had not to spit it back out on the sidewalk. "How much oil do they *use* on these?" he coughed when he'd finally managed to swallow. Now he needed a drink.

"It takes a while to get used to the food here. Especially when it comes in packages."

Zander took a long swig from his canteen, not brave enough yet to try one of the bottles of juice in the bag.

Linnea looked on warily. She needed sugar, though, before she could walk that far into town, so after Nathaniel promised he'd chosen only plain ones, she tentatively opened a bottle and took a sip. At first, she grimaced at the taste, but got used to it after a moment, and finished the whole thing. They did have juice in Deusterros. Not orange, or cranberry-grape, but after a few minutes Zander managed to polish off a bottle, too. Afterwards, they both felt up to sampling the sticks of beef jerky as they started up the road. These were similar enough to the type of dried meat they had at home to be palatable.

He wasn't sure potato chips were going to be on his agenda for a long time, though.

The gas station had been overwhelming enough, but walking into an enormous, air-conditioned discount store nearly undid him. There was *so much stuff* here. He had no idea what he'd ever thought people needed any of it for. Even the clothing aisles seemed comically absurd in the choices they offered.

He counted eighteen different types of packs of underwear in his size alone. *Eighteen.*

And poor Linnea stood and stared in awe at the racks and racks of clothing, not even knowing where to begin. Zander and Nathaniel started for her, picking out some shorts and summery tops for her to try on in the dressing room. He stood outside, wishing the whole time that Quinn was here with them so she wouldn't have to be in such an intimidating place alone.

Somewhere along the line, though, either the sugar and dry clothes kicked in or the rack of dresses they were passing called to her inner self, because she stopped and let out a little squeak before sorting through them.

She picked out a lacy-topped sundress that — though quite modest by this world's standards — made Zander's heart beat faster when he imagined her wearing it. After that, they actually had to steer her away from the makeup aisle by reminding her that everything they bought right now had to be carried. And if there wasn't room in the nearby hotel, they might be walking loaded down for a while.

He wouldn't have minded watching her pick out a few entirely unnecessary things, though. Watching her actually enjoy herself in his world gave him an unexpected feeling of pride and warmth.

This was a strange world, Linnea had to admit. All of the stories, over all those cycles, from William and Thomas, and then Quinn and even Zander could never have prepared her for some of the things she'd already seen here.

Some of it wasn't so different. The people might dress differently, but she had cousins who'd have great fun at a bedsheet party. Judging purely by Quinn and Zander, people were mostly the same in both worlds.

The *stuff* was overwhelming, though. The sheer amount of metal she'd seen tonight, just in benches and store shelves would have taken cycles to mine in Eirentheos. And the *lights*.

They hadn't walked far, at least not by her standards, when they arrived at what Nathaniel and Zander called a restaurant. In this world, Zander explained, there were places to go just to eat. Not an inn where you could stay while you were traveling and eat meals, too, but just somewhere to go to eat food.

"Even when you're not traveling?" she asked as they headed toward the door.

She could tell the experience was strange for Zander, too. He'd once been used to the way things worked in this world, but when he answered her question, he looked as bewildered as she felt. "Yes. People often leave their houses at mealtimes and come eat at a place like this just because they don't want to cook or have people over. It doesn't make much sense, I know."

She frowned. "It rather does, though. It has to be a nice option for someone who doesn't live in a castle and have servants to bring dinner each evening." She put her hand on his elbow. "You don't have to apologize for the world you came from at every turn, you know. I don't understand all of it, and there's a lot, but I'm a little excited to see what it's like."

The food in a restaurant was much easier to navigate than the gas station had been. Nathaniel pored over the enormous cards with massive lists of dishes until they found a kind of simple soup with vegetables and noodles and chicken. It was salty, but palatable. And the salad wasn't intimidating, either. There were vegetables she didn't recognize, but none she didn't enjoy tasting. After finishing the meal with soft, warm rolls of bread, they were all in better spirits to take up walking again.

This trip was a bit longer, but it was still only a short time before they were standing before the second gigantic building she'd seen tonight. This one wasn't boxy like the store had been, instead it was taller, three stories high, and laid out in what looked like an L-shape, though she couldn't see the other side. Rather than one large entrance, this building had lots of smaller doors on all three levels with windows next to them. Some of the windows were bright, casting light onto the flowerpots hanging from the iron railings in front of them. Many were dark.

She was really rather enjoying how easily Zander had adapted to the change in their roles. He was always ready with names and explanations of things she hadn't encountered before. Parking lot. Street light. Van. Skunk. (She wasn't disappointed they didn't have these in her world.)

"Is this something more like an inn?" she asked as Nathaniel began leading them through the parking lot.

Zander nodded. "This is called a motel, and there are rooms here people can rent to stay in."

"I'll go and see if they have anything available," Nathaniel said, setting down his backpack next to the two of them.

The new backpack they'd purchased for Linnea was getting hot on her back now, despite the fancy material it was made of that was somehow lighter and cooler than anything she'd ever seen in her world. She set it down beside Nathaniel's.

"Thank you for being so patient with me," she said to Zander once they were alone. "I've heard of a lot of these things before, but…"

"You couldn't have imagined. Nobody could. I don't even understand what half of these things are anymore. All that food on the menu…"

"*That's* the word I couldn't remember."

"Yeah, well, in your world that word would not mean that you had to decide between two hundred different things just to eat dinner."

"Didn't you miss it? All of this? You could do anything right now. That restaurant said it was open all night. You could go and eat any one of those two hundred things any time you wanted."

"True… But there are things I couldn't do right now, too. I can't whistle for Larya. And, honestly, as much as I missed my truck those first few weeks in your world… it's not anything compared to how much I wish Ember was here right now, carrying this dang bag for me."

She giggled. "You should have gotten one of these ones at the store. This is a lot lighter than leather."

"I may end up back at that store tomorrow."

"Good. You'll find me back over by the makeup a couple hours after you're finished paying. William never brought me back half the stuff they had in there. There were little tubes of gel to make your eyelashes sparkly and purple. He has some explaining to do when I get back."

He chuckled. "For what it's worth, I like your eyes just fine the way they are right now. Not even sparkly purple eyelashes could make you any more beautiful than you are like this."

A warm tingly feeling filled her insides and she had to catch her breath before she could answer him. "That doesn't mean I won't have fun with the sparkly purple. It's for me, not for you." But she reached over and took his hand, lacing her fingers between his.

"I think you should definitely have some of the sparkly purple stuff, then. And maybe blue, too. We'll go back to the store tomorrow." He bent his head and kissed her softly, right on her eyebrow.

Oh, she wanted this. She wanted to just melt into him, right then and there, to put her arms around him and pull him tight, and never let him go. But…

"We can't," she said, pulling back and letting go of his hand. "I shouldn't have…I'm sorry."

He frowned. "Why?"

"Come on, Zander, don't make this harder than it is. Look where we are. Look at what's in front of you, at the decisions you still need to make. You can't make those decisions just because of me. It's too big to get it all tangled up with a girl."

He looked shocked — more than he should have. He was smarter than that. She was half tempted to smack some sense into him. Maybe he was still in shock over actually being here, because he'd never been so thick about the situation before.

Before she could get really annoyed with him, though, he reached into his pocket. "I know you're right. I know I should be thinking the same thing, and taking a step back. And I *really* should be protecting you, not putting you in a position to get more hurt than you already are. I'm sorry I'm not. It's just…" He held out his hand and showed her what was in it, the little gold coin resting on his palm. "Just like that dandelion, Linnea. Even here, where we shouldn't be at all, it just keeps cropping up. And I keep hearing it's a weed, but…it's entirely too beautiful to ruin."

He meant every word he'd said to her. Every bit of it. It was just that reality kept getting in his way.

There was plenty of room in the motel, it turned out. Nathaniel was able to secure two adjoining rooms so that Linnea could have her own. She was as fascinating to watch as she was fascinated by the rooms. The lights and the little refrigerators, the ice machine near their rooms, the bathrooms with showers and running water she'd been missing in Philotheum…all of these things intrigued and occupied her. And then there was the television. He had a feeling that would be on in their room for as long as they stayed there. She'd never seen anything like it.

And then there were the telephones. One in each of the two rooms. He felt like they were staring at him as he sat on the bed next to Linnea to watch her press the buttons on the remote, flipping manically through the channels.

"You need to do it, Zander," Nathaniel said, settling into the chair by the little desk. "It's going to eat away at you until you do."

It felt like someone had put a metal clamp around his stomach and was beginning to tighten the screws. He glanced at the clock on the nightstand. "It's nearly eleven. It's too late tonight."

"They're two hours behind us, actually. It's the perfect time to call. They'll be at home and not in bed yet."

He stood and started pacing. The screws grew tighter, and he started to feel cold, though he was wiping sweat from the back of his neck. He imagined it had little to do with the air-conditioner blowing on him from near the window. "I don't know if I can."

"You can." Linnea walked over to him and grabbed his hand, moving it away from his neck as she pulled him toward the door that led to the other room. "It's this device?" she asked, pointing to the phone on the desk.

He nodded.

"How does it work? Can you send a message on it somehow, like a bird? That's kind of how William explained it, but I never understood."

He suspected that she might know more than she was letting on, but he was grateful for the distraction that came with explaining how a telephone worked, how you could actually talk to someone, in real time, even when they were hundreds of miles away.

"It's like magic," she breathed, just as she had when she'd understood the television.

He smiled. "It sort of is. Except when you're terrified of actually reaching someone on the other end."

She reached for the receiver and handed it to him. "Now show me how it works."

It took him three tries to read the directions for reaching an outside line, then making a long-distance call. It was all far more complicated than a cell phone. And, for a moment, he forgot the middle digits of his home phone number, but once he started dialing it all came back to him. And then, there was a click, and then the line on the other end began ringing.

He nearly slammed the receiver back down in fright.

But then it was too late. *"Hello?"*

He froze. It was the most familiar voice in any world, the first voice he'd ever heard. A tidal wave of familiarity and longing washed over him, but he didn't know what to say.

"Hello? Is anyone there?"

Now the overwhelming feeling changed to terror. He couldn't do this. He started to pull the phone away from his ear.

Linnea pushed it back. "Say something."

"Who is this? I can hear someone there."

"Mom?"

Silence.

Then, a strained whisper. "Zander?"

His heart was pounding so fast and loud in his ear that he almost couldn't hear her, but he pushed forward anyway. Linnea's hand between his shoulder blades helped. "Yeah, Mom. It's me."

There was a *clunk*, and he was pretty sure she had dropped the phone on her side. His stomach tumbled along after it. Then, some garbled scratching noises, as she picked it up again. "Is it really you?"

"Yes, it's me," he repeated. "I'm sorry I…"

"Where are you? Are you okay? Where are you?"

Linnea tapped him gently on the shoulder. "Do you want me to give you some privacy?" she mouthed, pointing toward the other room.

He shook his head, trying to stem the rising tide of panic. *No*, he didn't want her going anywhere. He had no idea how to do this.

"Mom, I… I'm fine. I'm in a hotel in New York. Everything is fine. I'm safe. It's fine."

"New York? What do you mean? Where have you *been*?" Her voice was no longer a whisper; Zander was certain Linnea could hear every word of the conversation. He stared up at her in helpless horror.

Linnea shrugged. "It's hard to go wrong with the truth."

He doubted that sincerely. It might be easy to tell the truth when it didn't involve alternate universes and timelines, but his did. He should have had a plan before he ever made this phone call. *What had he been thinking?*

"Who is that there with you? Is that Quinn?"

"No, Mom, it's not Quinn. Her name is Linnea, she's a…a *friend*."

That Linnea nodded encouragingly was a good sign, he supposed. At least for one of the messes in his life.

"Oh, is that why you're calling now? Things didn't work out between you and Quinn and *now* you've decided we're worth talking to about it?"

Wait. What? "Mom, I never was with Quinn. We broke up when I was still in Bristlecone." It was all too confusing and the only thing he could remember was the truth. "Why do you think that?"

"What else are we supposed to think, Zander? One minute, you were here, moping around about breaking up with her, then you run off with Owen for the weekend over something about her, and then Owen comes back and you didn't. The only thing we could guess is that you went off to wherever she was."

The problem was, this was sort of true. It was just as easy to lie with the truth as it was to be honest. He wondered exactly what Owen and Megan had told his parents, though he guessed it was just enough of the truth to make sense, but not cause problems.

"We called the police, Zander. But they said you were eighteen, and you were the one who ran off with someone else's kid. There was no evidence that you were in any danger or that you'd gone of anything other than your own free will — so there was nothing they could do. I don't even know where you went. Where did you go? Have you been in New York the whole time? Is that where Quinn is, too?"

The dam burst. "I didn't take Owen anywhere. I guess I sort of did, but he led me to this crazy broken bridge that led to another universe where Quinn is a queen and she's married to someone else, and then I got stuck there. And that's where I've been. Fighting in a war, becoming a knight, falling in love with a widow. It's been a crazy cycle…I mean year."

On the other end, his mother's voice was quiet again. "Zander, you've only been gone for six weeks. What are you talking about? Are you on drugs?" Now, in the background, he heard her yelling for his father.

This had been a terrible mistake. He didn't know what he'd been thinking. He slammed down the receiver.

Linnea sat down on the bed facing him. "So…that's how a telephone works, then."

He chuckled and held up a hand in defeat. "That's how it works. Although I've never seen it be quite so dramatic."

"What did you expect? You disappeared on your parents for…I don't know how long it's been to them, but overnight is long enough when it's your child. I disappeared once. My parents turned over the entire kingdom starting the next day. They're not just going to ask whether you slept well."

"She thinks I'm crazy. Or that I've taken something that's interfering with my perception of reality."

"Wouldn't *you* think that, too, if someone told you the same thing?"

She was being infuriatingly reasonable in the face of something that wasn't reasonable at all. "Of course I would! So why did you tell me to tell them the truth?"

"What else do you have that you're willing to own?"

"Wh—?" He closed his mouth choking off the word at its source.

"Exactly. They're your parents. Are you going to let them believe you ran off somewhere following Quinn after she broke up with you? Yeah. I heard that. Are you going to spend the rest of your life knowing that your mom thinks you would just leave and go somewhere without telling her, or that there's actually something wrong with you and they should be worried forever? I know you, Zander. None of those things make any more sense than what you actually told them."

"No, they don't." He buried his head in his hands. "But there's not a believable truth here, Nay."

"Doesn't matter. It's still the truth. Don't take on something that's less than what you've done and who you've become. You didn't run away from your parents because you were a desperate kid chasing a girl who didn't want you. You haven't been hiding from your parents like a rebellious vagabond, either. You left because Owen asked for your help, and you stepped up to give it to him. You saved William's life when you did that. And you stayed gone because you're an honorable man and you were trying to save a friend. You've done nothing ever since then but *be* an honorable man, standing up for a kingdom, serving your friends. Don't trade that. Honorable men don't lie to their parents."

He stared at her. "You make it sound so easy."

"Nothing is easy. We left easy behind a *long* time ago, I think. But, you know, this story was just as unbelievable when Owen told it to you. I have my doubts that you even believe most of it still, and you've seen it and lived there. But you found a way to handle it. Why not give your parents the same opportunity?"

"And if they don't handle it? If they never believe me?"

She stood and took the two steps to him, then bent and kissed the top of his head. "That's on them. Sometimes all you can do is plant the seed in the right place. You don't get to choose if starts growing or not."

He could suddenly feel the cool weight of the tiny coin in his pocket again. "You're kind of incredible, Linnea. You know that, right?"

"Not just kind of. I am. It's why you're falling in love with me. Yeah, I heard that too."

Before he could respond, the telephone on the desk gave a shrill ring, and she stepped away from him.

"They must have seen the number," he whispered.

For someone who'd never encountered phones or how they worked before, she seemed to understand immediately what he meant. He wasn't sure why, but this gave him hope that maybe his parents could understand more than he thought, too.

She picked up the receiver and held it up for him, pressing it to his ear.

"Hello?"

MESSAGE

WILLIAM WAS JUST CLOSING the nursery door behind him after tucking Samuel in when the door to the apartment flew open, making him turn in alarm.

Quinn was sweating and ashen-faced as if she'd run through the entire castle to get here. And perhaps she had, considering the state of the crumpled note he pried from her hand once she held it out, too out of breath to speak right away.

He unfolded it carefully, trying not to smudge the hastily penciled words on it. Maybe Quinn *hadn't* been running before she got here, he decided after reading it. Just looking at the thing made him feel as if he'd just lost a race. "Linnea's gone?"

That wasn't the only earth-shattering piece of information he could glean from the few words in the note — just the most gut-wrenching one. The rest of it — that there was actually a working gate, that they could travel away from this world, that there was apparently someone else who'd discovered this before they had — he'd have to acknowledge all of that after he'd had some time to think.

"This girl, whoever she is, just pulled her through and she was gone. Marcus and Thomas tried to get through for an hour before they sent this."

She was only repeating what he'd already read in the note, but he understood, knew she was trying to make sense of it all by talking it through.

"Yeah." He took a deep breath, trying to center himself and clear his head. She noticed and followed suit, rubbing her hands together to calm their shaking, too. "Okay," he said, trying to prioritize the issues. "Benjamin and Adeline are fine. They're here, we've got them."

She nodded. "We'll have to let Mia and Elisa know that Linnea won't be returning tomorrow as we expected, though."

"Marcus will like to hear that they're doing well back here at the castle. We should send him a message to reassure him." He grabbed his notebook from the table where he'd left it to begin making notes, which reminded him this wasn't the only crisis they were facing right now. This new issue was the more pressing one at the moment, though — if only slightly.

"How often did you decide you think this gate opens?" she asked.

"If I read it right, it's every twenty-seven days on our side, three days on the other."

"That's a long time. What if they're in a strange world and not Earth at all?"

"Don't, love. I know it isn't easy, but we're going to have to just *not* freak out for twenty-seven days. If she doesn't come back then, we can revisit that., okay?"

"Okay." She was trying, he could tell. He watched her pace between him and the fire for several minutes, giving them both a few moments to think.

He turned to a clean page to draft a note to Marcus and Thomas. "We can't leave that gate unguarded."

"No, we can't. But it's not like we can send a whole bunch of castle guards to stand around a gate they don't even know exists. Do you think those two would be willing to stay out there?"

"I've no doubt. I don't think Thomas will come back without Linnea regardless. He'll sit by that gate until she comes through if nobody stops him."

"True." Quinn finally slowed her pacing and came to stand by the table with him. He wrapped one arm around her waist as he wrote. Just touching her helped him focus and calm down. "At least Mia will understand."

"And…he and Marcus may end up with more company out there after we send a message to my father."

"Oh gosh…I hadn't even thought about that yet. Do we have to tell him right now?"

He knew she wasn't serious, that she would never keep something like that from Stephen, but he cleared his throat. "You really want to handle all of this alone without him?"

"Can we go back to the time when he was the only one who knew about bad situations and we got to remain blissfully unaware?"

He stopped writing and put both of his arms around her, pulling her close. "How about I take care of the letter to my father, and you get one sent to Marcus and Thomas? Then we'll have a few minutes to catch our breath while we wait for their responses?" *A very few*, he thought to himself as he kissed her.

For a few seconds, she leaned into the kiss, reveling in the reconnection they both needed after spending even a few hours apart during the day, but then abruptly, she pulled away and narrowed her eyes. "What aren't you telling me?"

"About that going back in time to when some people could actually keep things from other people…"

She jabbed him in the ribs. "You'd pick that?"

"No. Not for a moment, love. I was just hoping to give you a small break before I shared more bad news."

"You're going to have to find a wife who's not the queen of a kingdom that just went through a war, then. Because this one doesn't do breaks."

He chuckled and kissed her nose. "Entirely too much trouble to find a new one. You'll have to do."

"Thanks. Now spill."

"Before Nathaniel and Zander went through the gate, they were traveling around to villages, gauging the need for medical care…"

"And the receptiveness of the people there to actually *accept* medicine that seems so strange to them. As medicine from my world does."

"Right. Well, in one of the villages, he came across a small outbreak of a disease that concerned him, particularly since there were already three children who'd been affected."

The color drained from her face. "Not again…"

"No," he said quickly, knowing exactly where her mind was going. "It's nothing like that. At least, there's no indication that it's anything purposeful. It's just…normal. Horribly, typically normal for this world, unfortunately. Cold weather, people spending more time inside than out. It's worse, actually, during this season where sometimes the weather is reasonable and people get out and mingle with each other, and then go incubate things in closed spaces…"

She was putting on a good show of patience at listening to him, but he knew she was waiting for him to get to the point.

"Anyway, he sent me some samples of blood to analyze — don't ask me how he got anyone to agree to giving them to him. I finished that today, and I think it's Diphtheria."

There was a flicker of recognition in her eyes, but her stare was mostly blank. "And that's bad, I'm assuming?"

"It's not good."

She pulled away and started pacing again. "How bad are we talking, Will? Epidemic? People are dying? You said it was a small outbreak, right?"

"Yes. Currently it's small."

"Wait…what did you call it? Why does that sound familiar?"

"It's a disease you have in your world. Had. It's no longer common there, especially not in the United States."

"But we do have it here."

"I…" he had too much nervous energy to stand in one place now, too. He went to stoke the embers on the hearth and put in another log. "I don't know. It's not a disease I ever saw in Eirentheos. That doesn't mean it never happened, but it's not something I studied or thought I needed to. It's not unusual for diseases to be more or less common in different parts of any world — the two worlds I'm familiar with, anyway."

"Is it common here in Philotheum?"

"Enough that Nathaniel said one of the healers he talked to knew what it was. They call it something different, but the symptoms they describe are spot on. One of the children who had it died last moon."

She looked as stricken to hear it as he felt saying it. "Can it spread from the villages?"

"Yes. How quickly and how badly depends on whether the people in the kingdom have any resistance to the illness or not. I really have no idea. There were cases in your world where epidemics nearly wiped out entire populations that had never been exposed to it before. If it's been around for a long time, then maybe it won't spread as fast. I don't know. Even if there's resistance, though, it can spread and kill people."

"Can it be treated?"

"It can. Sometimes it does go away on its own. One of the children who had it weeks ago has apparently recovered, although it can cause heart problems and other issues that don't show up until later. The best treatment is an antitoxin. Antibiotics help, though they're not quite a cure. But nobody in the villages has either of those things."

"And Marcus and Thomas are out there, not far from where this is happening. And Zander and Nathaniel and Linnea…"

"Nathaniel, Zander and Thomas are not at risk. They're all vaccinated against it. As are you and I."

"Oh. Well that's…convenient. But it's not enough." She cast a glance at the nursery door that made his stomach turn.

"Exactly. It's not enough."

"And we don't have the vaccine here, I'm guessing."

"Even if we'd developed an efficient system for manufacturing and delivering vaccines — which you know we haven't — we didn't know we needed this one. Philotheum is new to us. Same goes for the antitoxin. We have antibiotics, but…"

"But you've been behind in producing enough of those since before the war. And a lot of your supplies are still missing and destroyed." She understood all the issues facing her kingdom remarkably well now.

"Exactly."

"We'd better hope that Nathaniel did actually end up on Earth and he can bring some things back."

"I know that was one of the reasons he was so interested in joining Zander on his little quest."

She nodded, then her eyebrows knitted together. "Wait… Why would Thomas be vaccinated?"

"Oh. That's a hard line of Nathaniel's. You don't bring back bugs from Earth, period. We have a hard enough time not killing off half the population in epidemics on a regular basis as it is over here."

Mouth agape, she stared at him. "Does that happen?"

He walked to her again and put his hands on her upper arms. "I'm not trying to scare you love. I'm trying really hard not to, actually, because it isn't helpful to anyone. But there really was a reason that Nathaniel and I were so desperate to study medicine on Earth. You've been here less than a cycle — you haven't seen everything yet. You've not been introduced to the reason our populations stay so small, despite the fact that some families have thirteen children."

"Well, now you are scaring me. I'm starting to wonder if I can get in on this gate that we've found."

"It does open in twenty-seven days."

"You're supposed to encourage me to stay here, Will. To take care of my people. To rule them even if some bizarre virus wipes out all but three of them."

"I'm supposed to, I know. Some days, though, I find myself thinking only about you and Samuel. Is that a crime?"

"Technically, it's treason, so, yeah."

"Point taken. You going to have me arrested?" He pressed his lips against hers, preventing her from answering for as long as he could get away with it.

"I might arrest you *myself* for entirely other…purposes," she said, grinning, when she finally pulled back away from him. "But only temporarily, because we'd all be in trouble without you. I can't get away with detaining the one trained healer in the entire kingdom who believes in germs."

"See, you need me."

"Well, that was never in dispute. Which is why this next question I'm going to ask is going to kill me."

He raised an eyebrow.

"You need to go out there, don't you? To see what's going on, and take medicine to those people?"

"I should leave in the morning."

SEEDS

"YOU'RE…DIFFERENT HERE," LINNEA said as Zander settled in across the table from her.

They were in a little area on the first floor of the hotel that served breakfast in the morning. Zander had said it wasn't a restaurant, though it had high, cushioned chairs on either side of the table the way the restaurant last night had. Linnea thought the whole thing wasn't so much different from an inn in her world where meals were always served. Apparently they didn't serve lunch or dinner here, though.

Several foods here she actually recognized — eggs, bread, meats. There was even a large metal container of hot grain cereal and bowls of toppings to put in it, one of her usual breakfasts at home, though, like everything, it was a bit different here.

She was most fascinated by the things that were very different. She'd brought several little containers to the table. They were white with some kind of metal/paper lids and had strange, colorful names on them.

"Different good, or different bad?" Zander asked, eyeing her as she tried to peel open one of the containers.

The contents made her gasp and frown over at him. "This is food?" It looked like small, brightly colored pebbles. Not ordinary colors for food, at all. There were vivid shades of purple, red, and blue.

"Some people think so," he said, chuckling. "It's cereal. It's designed for children."

This made sense. Some of her younger siblings would love such ostentatious food. "How is it made?"

"I don't know." He shrugged. "In a factory somewhere. It's actually just different grains mixed with lots of sugar and food coloring. This one here used to be my favorite." He picked up one of the other containers and opened it. "It has marshmallows."

"I don't know what those are."

"Here," he picked out a small blue piece and held it toward her mouth.

She took a tentative taste. "It's strange, but not bad. Sweet."

He smiled. "So, I'm different how, exactly?"

"I don't know...like this. It's interesting to see you in a place you know so much about, teaching me things. I rather like it."

He tossed a few pieces of the cereal in his mouth, and then made a face. "Would it be weird if I said I'm already missing...*home?*"

They were mostly alone in the little space, sitting at the table furthest from where an innkeeper was wiping the counters where the food was kept. She wasn't worried about their privacy. Besides, even if they were overheard, she doubted their conversation would make sense to anyone.

"I'm trying to just enjoy this and not think about how many days have passed there just since we've been here."

"It looks like you finally get your adventure."

"I guess so." She smiled over at him before taking a spoonful of the colored cereal. *Ooh... best to stick with the eggs.* "You ate this as a meal?"

"Don't ask me how. It's like candy now."

"I'll have to ask William if he ever got used to the food."

"So how come your parents never let you come here to visit? Even Thomas got to sometimes, didn't he?"

She nodded. "A few times. Honestly? I give everyone a hard time about it now, but it wasn't entirely my parents' fault. I wasn't the easiest child. If they'd have let me come here at the age they let Will, I'd probably have wandered off or gotten in someone's car or something. I was a bit distractible."

"You? Never…"

She kicked his foot under the table. "William and Thomas and I…we were an interesting combination. I still think my parents had to be a little bit off their pace to continue having children after us."

"If I didn't like your little brothers so much, I'd agree with you."

"Yes, they lucked out. At least until they got Emma — she takes entirely too much after me. Anyway, until I was probably fourteen or so, I wouldn't have actually wanted to be away from home for that long. I missed Will, but not enough to go away from my parents, and when Thomas told me I'd have to get needles before I went…"

He chuckled. "Count you out."

"Yeah, well, I'm stuck with it now. Nathaniel won't let me take anything weird back home."

"Weird, deadly, same difference right?"

She kicked him under the table again. "Once he finds a car and a way to get medical supplies and gets back here, that problem will be solved. I got over both of those issues, anyway, it's just that by the time I did, things were too fraught. I didn't *know* about everything with Quinn and William then, so yes, I was angry and very teenage-girl about the whole thing. But now that I know, I get it. I don't envy my parents having to handle all of that."

"So…teenagers are like that in your world, too?"

"Some of them. Me."

"And you know all of this, and yet you still let everyone feel guilty for not taking you?"

"This bread is so soft," she said, taking another bite. This, too, was sweeter than she was used to, but not as overpowering as the cereal.

"You never actually grew out of that 'difficult child' thing, you know that?" he said, narrowing his eyes, though his smile belied his real feelings on the topic.

"Yes, I know. I make no guarantees that I ever shall. Speaking of parents… Are you ever going to be ready to talk about how your second phone call went last night?"

She'd left him alone, to give him privacy last night after she was sure he was okay.

Nathaniel had nodded approvingly when she exited the room and pulled the door closed behind her. He'd shown her more about how to work the television. She had trouble settling on just one show, because it was all just too interesting, but eventually they'd come across the beginning of a program that featured a lot of young adults around her and Zander's age. A comedy, Nathaniel had called it. It had been funny, even if she didn't understand half the things they were doing or using. She'd never heard either Quinn or Zander use half those words. Of course, there were no "computers" or "cell phones" in her world.

The movie had been nearly over by the time Zander came out. She hadn't pressed him then; he would talk when he was ready. Besides, as easy as Nathaniel was to talk to sometimes, he also knew Zander's parents and had a little too much advice about giving them the benefit of the doubt. Not that Zander shouldn't do that — but he had enough to process without feeling like he needed to apologize for his feelings.

So they'd put on another movie. This one was supposed to be scary. There were furry creatures with big teeth and people with fangs that Zander called "vampires". This one had made her laugh far more than the comedy.

And then, when it was too late for anything but heading to bed to be reasonable, she'd been the one to struggle. Nathaniel had purchased two rooms so that she'd have her own space, but she wasn't used to this at all. She hadn't slept completely alone since before... And nighttime was the worst for missing her babies. It was hard to fall asleep without their little noises and grunts. Easier to stay asleep, maybe, but still she found herself reaching out for tiny fingers in the middle of the night.

She'd tried, and she'd been silent, but after a while, Zander had appeared in the doorway between both rooms holding a box of tissues.

She suspected that Nathaniel's look might not have been as approving when Zander didn't return to the other room, but instead grabbed an extra blanket and slept on top of the duvet she was under.

It was the best night's sleep she'd had in a long time.

Nathaniel had left early this morning in search of a car and to start whatever process he had for obtaining the precious supplies that would mean so much back in Deusterros. This trip might mean William and Nathaniel could finally return their laboratory and castle clinic to the way it had been before the war.

But Zander still hadn't said one word about the phone call.

He picked up the white mug in front of him and drank deeply. "There's like, an unlimited supply of coffee here. Think about that. I could have as much as I wanted. We should stay here all day."

She glanced over at the innkeeper — *was that the right word? She wasn't sure* — who was now scooping the leftover eggs into a large gray barrel lined with some kind of thick black bag. "I don't think they'll be serving breakfast much longer. Perhaps you should get more while you can."

Clearly, she was going to have to wait him out. He stood and went over to the glass pot where the coffee was kept and poured himself two paper cups full, making her feel both satisfied and bittersweet. She liked watching him have the things he'd missed so badly — but she knew that his happiness here meant she might lose him. This was his world. He belonged here. She would never ask him to give this up for her.

Once he finally returned with the cups, she helped him carry one and they headed back outside to go back to their rooms.

The midmorning sun warmed every part of her body. The foreign material of her new blouse and short pants was finally comfortable in the sunlight. "It was chilly in there," she said. "The room was last night, too. That's very strange when it's this warm out."

"Air conditioning. Here, we can heat entire buildings in the warm season and cool them in the summer."

She couldn't even imagine how this worked. "You mean, like a cold fire or something?"

His laughter wasn't at all mean-spirited, and she didn't mind. "There are fires and fireplaces in this world, of course, but we have machines that can heat every room in a house or a building at once, or cool them, if that's what you want."

"I can't imagine how much wood that takes to operate."

He closed his eyes and held his face toward the sunlight. "No, you can't. Even if we wanted to do something like this in Philotheum, I'm not sure we could. I doubt we even have the resources in the kingdom for all of it."

"Is there that much more here?" It was a stupid question; there had to be. She only had to look around to see it all, so she was startled when he shook his head.

"Not all in one place, no."

There was something about the way he said it, a tone in his voice maybe, that let her know it wasn't a topic he wished to discuss, so she dropped it, and for a few minutes they just stood together in the warm light, soaking up the lovely reprieve from the cooler weather in the other world.

"The phone call went fine," he said, breaking the silence. "In the sense that nobody slammed the phone down on anybody else, anyway. There was a pleasant good-bye at the end, from both of my parents."

"Did you speak to your sisters?" She was fairly certain phones worked that way — that he could talk to anyone on the other end.

He took a long drink from the cup in his hand. "No. My father said it would be too confusing for them, that they don't need me to stir it all up and upset them again if I'm not coming back home anyway."

"Is that — are you not planning on it? On going home?" She hated herself for asking.

"I don't know. I'm certainly not ready to hop on a plane and travel there today, which is what he would like me to do."

She wasn't sure it was quite the right thing to do, but she took a step closer to him, so the tips of their shoes were touching.

He smiled and tapped the toe of her shoe with his. "He did apologize, for pushing me to go to the college he wanted instead of where I wanted to go. And I told him that I forgave him for that a long time ago and that it had nothing to do with my being gone."

"What did he say then?"

"That kind of made him angry again. I could tell he was trying not to be, but he just thinks I'm crazy, Nay. I've only been gone for six weeks in his mind — that's not long enough to have done anything 'a long time ago'. So then — and I know it was because I'd already annoyed him — but he asked if what I wanted was for him to just fork out for whatever college I wanted to go to, if that would make me happy."

"Ouch."

"Yeah, because I don't even know how to deal with that, to think about it. College hasn't been on my mind for so long now. Is that what I'm supposed to do? Come back here and move into a dorm and... It's like I don't fit in anywhere anymore."

"That's not true, Zander."

He took another long drink of his coffee. "I know it's not. And I don't know what to do with that. Because it seems like a stupid reason to pick your world, like this decision should be harder or something. What kind of selfish and ungrateful son am I if I can't even come up with one reason to stay in the same universe as my parents?"

She looked down to the ground, to where their feet were touching on the sparkling pavement — she'd learned that word this morning, too. "Does anyone grow up and stay in the same universe as their parents?"

He nearly spat out his drink. "Well, in a literal sense, I'm pretty sure almost everybody does."

She laughed, too. "Yes, but you know what I mean."

"Yeah, I do. It just doesn't make it any easier."

"You don't want to feel like you're running off to a different world after a girl, do you?"

"Are we going to talk about that?"

"Well, if you're even considering coming back home with me, knowing that most likely it will be forever, then, yes, I'd rather prefer we actually talk about what that means for the two of us."

"And what if I go back just because I like being a decorated guard more than an undecided college student who's fighting with his father?"

She shrugged. "People do all kinds of crazy things when they're eighteen, Zander. Even in my world. Regardless, I'll still be there."

And then, for the second time in as many days, his lips were against hers. This time it was more his fault, although she wasn't objecting. The two cups of coffee did make it a bit awkward, though, so this kiss ended a lot sooner than the last one had.

"So... Not just the guard thing, then."

"No. Not just the guard thing."

Forgetting what it was, she took a sip from his cup. It took everything she had not to spit the bitter liquid back out onto the pavement. "Why do you drink this? I'd rather eat that cereal in there."

"More for me," he said. "Here, I can hold both cups. We should go back up to the room."

They were halfway up the metal-and-concrete stairs when she noticed something amiss. "Isn't that the door to our room?"

He followed her gaze up to the second floor, to the two doors that led into their rooms. Linnea was right; one of the doors was ajar, though he was certain he'd made sure both of them were closed before they left. It wasn't like there was much in there for anyone to steal. Nathaniel had left Zander with a couple hundred dollars in cash and a prepaid credit card before he took off, "just in case", but all of that was tucked safely in his pocket. Linnea had some bills stashed in hers, as well. Everything else, with the possible exception of his dagger, could be replaced at the discount store down the street.

"Maybe it's housekeeping? Hotels usually have someone come in and clean the rooms in the morning. Make up the beds and such."

She didn't react. Probably because living in a castle wasn't much different than staying in a hotel in that regard. Even as he said it though, he realized there was no supply cart in the hallway outside their rooms, although there were two outside of rooms on the third floor — and those doors stood wide open.

"Or maybe Nathaniel is back."

It was much too early for that. "Stay here, please," he said, dashing up the rest of the stairs to the second floor.

She stayed where she was — he wasn't sure he'd ever fully adjust to a girl who was used to being protected and escorted by guards wherever she went. Her eyes did flit from side to side, assessing the situation, though.

Once he reached the outdoor hallway, he tried to walk as quickly and silently to the door as he could, and then perched just outside of it, wishing his dagger was where it belonged. This morning he'd been certain that carrying it on himself was far more dangerous than going without — but he hadn't expected a situation like this.

With as much stealth as he could muster, he pushed the door open in one swift move.

It was a small room, small enough that he could see nearly every inch of it from the doorway. Enough of it to know that nobody was in there.

Someone had been, though. The three of them hadn't bothered to put anything away last night, but two of the drawers were open, and the closet door stood open at an odd angle.

The beds were torn apart, too, even though nobody had slept in one of them, and Nathaniel had smoothed the covers over the one he'd used before he left this morning.

The one thing he knew they'd left open, though — the door that connected the two adjoining rooms — was closed.

Full of adrenaline now, he rushed over to it and pulled it open, revealing only a sealed door on the other side. He couldn't get in to the other room.

He'd barely turned from the locked door when he heard a loud *slam* that made the mirror on the wall across from him rattle.

His reaction was immediate. He took off at a run back toward the hallway. Someone had just exited the second room.

When he reached the top of the stairs, he froze. It was *her*, Leah. Right there on the stairs. She stopped running on the step just above Linnea. "Where is it?" she demanded.

Linnea's confused gaze flicked up to meet his.

Blood pounded in his ears, flowing to every muscle, preparing him to intervene in an instant, but he stayed where he was, watching.

"Where is what?" Linnea asked.

"The stone. Where is the stone?" Leah's eyes traveled the length of Linnea's body, lingering the longest at the silver chain she wore around her neck.

He was sure his confused expression mirrored Linnea's. "What stone?"

"The stone! Don't play stupid! You went through the gate! You must have the stone. Where is it?"

As soon as her hand made the smallest move toward Linnea, Zander sprang, making it to them in the same second Leah's fingers touched the chain. As soon as she'd pulled the silver pendant from under Linnea's shirt, though, she dropped her hand again. "You're a royal."

"Yes." Linnea's own fingers closed over her silver birth-gift pendant. Zander moved closer to Linnea, forcing Leah away and to the step below them. "This isn't a stone. I don't know what you're talking about. We don't have any stones."

Leah stared at both of them. "How did you get through the gate?"

"What do you mean? You're the one who pushed me through. I wasn't even expecting it. I brought nothing with me. I definitely don't have a stone."

Leah's scrutiny turned on Zander; he felt like he needed to protect his own — bare — neckline from her fiery stare.

He held his hands up. "I don't, either. You're not making any sense. What stone are you talking about?"

Leah was already backing away, moving slowly down the steps. "What did he do?" she muttered under her breath, and then she turned and ran.

Zander was too stunned to follow her before she reached the bottom of the stairs. Almost as soon as her feet touched the pavement below, he lost sight of her. "Where'd she go?"

They both ran down the stairs after her now, but when they reached the bottom, she was nowhere. Not on the walkway, not in the parking lot, not anywhere. There were a few cars in the parking lot, sun glinting off their windshields, but none of them moved.

"Can I help you with something?"

The voice made him jump. Linnea whirled in surprise, too. It was one of the housekeepers, a young man in his early twenties.

"Is everything all right?"

"Did you see anyone run through here just now?"

The man frowned. "Just you two. Nobody else. Is there a problem?"

"Uh... No. We're fine. Thank you, though."

Back upstairs, he hung up the "Do Not Disturb" signs and latched the security locks on the outside doors of both rooms.

The second room had been ransacked just like the first. Linnea's new clothes were strewn everywhere, and both of the backpacks had been emptied. But nothing was missing. Zander found his dagger under the edge of the bed, which wasn't where he'd left it, but it was there, unharmed.

"What stone is she talking about?" he asked as they began picking up the clothing and straightening the mess.

"I have no idea. I've never seen any kind of stone or heard of one."

He carried his backpack over to the table and began sorting and organizing the contents. "She thought you couldn't get to this world without it."

"Which is weird and doesn't make any sense. The gate was open. Anybody could have gone through it."

The doorknob started making clicking and rattling noises, making them both jump to their feet. Zander grabbed the dagger and held it out of sight against his forearm.

If it was Leah again, he didn't want to miss her, so he edged his way over to the door and undid the latches as silently as possible. As soon as he did, there was another click and the door popped open.

"Thanks, I..." Nathaniel stopped and frowned as he took in their posture and positions. "What's going on here?"

It took Zander a moment to collect his thoughts, and Linnea didn't respond right away, either, although she did slide over and take the dagger from him, setting it on a night table before locking the door back up.

"We weren't expecting you back so soon," Zander said.

"Turns out I'm going to have to travel out a bit further to get all the supplies I'd like." He set an enormous pack and his medical bag down on one of the beds and then pulled the rolling desk chair over by it. "I thought now that we've got a car, you two would rather come and see some things than be stuck here in the room waiting for me. Linnea, come have a seat here while you two tell me what's going on."

Linnea did as she was told, and Zander went to stand in front of her in case she needed some reassurance or a hand to hold. They told Nathaniel everything that had happened while he finished getting things ready.

"A *stone*?" Nathaniel was just as confused as they had been. "Do you think she means a magnet, like the one Owen removed from the other gate?"

"Maybe, but he didn't have it on him when we went through," Zander said. "He buried it in the ground on the other side."

"I want to know how she's so good at hiding," Linnea said. "It was really like one minute she was there and the next minute…nothing."

"Maybe she has a room in the hotel and she went in." Nathaniel sounded as concerned as they were, but he shrugged. "I guess all we can do is hope she shows up again — and make sure we don't leave any valuables in the room."

SAFETY

QUINN WAVED GOOD-BYE FROM the door of the stables until William and Kian reached the gate and then disappeared on the other side. She didn't like it, having him away from her. Raeyan seemed to have sensed her discomfort this morning and was pacing between her feet, not even begging for a treat.

"Is everything all right, Your Majesty?"

The voice didn't even startle her anymore. She was so used to him turning up at odd and random times, apropos of nothing, that this time she just turned as if she'd been expecting him. Maybe she had been.

"Not especially, no. But then, I suppose you knew that."

"I had heard that His Majesty was going to be heading away from the castle this morning to attend to some of his people."

"Yes, well, between that and Linnea disappearing through a gate by accident, it's been quite the week here."

"What do you mean she disappeared through a gate?"

Quinn's thoughts spun rapidly. They'd told Alvin about this, hadn't they? Maybe not about Linnea, since that had just happened, but...

"The gate that Zander was searching for. They found it, with the help of some old book Linnea and Thomas found here in the castle. She never intended to go, to leave for that long, of course. But apparently last night, just after Zander and Nathaniel went through, some girl appeared out of nowhere, grabbed Linnea, and pulled her through. Now she's gone, and can't get back for twenty-seven days."

She'd never seen such a look on Alvin's face. Not ever. Usually, he was the one telling her things she hadn't yet even imagined. Sometimes, she was almost sure he was telling her about things that hadn't happened *yet*.

But if current expression was to be believed — and the fright in his hazel eyes made her think he was genuine — he hadn't known about any of this until right now.

"Is it the gate near Oak's Hollow?"

"I don't know. I think that sounds familiar from the map I was looking at." *How many gates could there possibly be nearby that they needed labels like that?* Raeyan stopped pecking around at the ground and flew up to perch on her shoulder. Usually, she took issue with it when the bird tried this, as he was still young and not always in control of his talons. But right now, his weight was reassuring.

"Who is this girl you're speaking of? Have you seen her before?"

"I've never seen her, no. Zander has. He found her sneaking around the castle one night, and found her another evening in town. I don't know anything else about her, I'm sorry."

She'd had her share of strange experiences with Alvin. Enough that she expected strange as standard when dealing with him. But this topped all the rest of them. Without so much as another word, he turned and left. One minute, she could see him in the middle of the stable, walking down the row between the horses, and the next he was gone, as if he'd disappeared into thin air.

"Really?" *she muttered after him.* "You have to do that when everyone I'd prefer to talk to about it is gone?"

Raeyan let out a soft chirruping sound, which made her smile.

"You're right. You're still here. Up for taking a message to Will for me?"

"So, what do you think of my world now?" Zander asked, as they stepped out of a restaurant and into the warm sunlight of a beautiful late afternoon.

She turned and smiled at him. "At the moment, probably because I'm all full of good food and maybe a bit tired, I'm going to say that I don't think it matters what world we're in. I like the company I'm with."

Her words did things to his heart that he hadn't known were possible. Still, his stomach churned in skittish circles as he reached to take her hand, calming only when her fingers closed around his. It didn't make sense that he should be so nervous about this after everything they'd been through together, but he was. "I'm rather fond of the company tonight as well."

This morning, when Nathaniel had asked if they'd like to be dropped off to do some shopping and sightseeing, part of him had hoped that he meant going to New York City, a place that Zander had never been. But now, he was happy that Nathaniel, in his wisdom, had instead chosen a bustling mountain town in the Catskills. Earlier in the afternoon, they'd wandered through a bookshop and just the sheer selection of maps and pictures of the city they'd seen there were enough to let him know that a person didn't always have to travel through a supernatural gate to enter a different world. Bristlecone had more in common with Philotheum than New York City did.

This small city was almost too much for both of them, although they'd certainly had fun. The constant traffic of cars, trucks, and other vehicles was the hardest to deal with. Poor Linnea nearly jumped out of her skin every time one passed close to them on the street.

He couldn't blame her. Although he'd grown up with cars, after so many months in a world without them, climbing into one this morning had been an almost terrifying experience. Humans were just not supposed to move so *fast*. Although he'd adjusted, and even begun to wish he could drive for a bit, Linnea's knuckles had stayed white on the edge of the seat for the whole trip.

"This world does have everything, Zander. I never realized...I can see why you'd want to stay here."

He nodded. It was harder to consider leaving it today. He'd been comfortable indoors, eaten foods he was familiar with, and drank more coffee than he probably should have. And there was the heady, familiar weight of a cell phone in his pocket. A prepaid one Nathaniel had picked up somewhere, but still, the feeling of it buzzing, as it was doing right now, made him feel safe. He pulled it out and flipped it open.

"It's a text from Nathaniel," he said. "He's heading back now, should be here to find us in half an hour."

As nice as the instant messages and the buzzing were, though — it was strange to receive a message from someone without an accompanying rush of feathers. The phone didn't peck affectionately at his neck or beg for a treat. Though it was less annoying than those things, he couldn't help missing Larya as he slipped it back into his pocket.

"We should have waited until he got here to eat," Linnea said. "I'm sure he'll be hungry."

"No, he said in the message that he ate already. I'm sure we'll want to do something again later for dinner, too."

"That sounds nice." She yawned, which she'd done a couple of times during lunch, as well.

"Are you doing okay? Your arms hurting?" He rubbed his finger over one of the spots she'd peeled a bandage from hours ago.

"A little, but it's fine." She picked up his hand and wrapped it around her waist, instead. "Now it's even better."

The electricity running through him now was so much more powerful than lights or televisions.

"Is this what it would have been like?" she asked as they walked down the sidewalk together.

"What?"

"If I was just a girl in your world, and there were no such things as gates, and you wanted to court me — would you have asked me, and taken me to eat in a restaurant and to look in shops, and to take a walk with your arm around me?"

He smiled, picturing that for a moment, what it would be like to have her as his girlfriend here in his world. To do normal things, the way they were doing today. But even actually imagining it was difficult.

"I'd have done those things, maybe. Asked you out, taken you to dinner and a movie, sure. If you had agreed to go out with me in the first place — which you would not have."

"Why do you think I wouldn't?"

He liked it, the way she crinkled her nose, as if he'd just said something too absurd to entertain. It made him want to kiss her again. But he was serious.

"If there were no gates and I'd never been to your world...I wouldn't be the same person I am now. I don't think you would have liked me nearly as much." The thought surprised him — he realized that he hadn't liked himself nearly as much back then.

"Quinn liked you."

"Well, I wasn't an axe murderer or anything."

Linnea's giggle could have kept him warm and comfortable in a blizzard.

"And Quinn only thought she liked me as anything more than a friend. It would never have lasted. Even if William hadn't entered the picture, and she'd never found your world, who I was then — I still would never have been enough for her. I'd have maybe matured enough in ten or fifteen years to be the kind of man who deserved a girl like her, or like you, but I can't guarantee even that."

"My father says it's your choices that shape who you become."

"I know." He smiled. "He's said that to me, too. There was a time it made me angry, because I didn't really choose to go to your world, or especially to get stuck there. But he just said it didn't matter — that my experiences had given me *different* choices to pick from, but what still really mattered was what I chose. I kind of thought that was a cop-out answer."

"But now?"

"Now, I still admire and respect your father, and I know he was right about the choosing part. But I think I understand something that maybe he didn't. That it matters that the choices were different. It changed me. I can't go back to who I was before I made those choices."

The phone in his pocket buzzed again, this time accompanied by a loud ringtone. He pulled it out, pressed the button, and held it up to his ear. "Hey, Nathaniel."

There was a long pause, and then a woman's voice said, "Zander?"

He frowned. The voice sounded familiar, but it wasn't his mother's.

"What?" Linnea whispered.

He shrugged. "Yes. This is Zander. Who is this?"

"Sorry, of course. It's Megan…Robbins?"

"Megan! Wow. I wasn't expecting to hear from you. How are you?"

"I know. I'm sorry. I didn't mean to startle you. Of course you weren't expecting me to call."

"How did you get this number?"

"Well, first I got a very interesting phone call this morning from *your* mother. I had a bit of a hard time believing she had actually talked to you."

"You and me both."

"But then Nathaniel called me this afternoon and we had a nice long talk. He told me how Quinn is doing and that things are going well there…"

"So, he fudged a little on the truth, then?"

She didn't laugh. "If he did, I'd rather not know from here. It already took me long enough to convince myself not to hop on the next plane and go find this gate, wherever it is, and meet my grandson. I just want to know that everyone is healthy and happy."

"Well, they are."

"And you, Zander? How are you doing?"

"I'm…all right, I think. It's weird to be back here, but nice, too. It's good to talk to you."

"Are you back to stay?"

"Can I get back to you with the answer to that in a couple of days?"

"Sure. And if you don't, will you please give Quinn an extra hug for me and tell her how much I love her and how proud I am?"

"Even though you already asked Nathaniel to do all of that for you?"

"She could never hear it enough."

"I know that she misses and loves you."

"Thank you, Zander."

"Of course… Megan?"

"Yes?"

"Is there any chance I could speak to Owen?"

"Um… he's not home right now, I'm sorry." Something in Megan's voice made him wonder if she was telling the truth, but there was little he could do about it. He supposed she might have good reasons for not wanting to bring him into the middle of it. Still, though, there was something he needed to say. He didn't know where the thought had come from; it had just appeared, unbidden as they talked. "Can you do me a favor then?"

"Probably."

"Tell him that he needs to keep the stones safe."

"What stones?"

"He'll know. You don't even have to tell him that you talked to me, and you don't have to do it today, but just please, will you tell him that?"

"All right, Zander, I will. You travel safe, whatever you decide, all right?"

"Tell His Majesty to come back. Right now."

Her brow furrowing, Quinn looked up from the paper she was writing on to see her uncle, Charles, standing in the doorway of her meeting room. "I was just preparing to send a message to him right now. You want him to come back? Why? Has something gone wrong with an arrest?" Charles was overseeing the remaining troops who were conducting searches of the villages rumored to have leaders who'd opposed her during the war.

Although most of the nobility had taken the opportunity to flee that Quinn had offered, there were a few who were trying to hold onto their lands and estates. It wasn't going well for them, but so far things had been peaceful — as much as they could be.

"No. It isn't that. It's…your grandmother has fallen ill."

Over the many moons Quinn had been in Deusterros, she had experienced many different kinds of terror, sometimes even at the hands of her grandmother, but the cold panic coursing through her veins at the moment was something new altogether. "What? How sick is she?"

Charles didn't look all that well himself. Beads of sweat were collecting along the line where his dark hair met his forehead, and his cheeks were sunken in more than they should be. "Quite. I received a message from her by bird this morning asking for me to call on her. I didn't think it was urgent, so I waited until after our morning meetings, but now, I've just returned and…I don't think she's well at all. By the time I left, she was having difficulty breathing. I didn't want to leave her, actually, but she insisted on it, said I should be at the castle, performing my duties."

She doesn't sound that sick, Quinn thought, but then immediately mentally kicked herself for it. Sophia would probably be attempting to direct her sons and run things in the castle even if she was unconscious.

"I will let William know and ask him to return."

"We should have your grandmother moved to the castle as well."

Instantly, her eyes narrowed and muscles tensed in places she hadn't known existed. Her suspicion was matched only by the guilt she felt for *being* so suspicious. Charles sounded so worried, and if Sophia was truly ill… She really didn't like that this was happening when almost every soul she truly trusted and could talk to was away from the castle — all but one, anyway. "Excuse me?"

"She's so isolated out there; it takes a half-hour's travel just to reach her. And she's not used to it, it's so confusing and disorienting for her… If something happens…"

There was a reason her grandmother wasn't at the castle. And it was because if she *had* been here, it would have been because she was a prisoner in the dungeons. The tidy little guarded cottage out in the woods had *been* Quinn's concession.

She tried to hold her ground against both the rising tide of guilt and her uncle's plaintive, worried stare. "You're welcome to go out there and stay with her if you'd like, Charles. We can manage here at the castle in your absence so that you don't have to be worried about her."

He blinked and stared for a moment, and then cleared his throat. "Are you dismissing me, Your Majesty?"

In truth, she was. She didn't quite know how to feel about him asking her to invite Sophia into the castle. But she didn't know what kind of battle it was going to cause, and she did value her uncle's input and skill at helping her manage the kingdom when there were so many new things she didn't know how to deal with. "Of course not. I just think that someone should be with her if she's ill. I will send for William, as you've asked me to, and I will let you know by bird when he's arrived back here. Please give your mother my regards and tell her I will visit as soon as I am able. Travel safe."

Charles stared at her open-mouthed for several seconds before bowing his head. "Thank you, Your Majesty."

And then, so he didn't see how hard her hands were shaking, she swept past him out of the room.

She went straight from her meeting room to her apartment, grateful that Ethan, the guard who followed her, was one she liked, but also glad her destination wouldn't seem out of the ordinary.

Inside the master apartment, the three babies were all on the floor of her sitting room — the twins on a blanket in front of the fire while Samuel systematically pulled wooden toys from the built-in shelves under the window. Despite her son's best efforts, the toys were the only mess in the immaculate space. Mia looked up from folding a basket of diapers as she entered. "I've just made some fresh tea. Can I pour you a cup?"

"Yes, please." Quinn sank into an armchair, prompting Samuel to make a beeline for her. "Hello baby," she said, lifting him into her arms. "Where's Elisa?"

"She fed the twins a little while ago, then went to attend to their laundry." Mia brought over the tea and set it on the side table next to her. "Would you like me to fetch her?"

"No, actually. I was hoping to find you alone. I could use your ears for a few minutes."

"Let me get a cup for myself, then."

Although she'd expected her support, she was relieved when Mia's expression registered the same alarm she'd felt upon hearing Charles's request. "Do you think Lady Sophia is truly ill?"

"Quite possibly. If she is, should I bring her to the castle?"

"Of course, you're the only one who has the power to make that decision."

"That's not helpful."

"I know. I'm sorry. All right. What's the worst thing that could happen if she were brought here?"

"She'd have access to talk to all of the servants and guards and everyone. She might have visitors who could undermine castle security…I don't know, the last time she lived here she betrayed me and we all nearly died and we ended up in a war for my throne."

"Well, there's your answer."

"But she also saved my life at the end, and she is the only grandmother I have."

"So?"

Mia's abrupt answer nearly made Quinn spill her tea. "So…doesn't that count for anything?"

"Sure it does. Although I think you've already counted it for more than it's worth. She's alive, isn't she? And she's in a lovely little cottage rather than downstairs. What more do you owe her?"

Quinn was silent for a moment, sipping at her drink.

"Don't tell me that all these same thoughts didn't go through your head the moment Charles made that ridiculous request."

"Why do you think I came running straight for you? I don't have any idea what I'm doing here."

"Well, that's not true. You've got the crown, right?"

"Yeah, I can win over a kingdom, just not my own family."

"Families are far harder than kingdoms, Quinn. They can be wonderful sometimes, but they can also destroy you if you're not careful. Don't let Charles find a weakness when he presses your boundaries. You'll regret it if you do."

"I could regret it if I don't, Mia. What if it's really bad?"

"You mean what if the old capiya dies and you didn't let her back into your castle to push you around?"

Quinn snorted. A capiya was a horrible little animal they only had in this world. It was…oddly appropriate as an insult.

"And now you feel bad for laughing, don't you?"

"Hey now… Yes. Kind of."

"Well, don't, Quinn. I realize I'm being insubordinate bordering on treason right now, but…"

"But if you weren't willing to do that I wouldn't be coming to you for advice, right?"

"Exactly." Mia smiled. "If you want to be a good ruler, Quinn, then you have to afford people the privileges they've earned. I'm being entirely too forward in saying I think you've done exceptionally well in the area of rewarding those who've earned your trust through their actions. Now you need to trust yourself to do the same to those who've chosen the opposite."

CONTRETEMPS

WHEN NATHANIEL RETURNED WITH the rental car, the trunk was too full for Zander to even squeeze the meager purchases they'd made that afternoon inside. "Where did you even get all of this?" There were hundreds of vials of different kinds of medication, along with the kinds of supplies they couldn't easily produce in the other world. "Is this even legal?"

"Do you think I would break laws, Zander?" Nathaniel asked once they were all inside the car.

"Kind of. I mean, I assume you've had to break at least some to establish identity and get a medical degree and all of that."

"I suppose that's true. Most of that was so long ago I don't really think about it anymore. But none of that was necessary today. This was all just money. I suppose if I was trying to take controlled substances, like pain medication, back with us I could be asking for trouble. But some of the smaller hospitals and clinics I visited today will be able to do a lot of good for a lot of people considering the price I was willing to pay for the supplies they had on hand.

Zander stared. "And *that* wasn't suspicious?"

"I told them I was on furlough from my time as a doctor abroad, working in countries where basic supplies are desperately needed — that I was short on time, but not on funding."

"So, basically the truth, then."

"Close enough. Two private clinics actually donated boxes of medicines that were close to expiring. I should be able to either use them up quickly, or they'll be a boon to William's and my research."

Linnea cleared her throat. "So, how exactly are we planning to get all of this through the gate? We can't drive the car over there."

"I thought we would start working on that right now."

"Shall we stop in Rock Ridge for a midday break?" Kian asked as they rode.

It was already well past noon and the horses were looking as hungry and tired as William felt. Ordinarily, he would have eschewed stopping in any town and dealing with the recognition, but Rock Ridge was an exception.

"Yes. There's someone I'd like to see."

Only fifteen more minutes of hard riding brought them to a lovely stone house surrounded by pastures and orchards. Although the land was vast, and William knew there were other barns and a neat little cottage far back in the trees, the main house on the property sat close to the road, granting easy access to visitors facing emergencies.

He and Kian rode straight up to the trough in front of the large porch and dismounted.

No sooner had his feet hit the well-kept gravel walkway than the front door opened and a familiar woman stepped out. Just the sight of her made him smile. "Hello, Lily!" he called.

"Your Majesty!"

"Now, now, none of that," he said, hurrying up the stairs to wrap her in a giant hug. "Time with you is too precious to waste on formalities."

"I think I would be remiss in my official duties as your older cousin if I didn't remind you to behave as the king you are," she said. But her hug was too fierce and her smile too broad to take very seriously.

"It looks to me like you haven't been remiss in much of anything," he said, waving a hand around at the impressive grounds. "Are you still enjoying the new place?"

"I still have trouble believing it's all ours. The land, this clinic. You and Her Majesty have been more than gracious."

"It's less than you deserve. We could never thank you enough for all of your support and love. I'm just glad to see you happy here."

"To what do we owe this pleasure?" Lily asked as she led them around the wraparound porch to the back of the clinic where the living quarters were. William wouldn't have minded going through the clinic first, although he did have to admit he'd likely be distracted by it for a long time.

"I'm on my way out to a village called Yellowtree. There's a small outbreak there. Nathaniel and I have diagnosed it as what you call grey throat here?"

Lily instantly spun around to face him, her eyes wide. "Are you sure?"

"Unfortunately, yes. One child apparently succumbed to it last moon before we knew."

"Well, the healers out there wouldn't think to contact you."

"No, not yet. We're hoping to change that in the future, but we're not there yet. But now there are at least three children sick in the same village. All confirmed cases. It sounds like there may be some adults with symptoms too, but that's harder to confirm. I'm hoping to get out there and convince the village to quarantine before it spreads any further. There could be people who've been exposed but aren't symptomatic in…I don't know how many villages by now."

"Will…"

"Yes?"

"I just admitted a child to my clinic this morning with a high fever and a sore throat."

It *was* fun, Linnea decided. Moving this fast in a closed-up vehicle. The seats were far softer and more comfortable than anything they traveled in at home — although she supposed the smooth black roads had something to do with it. The softest pillow wouldn't be comfortable forever on the bumping, rocky roads in her world.

Cool air blew on them from slits on the — *what was it called? Some kind of board?* at the front of the driving compartment, making the car comfortable even in the late-afternoon heat.

Zander had tried to insist that she sit up front again, so she could see everything better, but up there the unfamiliar cooling was just a little too much for her. It was better when the direct stream was blocked by the seats. Besides, his legs were so much longer than hers, he ended up with his knees pressed against the back of her seat the whole time, making her feel terrible.

The music Zander turned on was strange to her. Unusual beats, odd instruments that didn't seem possible (probably they weren't in her world), and lots of loud young voices. But she liked it. She could picture herself singing like that, having fun. Maybe it was time for some more new traditions at home.

The whole thing was so pleasant that all she could do was lean back against the seat and enjoy it. The scenery here was so pretty — reminiscent of home, really, with all the trees and rolling hills, and watching it speed by the windows was fascinating. So incredible…

For several seconds, she didn't remember where she was, she just knew that she was moving and everything was slightly off-kilter. Then, the tires of the car rolled over a huge patch of bumpy gravel, jostling her to reality before everything came to a stop.

"Did you have a nice nap?" Zander asked as Nathaniel turned off the car.

"Did I really fall asleep? I was trying so hard not to. You should have woken me!"

"No way." Zander opened his door and then walked to Linnea's and opened it for her. "You needed the rest. I was glad to see you getting it." He held out his hand to help her out of the car.

"This isn't fair," she mumbled.

"What?"

"You're making it too hard for me to not fall all the way in love with you."

The hand that was holding hers grew very warm, very quickly as she looked up into his brown eyes. "Is that a problem?" he whispered.

"It's going to be when it's time to say goodbye." Even thinking it ripped at a too-familiar fault line in her chest. She was being stupid, she knew. And she needed to stop. To think about what was really important.

"I'm not going anywhere, Linnea."

What? She stared up at him. "What do you mean?" Her mind spun in a thousand directions at once, making it impossible to capture and hold a complete thought.

"Hey," Nathaniel called from the rear of the car. "Can you two help me load these backpacks? I'd like to get in there and back here before dark."

Nathaniel's plan was to carry in as many supplies as they could back into the woods near the gate and hide them there, hoping there would be enough time to toss supplies through before they carried the rest through when they went.

"So, where are we, exactly?" Linnea asked, wondering if she'd slept through the conversation. There were a few other cars parked in the gravel area where they were, but she didn't see any people.

"It's a hiking trail," Zander said. "We never ran into it last night because it was so dark, but this trail will actually get us close to the place where the gate is."

"How close?" She didn't like the sound of a well-used trail so close to the gate.

"We'll have to trek off the trail almost a mile," Nathaniel said. "So we'd better get started now."

Zander held up one of the backpacks so she could slip her arms through the straps. "And, you're right," he said, though she hadn't actually said anything, "it's not good that it's so easy to get so close to the gate. We have to make sure it never opens again after this."

"How do we know nobody's ever accidentally gone through?" Even now, there was what looked like a family, hauling some kind of box with handles off the dirt trail and toward one of the cars in the parking lot.

Nathaniel shook his head. "We don't."

After her talk with Mia, Quinn kissed all three babies and then headed back to her meeting room where she'd left the note she was writing for William, figuring she'd finish it and then head out to one of the balconies and summon Raeyan.

Just as she made it to the doorway of the room, she froze. Charles was still in there.

"Is everything all right, Your Majesty?" Ethan was already by her side, his hand at his waist, scanning both the interior of the room and the hallway. If he thought it was strange that she'd frozen at the sight of her uncle, he didn't show it. Her guards were nothing if not responsive.

"Yes, thank you. It's all right." Then, under her breath, "If you could just give us a moment, but stay close?"

Ethan bowed his head and stepped back as if she'd just made a completely unremarkable request. She made a mental note to review his salary and rank soon.

"Quinn, would you close the door please?" Charles said as soon as she entered the room.

Every hair on her arms and the back of her neck stood up. She liked Charles, had spent most of the last cycle trying to cultivate a relationship with her uncle, despite having grown up without knowing he existed. And she'd told him, many times, at family dinners, and games in the arena, and other relaxed events, that he was free to call her by her name, rather than her formal address. But this was different. This time it was meant to put her in her place.

It took everything she had to keep her voice from shaking. Her hands were a lost cause, but she hid them in the folds of her skirt, feeling for the reassuring weight of her dagger. "It's fine where it is, Charles. Is there something else I can help you with?"

His eyes flicked up and down the length of her, though he made a wise choice in staying on the other side of the long table in the center of the room. "Don't you think you've punished her enough?"

Quinn blinked; for a moment she didn't understand what he was talking about. "Who?"

"You only have one grandmother."

She took a step back, trying not to laugh at the absurdity of the thing. "You think this is my *punishing* her?"

"She's trying to help, you know. She loves you, and she's trying to help you be a queen and rule this kingdom. She's done it before, she knows what it takes and how to do everything that you have no idea about. You should be thanking her, and instead, you're kicking her out of the only home she's known since she was sixteen!"

It was hard to breathe, and even harder to speak. Her jaw felt like it had been encased in quick-drying cement. "Should I be thanking her for nearly allowing me to be killed?"

"She saved you! She was doing the best she could at the time. If you're going to succeed as a queen, Quinn, you need to learn how to forgive people for not being as perfect as you want them to be."

A burning sensation threatened behind her eyes, and her throat grew so dry that she desperately needed to cough. But she wasn't going to let those feelings win. Not this time. "You're taking some serious liberties with the truth right now, Charles." The warning tone in her voice was as explicit as she could make it.

But he didn't let up. "This is unbecoming of a queen. I'm not sure you're qualified for the job at all. I think we've made a serious mistake."

She felt like she was spinning even though she stood perfectly still. It took everything she had not to reach for one of the chairs for support, but she managed it, managed to stay upright and stare right back at him.

"You are dismissed, Charles."

He didn't move. He just stood there, continuing to stare down at her. She could feel herself growing smaller.

It wasn't true. She knew it wasn't true. *Was it? No.* Sophia *had* saved her life, by giving her a dagger. Sort of saved her life, anyway. It wasn't as if the woman had been there on the stage, speaking for her. Quinn could have died anyway. Sophia wouldn't have stopped it — would she?

Was she really taking it too far? Was she an unforgiving person? Was she making the wrong choice?

But…that hadn't even been the first time she'd almost died. The very first night of the war, the night the castle was invaded. Sophia had known, done nothing to warn her. Charles's words were getting inside her brain, making it hard to remember.

She held on to the one thing she knew was true. She *was* the queen. "I said you are dismissed, Charles. Go and tend to your mother. *At her home.*"

Again, he didn't move.

So she did.

"Ethan?" she called into the hallway.

"You wouldn't…"

But Charles's words were cut off by the guard's entrance into the room. "Yes, Your Majesty?"

"Would you please escort the prince to the stables to prepare for his journey to Lady Sophia's home?"

"Certainly, Your Majesty. Prince Charles?"

They were all exhausted after hiking all the way back to the gate with the heavy backpacks, hiding them as best they could, and then making their way back to the car.

Zander could tell that Linnea was struggling especially. He carried both their canteens and hiking supplies back out of the state park. But she wasn't ready to give up.

"Show me something else from your world. I know there's more. Somewhere fun for dinner?"

He raised an eyebrow at her. "Dinner is rarely much more exciting in this world than in ours," he said. "Actually, dinner with *your* family is way more fun."

She elbowed him in the ribs. "Don't," she muttered. And he knew she meant talking like he'd made a definite decision, like it was a done deal.

"I have an idea," Nathaniel said, interrupting them.

He wouldn't tell them. Linnea fell asleep in the back seat of the car again, and Zander rather hoped they'd just go back to the hotel and let her rest. Especially when Nathaniel pulled up outside of a large building covered in pictures of cartoon animals and slices of pizza.

"I don't think this is the kind of *fun* she meant," he said as Nathaniel turned the engine off.

"This is *exactly* what I meant," she said, sounding suddenly wide awake behind him.

Despite the vinyl seats and oddly named entrees, Zander discovered that it wasn't quite as hard to readjust to the food as he'd been afraid it would be. Tonight, he got daring and went for a big plunge — ordering a cup of soda.

Linnea frowned at the bubbles drifting up the sides of the red plastic glass. "What makes it do that?"

"Carbon dioxide," Nathaniel said, smiling. "It's a harmless gas, just a kind of air. You should try it."

She, of course, was never one to back down from any sort of adventure, so she carefully took a small sip.

Zander and Nathaniel both waited for the verdict as she pursed her lips and knitted her eyebrows, then, finally smiled. "It tastes like tiny, sweet fireworks."

It was such an apt description that Zander couldn't even laugh. He took a swig of it himself and closed his eyes, imagining the brilliant fireworks on the night they'd set them off over the castle, signaling the end of the war.

So many times he'd seen fireworks here in this world, but they'd never meant what they had there that night. That night, the fireworks had signaled the return of peace. Sparks had flown for the accession of the rightful queen, his friend, the family that had somehow become his own.

No fireworks here could ever mean what those ones had.

Linnea quite enjoyed the pizza, at least for a few bites. She was far more fascinated by the small children running around, dropping tokens into machines and earning tickets to trade for stuffed animals and plastic rings. "I want to try."

An hour later, they were loaded down with tickets. Zander's sword training had apparently improved his Skeeball skills as well, and he beat Nathaniel soundly in an impromptu tournament. Linnea turned out to be brilliant at a game that required "catching" a little flashing light as it danced around in a circle.

As they approached the glass counter full of prizes, though, a young woman accidentally pushed a stroller into their path, nearly tripping Linnea.

"Sorry," the woman said. "They're just…" she pointed to two small children, twins, from the looks of it, who had just taken off running toward a large slide all the way in the back of the restaurant. The little girl was taking off a coat, while her brother left a trail of his shoes as he ran.

"It's all right," Zander said, chuckling.

"We're trying to leave." The poor woman looked exasperated. "Could you watch her for just a second?"

"Uh…sure," Zander mumbled, before realizing, too late, that the woman had been talking to Linnea.

The "her" needing watching was a small baby nestled in a car seat in the stroller. Her pink bow was askew in her thick brown curls, and the bunny on her little bib was obscured by spit-up. A clean bib lay over her snuggly blanket, ready to be changed — perhaps that was the distraction her older siblings had taken advantage of. The baby was loving it. She smiled and cooed, showing off huge dimples and delight in her brown eyes.

He didn't need to see Linnea's reaction; he could feel it in the way the air between them became heavy and thick with a kind of longing that could never be fulfilled here in this universe. Immediately, he reached for her hand, though he was completely shocked when she allowed him to take it.

"Just one more night after this one," he murmured against her hair. "They're fine, they're safe, and it's just one more night after this, and then you'll be back with them."

She pulled it together quickly. No tears fell, though there was palpable relief when the woman retrieved her baby.

Linnea had lost her interest in spending the tickets, but Zander took them up to the counter anyway. He returned with two small stuffed bears, one pink and one blue, and left behind three children who were very happy with the bounty of leftover tickets he bestowed upon them.

"You need to call your mother again tonight," Linnea said, as she clutched the bears in her hands on the way back to the rental car. "It doesn't matter what she says, you just need to let her hear your voice. I know you haven't decided yet, but if you don't go back to her…"

"I have decided, Linnea. I know you're not ready to believe that, and I understand, but I have decided. But I'll call her," he promised. "As soon as we get back."

EMBROILED

QUINN HAD TOLD CHARLES she would send the note to William immediately, to demand that he return at once. And, of all the crazy things he'd said to her, this was the lone one she agreed with. If her grandmother was sick, then William needed to check on her.

And she meant to. The note was already written, folded, and tucked into her pocket. When she left her meeting room, she turned to go straight to the nearest balcony and summon her bird.

But somehow, she ended up in the stables instead, grateful that Charles's horses were kept in a different building than hers and William's. Now she was wondering what had made her think it was a brilliant idea to let any of her extended family live in the castle at all.

Which probably also made her unforgiving and spiteful.

Again, Ethan didn't say anything. He followed behind her at a distance that allowed her to feel almost as if he wasn't even there, but also left no doubt he'd be able to respond to any situation that came up. He stood just outside the door of the stables as she made her way to the center of the barn, to the place she knew she'd find some calm.

Dusk poked her head over the gate of her massive stall before she even reached her, making a sound that Quinn liked to think was delight. Whether it was over seeing her or the apple she plucked from a nearby barrel was up for debate.

"Hello girl," she said, walking right up to her.

For once, Dusk ignored the apple in favor of nuzzling Quinn's neck for a moment, allowing her to put her arms around the mare's neck and breathe in the heady, earthy scent of her. Immediately, she felt less overwhelmed and more human.

Then Dusk grabbed the apple.

Quinn laughed and rubbed the horse's withers as she ate her treat and then began searching for more.

"Give me a second, greedy thing. I know you've been fed." And not ridden enough recently. Maybe it was time to change it. A nice ride around the grounds would really clear her mind.

She knew she couldn't, knew she had responsibilities, things to do. Uncles to — apparently — fight. But even entertaining the fantasy felt good right now. Imagining the smooth motion of the horse underneath her, the biting wind against her cheeks making her feel less…whatever it was she was feeling right now.

Dusk seemed to sense something was off now, because she stopped begging for another treat and rested her muzzle on Quinn's shoulder for a longer time than before. It was the closest thing she could imagine to a hug from a horse.

It was so tempting. She didn't even have to find a stable hand to saddle Dusk. The tack room was right there — a private one just for Quinn and William's horses, heated by its own stove.

Dusk whuffled and looked over at the empty stall next to her, almost as if she was saying, *"Skittles gets to ride today. Why don't I?"*

And she might have just done it, if right that moment a large bird hadn't swooped in through the open doors at the end, nearly grazing her face in its haste to land on the wall separating the two stalls.

"Aelwyn?" She frowned. "What are you doing here?" There was only one possible reason — the bird carried a message from William. She scrambled into the stall to get to the bird's leg and open the canister. Dusk stepped politely out of the way.

But the little metal cylinder was empty; there was no message inside. She looked up, confused, and that was when she saw.

Another animal was coming in through the large double doors, this one accompanied by the most wonderful sight she could imagine right now — or ever, really.

"Will!"

Whether he heard the need in her voice, or his own urgency to be with her was just as strong, he dropped Skittles's lead and left the horse standing there as he ran toward her. She barely made it back out of the stall in time for him to catch her, scooping her into his arms and holding her there for a long moment, his lips pressed against her cheek as if he meant to keep them there forever.

Even when he did finally set her feet on the ground again, he didn't let her go — or maybe it was her own hands that refused to relinquish their hold.

"What's wrong?" The words came from both their mouths at the same time.

She shook her head. "You go first. Why are you back?"

His gray eyes traveled up and down her face several times, lingering on the hot flush of her cheeks and the tight corners of her mouth. "No, love. Mine can wait for a moment. I'm here now. Tell me what's going on, please."

It was the gentleness of his voice that did it. The utter, complete softness and understanding, the way she knew he could see deeper into her soul than she even could. The vague burning she'd been able to keep behind her eyes leaked out as two hot tears, one trailing down each cheek.

He didn't ignore them. He released one hand from around her

and wiped each one gently with his thumb, drying the salty moisture on his own cloak. "Tell me."

It took her a moment, but she managed to free one of her own hands to reach inside her pocket. She pulled out the folded note and handed it to him.

By the time they returned to hotel, Zander's pledge to call his mother was more than just a promise to Linnea — though he'd have done it for her alone. He was beginning to realize there wasn't much of anything he wouldn't do if she asked him to.

But the long drive through the twisty mountain roads under the starry sky, the beat of familiar music thumping through his chest, had given him time to think, to really clear his head and wrap his mind around his decision.

And he couldn't leave this time without saying a proper goodbye. Especially knowing it was likely to be forever. His last chance to ever talk to his mother.

She might not understand. His father might not even get on the line. But it wasn't about them. It was what he needed.

So when he sat down in the hotel room, alone, and picked up the phone and dialed, the last possibility on his mind was that nobody would answer.

The first time the phone clicked over to voicemail, he thought it was probably just a fluke. They hadn't made it to the phone on time.

But when he called a third time and still only reached a musical tone and, "Please leave a message for *Jack and Maggie*," he had to admit defeat.

He must have slammed the receiver down hard enough for Linnea to hear, because a few seconds later, she appeared in the doorway. "Already?" Her thick black eyelashes nearly covered her eyes in her frown.

"I didn't reach them," he said. "They didn't answer."

"I still don't understand how those things work," she said. "Can't you just…*call* them again?"

"I've tried. Maybe they're not home." He glanced over at the clock, realizing it was only quarter to nine. "It's earlier there. They might just be out."

"And you can only call them when they're home? It's a different kind of phone than the one in your pocket?"

He smiled. She really did pick up on things quickly, even when he failed to realize she might need an explanation for one of the strange things in this world. "Actually, they do have this kind too — but I never memorized their numbers. They were always just saved in my phone."

"I don't know what that means, but… Can you call them again in a little while on this phone?" She nodded toward the hotel phone.

It was only then he realized that he was missing plenty of his own beats this evening. Although money wasn't an object for them, at all, there was no reason for him to be running up the hotel bill even higher with phone calls when he had a perfectly good cell phone in his pocket.

As far as he could tell, Nathaniel had put enough minutes on the thing to get them through the next decade.

"I'll try again in a while. You want to go and get some ice for our drinks?"

The hotel's ice machine fascinated Linnea, and he loved to watch her smile as the cubes came tumbling out of the machine into a bucket, "like magic", as she said.

He understood it. While things like televisions and phones were amazing in a way she'd never imagined anything could be, it was the simpler things — like readily available ice that would completely change their lives in Deusterros if they had them.

Refrigeration in Philotheum would mean that all the milk Linnea had expressed on their journey to maintain her supply could have been saved for the babies, rather than just tossed.

Bigger than that, it would mean that so many more medications could be transported and stored between the worlds, that unused doses could be saved after they were mixed rather than tossed within a few hours. Sometimes, people there literally died for lack of something so simple he'd once taken for granted here. Pressing a button and getting ice.

It was just one more reason he knew he had to go back. If there was anything more precious than the technology itself, it was the knowledge he had about it.

No longer did he question all of the hours William had spent here with his nose buried in books, gleaning every bit of knowledge he could, carrying as many precious facts as he could back through the gate.

"Sure," she said. "I'll get the bucket."

Over in the other room, Zander did a double-take when he saw Nathaniel sitting at the desk, clicking away at the keys of a small computer. "A laptop? You bought a laptop today? We're leaving the day after tomorrow!"

Nathaniel barely looked up at him. "Hopefully by the day after tomorrow, I'll not only know how to best treat Diphtheria, but also I'll be able to produce the vaccine over there from the supplies we're taking back. We can't take enough with us."

"How to treat *what?*" Linnea asked.

It was then Zander remembered they'd never told her about the outbreak. About the little girl he'd seen in his dreams last night after falling asleep wondering if she was okay — knowing in the pit of his stomach that she might not be.

The gate couldn't open again fast enough.

Or slow enough for them to get everything they needed across.

"Let's get the ice," he said.

William wasn't sure he'd ever been quite as angry as he was right now. At least not with this kind of slow burning fury. He'd been mad before, furious even. And on Quinn's behalf, too. After Tolliver and some of the things they'd all experienced in taking over and then fighting for the kingdom, he thought he'd seen the outside limits of his rage.

But this was wholly different. What Charles had said to Quinn earlier was so far beyond the line of acceptable he didn't even know how to *begin* to wrap his head around it. He had to take several deep breaths just to listen to Quinn finish telling him the story.

They'd trusted Charles. Given him an advisory position. They'd even left him in charge of running the kingdom when Samuel had been born unexpectedly while they were on a trip.

His thoughts had never been quite so full of words a king shouldn't say aloud. (Although he said some of them, at least under his breath.)

And it wasn't even so much that Charles wanted Sophia to come to the castle. Although William could never have in good conscience have supported such a decision, he wasn't mad that Charles had dared to ask. He could have understood that.

But for him to speak to Quinn that way, for him to take the events that had transpired during the war and twist them around, to retell the story in a way that not only was blatantly untrue, but that made Quinn doubt if she was remembering it correctly…

There was a special place for people who dared treat his wife that way.

Or he wished there was.

If nothing else, he would restore her safety and her confidence with him. "None of what he said is true, Quinn. That's not how it happened."

"Are you sure? Am I really just being ungrateful and unforgiving? Am I doing the wrong thing?"

He wanted to vomit.

"Quinn, no. You did everything you could from the beginning. It was never enough for her. Nothing would ever be enough — clearly. Now she's sending Charles after you, and he's…" He rubbed at his temples, trying to stave off the impending pounding. "I don't even know. I don't know what he thinks he's getting at or what he's going to try. But you? You *have done nothing wrong.* I'm starting to think we should have dropped that woman off a parapet and into the moat when we had a chance."

She raised an eyebrow. "We don't have a moat."

Her tiny smile sent a tidal wave of relief washing over him. Hopefully he'd still be able to undo the damage Charles had attempted to inflict. He held her in his arms and kissed her forehead. "We need to get a moat."

They didn't *need* this much ice. The drinks they'd bought were already cold from the refrigerator in their room. But pressing the button and watching an endless supply clatter into the little plastic bucket was just so satisfying, Linnea couldn't stop herself until the bucket was overflowing.

She probably should have stopped before quite so many fell on the floor, though. She laughed and turned to hand the bucket to Zander so she could clean up her mess.

But he wasn't paying any attention to her at all. He was just standing there, absolutely still in the doorway of the little alcove, staring down the hall.

Quickly and silently, she set the bucket down on the floor, appraising him as she did so.

Though the muscles in his arm were tense, his hand was not near either place he'd normally keep a weapon. He was listening intently to something, but he didn't look about to spring, he looked… Petrified didn't seem the right word. He wasn't crouched protectively; he wasn't expecting an attack or anything of the sort. And yet, his frozen stance was exactly that. Petrified.

Linnea craned her neck and tried to listen over the low hum of the machine.

After a few seconds, she did hear something. The noises were distant; they came far down the hall, probably not even from the same floor they were on — somewhere below, she thought.

They weren't scary sounds at all. It was the noise of children playing somewhere. Laughing, shouting…*splashing*?

Now she ducked her head around the door, too, looking up and down the hall both ways. The sounds were louder here. She could almost make out distinct voices. But there was nothing else.

"Children?" she asked him.

He nodded slowly, not looking at her.

For a brief moment, she thought it was her fault, that he was reacting this way because he was worried about her.

While it was true she was aching today missing her babies, she didn't mean for it to be like this. She had to hold it together for them, to return to them. She'd finally managed to remember how often Ben would have been separated from their children, even if he'd lived — and she'd never have expected or wanted him to feel guilty about it, or thought they'd love him any less.

She hadn't chosen to be away from Ben and Adeline for this long, but she had to be strong for them, to make it okay.

And then she realized this had nothing to do with *her*. "What's wrong?"

It was as if he couldn't even hear her over the call of something too powerful to resist. There were stories about such things in her world — creatures with voices too powerful to ignore; so strong even a soldier could be lured away to his own death.

The short hallway ended at another, with a railing that overlooked a courtyard in the middle of the hotel. It was quite beautiful, Linnea wished they'd thought to explore the whole building sooner. There were flowers and plants everywhere, and the whole thing was lit by gorgeous glass lanterns, though unlike in her world, these lanterns held light bulbs. And down in the center of the courtyard, was the clearest, bluest pool of water she'd ever seen.

This, of course, was the source of the noise. There were several children in the pool, laughing, shouting, climbing the steps to get out of the water and then turning around and jumping back in, splashing water everywhere. Adults were scattered around, too. Some were in the water, playing with children.

One man held a little girl high over his head and then tossed her. She screeched before she went under and then bobbed up again, laughing hysterically. "Again!"

William had told her about swimming pools before. She'd been envious just at the description, especially during the long cold moons when swimming was impossible in her world.

Swimming pools, too, were impossible in Deusterros. They sometimes filled big barrels of water for children to play in during Eternolis, but something this size would have been filth and rashes waiting to happen. She wondered how they did it here.

And if they could go in.

But Zander still wasn't hearing or seeing what she was, or at least not in the same way. His mind had no room for the warm evening, or the sweet smell of flowers, or the idea that it would be fun to go swimming themselves.

His eyes were firmly glued on the smiling man with the happy, shrieking little girl. The man who said something to the little girl that she couldn't hear, but ignored her request to do it "again". After a second, she saw why. There was another little girl, hanging on the wall of the pool nearby, eagerly waiting her turn to be tossed in the air by her father.

As the man picked up his younger daughter, Zander whispered the first word he'd uttered since before the ice room. "Sophia."

Confusion mingled with a cold thrill of fear twisted Linnea's stomach into a knot. *Sophia?* She wasn't here, couldn't be here. Quinn's grandmother didn't even know about the gates, she was certain. Nothing in this world could possibly be associated with her. *Could it?*

She looked furiously all over the courtyard, feeling naked without her own dagger, wondering how Zander could even say such a thing, here, without his hand reaching instinctively for one of his own weapons.

And then she remembered.

Quinn's grandmother wasn't the only Sophia Zander knew.

He didn't speak of them often. The two little girls he'd left behind in Bristlecone. It was too hard, brought up too many conflicting emotions, got in the way of accepting his life in Deusterros.

And Linnea understood that more than anyone. Missing her younger siblings who were still in Eirentheos was sometimes worse than missing her parents.

"Is that them?" she whispered. "Your sisters?"

She felt lucky to even get a nod out of him, the way his attention was so completely absorbed by the scene in front of him. She leaned against the cool metal railing so she, too, could stare, fascinated.

The little girls, Ashley and Sophia, were gorgeous, of course. Both with brown hair and big brown eyes and smiles that could have powered all the lights in a castle. She wanted to hug them both, even in their wet clothes — she didn't care — and to hear those voices up close.

Zander's father… She wasn't sure what she'd expected. The things she'd heard about him had made her feel that he must be much different than her own father. And in some ways, he was. His skin was a much lighter color, and he was shorter. He was balding on the top, but the hair he had was well-groomed, at least in line with the styles she'd seen on the television.

But the way he played with his little girls — the way they shrieked and hugged him in delight, clamoring for "again" and "more" and "higher" … now she understood the depths of Zander's hurt and his own confused feelings on the way things had been left between them.

She looked around at the rest of the people down there, wondering if his mother was there, too. Eventually, Ashley, the older of the two, got out of the pool and ran over to where a woman was sitting on the side and dug into a bag next to her chair.

Even from this distance, Linnea loved Zander's mother immediately. She was beautiful, a bit zaftig in a way that made her hope to blessed with a hug. Her children couldn't resist, anyway. Ashley launched a full-body wet cuddle at her mother before running back to the water. The girls got their darker hair and eyes from her.

"Should we go down there?" Linnea asked after a while. "And say hello?"

Zander shook his head, which she realized she should have expected. He was a quite private person. Making a scene like that would bother him.

"Then we should probably step back a little," she said, "before…"

"Zander! Daddy look! Mommy! Look up there! It's Zander!" Sophia's little fingers were waving in ten directions at once as, suddenly, the eyes of his entire family were on the second floor, staring at them.

"I didn't know Zander was going to be here! Mommy! Did you know Zander was here?" Ashley was already out of the pool again, this time running for her towel before dashing toward the stairs.

Quinn didn't know why it was so much easier to believe William than the reasoned arguments and voices in her own head, she just knew how grateful she was that he was here. He held her for a long time, just letting her rest her head against his chest as she regulated her breathing with his.

Finally, she was ready to ask the question she knew she didn't really want the answer to. "So… Why are you back?"

He sighed, which didn't boost her confidence at all. "Because I'm afraid that the outbreak has already spread as far as Rock Ridge."

"You're afraid it has, or it has?"

"Well, I've got two vials of blood in my bag that I need to test in the lab to be sure, but…"

"You're already pretty sure. So, what do we do?"

"We have to keep it from spreading further. If it reaches the city…" He glanced over her shoulder. There was nothing there, but she knew what he was thinking. The castle. The babies inside.

Her heart thudded in her stomach. "How do we know it hasn't already gotten this far?"

He didn't answer, but he didn't need to. "We just have to stop it in any way we can. We need to order the affected towns under quarantine and then restrict travel into the city, particularly into the castle."

"I don't really know what that means, Will."

"It means isolating the people who are sick, or who have come into contact with anyone who has symptoms. They need to not be traveling anywhere in the kingdom, exposing anyone else."

"You mean locking people in their homes?" For the second time today, everything was spinning. "Some of these people don't even believe in germs, Will. They're not just going to be okay with that."

His Adam's apple bobbed up and down, and he looked at the ground.

"You think we should send troops."

There was so much surprise in his expression she immediately grew warm. "I didn't say that. "I don't actually have an answer here.

I'm just telling you what I know, and that if this spreads much further, we're going to have a serious problem. Let's not forget we don't have any way to protect *them*, either. We'd be risking every soldier we sent out there."

She rubbed at the side of her neck; she needed her head to be clear for this discussion. William was so good at what he did, but this part here was hers, she was in charge, these were her decisions, her people to protect. "Most of our troops are already deployed around the kingdom. They're already out there, in the villages, helping rebuild, doing what I asked in identifying those who fought against us in the war."

"Maybe we should call them back?"

"And what, William? Tell the rest of the people, that we're sorry, but rebuilding their lives doesn't matter? Sorry about your children, but we don't want our soldiers getting sick?"

He gaped at her, half in horror, half in what she recognized as admiration. "I'm sorry, Quinn. That's not what I meant. I'm just... I don't know what I'm doing with that part, at all. You... Learned a lot during the war, I think."

"I'm still learning. But I do see situations better now. I mean, I actually know where my troops are and what they're doing right now. That's a start, right?"

He laughed and leaned in to kiss her cheek. "It's more than a start, my love. My queen."

She smiled and took his face in her hands, kissing him on the lips instead, letting it go a little longer and deeper than maybe they had time for at the moment. But, oh, his kiss...his love...the way his arms wrapped around her and she never wanted him to let go... By the time she did finally pull away, she felt better than she had all day, and her head was much clearer.

"I do need your help. You know more about the risks and what would make the situation worse."

He nodded, looking calmer now, too. "You're right about not recalling the troops. That would cause more panic than attempting a quarantine will. But troop movement wouldn't be good, either, Quinn. That's a lot of exposure and bodies and movement."

"So what we need is to freeze movement, wherever anyone is sick."

"Yes."

"All right. I'll draft messages to the troops immediately, anyway. And ask them to immediately report any sickness in any village. And, then, I hate to do it, but if anyone in a village is sick, we'll need to quarantine. But we have to make sure they're cared for, William. We need to make sure they're supplied with everything they need, and that we provide the best care we can to anyone who is sick."

The look of admiration in his eyes had overtaken the fright completely now. "And that, my love, is why you're the queen."

"I just wish Marcus and Zander were here. I have a feeling Charles is going to fight me on this. Also, I don't like that Thomas and Marcus are out there. It just feels wrong now."

"You know we probably won't be able to convince them to come back. People out there need so much right now, and the gate. Defending the gate is important, Quinn. Linnea and Nathaniel are over there, and if this girl makes an appearance again…"

"I'm still going to send them a message. Thomas might not be at risk of getting sick, but Marcus…maybe I can at least convince him to be careful. Stay away, wear a mask, something."

He nodded. "And I think we need to restrict access to the castle immediately. We can talk to the staff about the best way to do it, but we can't allow anyone who's been traveling anywhere to be near the babies. I feel wrong about saying it when other people's children are at risk, but protecting Samuel is also protecting the future of the kingdom."

Her hands were shaking again, so he reached for his, to steady herself. "For how long?"

He shrugged. "I wish I knew. With any luck, Nathaniel will be able to bring back enough vaccine to at least protect the children in the most vulnerable places."

"And Samuel," Quinn interrupted.

"And Samuel, for sure. And Benjamin and Adeline as well. Then, hopefully we can begin making the medicine here and convince people to take it. That's going to be the hardest part."

"Maybe it won't be. Maybe when they see what a difference it makes. Maybe if we can stop the spread with the quarantines and your medicine."

"Hopefully. I'll do what I can in the coming days to go out there and visit any patients as well. I'll gather as much medicine as I can before I make any trips."

"We should have left with Zander and Linnea." It was the kind of joke she made often, but only rarely was she as serious about it as she was right now.

"But we didn't. So, lucky us, instead we need to prepare for a trip to your grandmother's."

CONCESSIONS

THAT THE LITTLE BODY in his arms was sopping wet and the water was soaking through his shirt didn't faze Zander in the slightest. All he knew was that she was heavy and real and warm in his arms. He'd never expected to see his little sister again, not ever. The weight of that fact had never truly sunk in until right this moment.

"Were you on a trip, Zander? Like us? Did you get me anything?"

He brushed the damp tangles off her forehead before kissing it. "I have been on a trip. Kind of."

"Did you go on a plane like we did? We got to fly on an airplane. Mama made me share the window with Soph. Daddy didn't have a window."

"It sounds like you had fun. Did you like the plane?"

"Yes! The man — the flight attendant? He gave us pretzels and soda. Even Sophia got to drink a whole can herself! It hurt my ears when we landed, though."

"I'm sorry." He leaned in and kissed the spot just in front of her ear. "There?"

She nodded. "It's better now, though."

"Ashley!" His father's voice boomed loudly from somewhere behind them. Zander turned around, still holding her. There he was, his father, standing a good ten feet away, not moving toward them, just calling for his little sister. One of his hands was clutched firmly around Sophia's wrist. "You're all wet. Come down now and get dressed."

"Zander doesn't care if I'm wet! Do you?"

He shook his head. "She's fine."

"Now, Ashley. You don't need to be standing out here in your bathing suit. Come and get dressed."

"But I want to go swimming again!"

"Me too, Daddy! And I want to see Zander!" Sophia twisted and tried to break away from their father, but he scooped her up into his arms.

"If you don't come right this second, Ashley, I'll come pick you up and take you to the car instead, and we can just go home. No more swimming at all."

Even his little sisters knew better than to ignore the voice their father was using now. Ashley slunk down from Zander's arms and ran to catch up with his father who was already walking quickly away, with Sophia looking backwards over his shoulder.

Beside him, Linnea let out a low whistle and she stretched her hand toward his until the tips of their fingers were touching.

But he didn't take her hand or say anything back. He was too busy staring at the stairs. Because there, almost to the top, was his mother.

After the way his father had just reacted, he had trouble breathing as he watched her approach. He wondered if she would even say anything to him, or if she would just disappear down the hall, like the rest of his family.

When she didn't disappear, when she reached the top step and then took another, tentative step toward him, he couldn't manage to force any air into his lungs at all.

She stopped when she was still two feet away. "Zander. It's really you."

He nodded.

"Can I…?" she held her arms open.

He bridged the gap between the two of them in a single step and stepped into her arms, wrapping his own around her back.

The smell… There was nobody else in any world who smelled exactly like his mother. It was the smell of her shampoo mingled with her perfume and a mixture of love and trust he'd never feel in any other arms.

Moisture welled in his eyes, reminding him… "I'm getting you all wet." His shirt was drenched after holding Ashley.

She acted like she hadn't even heard him; her head stayed buried against his shoulder, holding him tight.

When she finally pulled away slightly, it was with a confused frown as her hand traveled up to his right bicep. After feeling the muscle there for a moment, she took a step back. "That's not from football."

"No. It's not from running across the country and doing drugs, either."

"Your father didn't mean that last night, you know that. He was upset."

"We're all upset. Clearly." He looked down the hallway where his father had gone. "You didn't tell the girls I was here at all, did you?"

"We didn't know for sure that you would be. It was a crazy, last-minute trip banking on the off chance that you might still be at the hotel you called us from last night. You don't want to ask how expensive it was."

She wasn't complaining. He could tell by the way she kept her hand on his arm, by the way her expression remained a longing one as she looked at him. "I can help with the cost, Mom." He reached into his pocket and withdrew the hundred-dollar bills that were stuffed in there.

Her eyes went so wide he thought they might fall out, and she covered up the wad of cash with her other hand as if he was showing her a gun or something. "Where did you get that?" she hissed. "You're not actually dealing drugs or something, are you?" She eyed his biceps with suspicion before turning a wary gaze on Linnea who was still standing beside him.

"I'm going to go back to the room," Linnea said in a tiny voice. "Come get me if you need anything."

He nodded, though he couldn't much concentrate on her right now. "I'm not selling anything. I…" he realized why it looked that way. "Mom, it's just paper to me. I can't even use it where I've been living. There's nothing there I need to buy, even if I could."

"It's not that girl, is it? Is she giving you the money for something?"

"Mom, no. That's Linnea. She's… She's my friend. We've been through a lot together. Her husband died shortly after I met her, and… I don't know. She doesn't have any money, though. Not this kind."

His mother grew silent, her eyes flicking from his face to his bicep, then to the fistful of money before starting the whole cycle over again.

"So this story you told us last night. Other worlds and some kind of gate and Quinn Robbins…"

"Her name is Quinn Rose now."

"She's married? To some boy she met five minutes ago? Megan let her get *married?*"

"Time doesn't work the same over there as it does here, Mom. You think I've only been gone a few weeks, and for you that's true, but for me… Well, for example, yes Quinn is married. I think the courtship was short but not crazy short. They were together for a while first. Now they have a son. He's crawling."

"Wait… *Rose?* You don't mean she married that weird nephew of Doctor Rose's?"

Once upon a time, Zander would have laughed. He, too, had thought that William was a bit strange. Normally, though, his mother would have put a smackdown on him *saying* so. That she was running her mouth this way right now was a testament to just how upset she was.

"His name is William. He's not actually Nathaniel's nephew. He is Linnea's brother, though." He felt like he was speaking nonsense. Gibberish. Gobbledygook. *Great, now his brain was stuck. On mumbo jumbo.* He took a deep breath. "Do you want to go somewhere, maybe? Where we can sit and really talk?"

The rooms directly around them appeared to be empty — or there were no lights coming from the windows at least — but they were still standing at the railing nearest the courtyard, and though they'd kept their voices relatively low, this wasn't a conversation that should be overheard.

"Maybe we could go for a walk?" she suggested, following his gaze down toward the people in the pool.

"There's a little coffee shop across the street and down a little way. The sign says they're always open." *Not that he'd paid special attention when they'd passed the sign or anything.* "My treat?"

They walked in silence down the hall to the front of the building and down the stairs. Once they were in the empty parking lot, his mother spoke again.

"I thought William was her cousin, or something. If Doctor Rose was really her uncle, too."

He almost had to laugh. That seemed like such a small detail in the grand scheme of the situation. It didn't even *matter* right now.

Also, he had a lot of trouble thinking of Nathaniel as *Doctor Rose* anymore. In his mind, they were almost two different people, the doctor he'd known back in Bristlecone and the man he knew now.

"Nathaniel and Quinn's biological father were brothers. Quinn is his niece. But Nathaniel also grew up extremely close to William's father, almost like brothers, so when William's father had children, they all considered Nathaniel their uncle, and that's what they called him. They still do."

"Why wouldn't Megan have just told Quinn that? She knew, didn't she?"

"I don't know. I think maybe because it's not at all easy to talk to someone about another world that you go through a gate to get to. They tend not to believe you." He looked at her pointedly.

"You're saying Megan knows about that, too."

"She always knew, Mom. She even took Quinn there once when she was a baby. But then, after Samuel died, she didn't want Quinn to know about it until she was an adult and she could handle it or something. So she… Well, she lied to her. And she kept her from knowing who Nathaniel really was."

"Until Nathaniel, what? Decided to go back to this other world and he took Quinn with him?"

The hairs on the back of Zander's neck stood up, warning him. He couldn't let the conversation keep going in this direction. If they kept talking like this, he was going to have to tell her that there had been a gate in Bristlecone that was open all the time, that people could have passed through any day they chose. That would open up too many questions about all the gates. And if his mother — or his *father* — decided to get too persistent with getting information about the gates…

He wanted to be honest with his mother, he didn't *want* to lie, but he now understood just how important a lie could sometimes be. And just how different *the truth* and *the whole truth* really were.

"Something like that, yes, Mom. It was a little more complicated than that, but yes. Quinn chose to go, though. Nathaniel didn't kidnap her or anything. It was a really difficult decision, and her family on both sides supported her."

"The last time I saw you, Zander, you were still brokenhearted over that girl. I didn't think you'd ever forgive her."

They'd reached the door of the coffee shop. Zander held the door open and ushered her inside, earning a look that made him wonder if he'd ever held a door for her before. He knew he'd changed in some ways since leaving this world, but he didn't know what would be noticeable to someone else.

It was a cozy little café, lined with high-backed booths along one wall, while the opposite wall was made up of built-in bookshelves, filled with games and used books. One table in the middle of the floor was a chess board, and two young men, probably college-age were in the middle of a game. Soft music played from the speakers overhead. It was perfect.

"Here, Mom," he said, leading her over to the booth furthest from everyone. "What do you want?"

"Are you ready for this, love?" William asked as the carriage rolled to a stop outside Lady Sophia's cottage.

Quinn had never actually been out to her grandmother's new home. Jonathan, one of her other uncles had handled securing the property and getting Sophia settled here. Of course, as soon as he'd done so, he took off again to roam the kingdom, as always. He never stayed close to home. Of all her relatives, he was the one she liked the most, but trusted the least.

Of course, that had been before what Charles had said to her yesterday. Now she wasn't sure she there was anyone she could trust.

Now that she was here, she wondered if calling the place a "cottage" was yet another way to make her feel guilty for "banishing" Sophia here. Or else cottage was a word that meant something completely different in this world.

This was more like a villa or an estate. Possibly even a smaller version of a castle.

There were at least as many footmen here as Quinn had. Two of them opened the enormous wrought-iron gate to let their carriage pass through.

"I don't have a choice but to be ready, do I?" And she was ready. Yesterday's meltdown had been temporary. She could do this. She was the queen. She had won the fight for her kingdom — she could handle her family.

Even if they weren't going to make it easy for her.

Despite all of the servants at the "cottage", Quinn's own guards, Kian and Ethan, opened the doors of the carriage and stood ready to assist.

She nodded to them and they stepped back, just standing guard as Sophia's footmen handled their exit onto the carpet laid out for them. There was no need to start a new battle today over etiquette.

Charles stood on the top step, stoic and unmoving, still angry. Something wasn't quite right, though, Quinn couldn't quite put her finger on it until he swayed slightly as he stood there, though he still kept his eyes staring straight ahead.

"How is Lady Sophia?" she asked the nearest footman.

The man's cheeks turned bright red and his eyes widened, but he said, "Resting comfortably, Your Majesty."

"Thank you…" It always took a moment to get people to say their names when she pressed, but she intended to be known as a leader who cared about her people personally.

"Arlen," he finally stuttered.

"It's a pleasure to meet you, Arlen. Thank you for your service." She held out her gloved hand, and when he took it to kiss her fingers, she transferred a small gold coin from her hand to his.

When he pulled back from her, he no longer seemed nervous or uncertain about her. Instead, there was admiration in his eyes.

She could do this.

William held out his elbow and she looped her arm through it as they made their way slowly up the carpeted walk. It was snowing lightly today, not enough to stick on the ground, but just enough to dust the branches of the hundreds of trees surrounding the estate, making them look like icy, magical wands.

"Are you feeling well?" William asked Charles when they reached the top of the stairs.

Charles looked as if merely being spoken to was painful, but he nodded and said, "I'm just fine, thank you. Please just tend to my mother."

That it was apparently just shy of torture for Charles to even be in the same kingdom as Quinn at the moment didn't stop him from following them through the house, up to the third-story master bedroom and inside with them.

The room was all windows; a three-sided panoramic view of fairy-dusted orchards and fields that stretched for miles until fog finally obstructed the distant landscape. Two roaring fires, one on each side of the room kept everything at a cozy temperature for the woman sitting propped up against dozens of pillows in the enormous canopied bed in the very center.

Quinn felt strange wearing her shoes over the rich carpets as she walked in.

"Your Majesties." Sophia said before they'd made it halfway across the room.

"Lady Sophia." Quinn dropped a curtsey while William bowed in respect.

"To what do I owe the pleasure of your company?"

William's hand twitched next to hers, offering a quick, reassuring touch before he spoke. "We heard you weren't feeling well, Lady. We thought we would come and see what we can do to help."

"Who told you that?" Though it was quite obviously true, emphasized by a horrible, dragging cough at the end of her question, she sounded genuinely surprised.

Quinn's eyes shot to Charles.

"I did, Mother. I asked Quinn to send for William yesterday."

"You bothered their Majesties with *this?*" Sophia coughed again. This time it took her several minutes to recover her breath, and

Quinn thought she saw a spot of something red on her grandmother's handkerchief before she tucked it out of sight.

"Not to worry, Mother. They didn't see your health as an important enough issue to address yesterday. Her Majesty sees fit to leave you out here in the wilderness to rot rather than securing the best attention in the city."

Sophia turned her gray eyes on Quinn. "He asked you to transport me to the castle yesterday and you refused."

It felt like her stomach was inside a slowly tightening vise, but she managed to keep her own gaze locked on to her grandmother's. "He seemed to think that putting you in a carriage and making you travel on bumpy roads for over half an hour was better than leaving you comfortable in your own bed."

William set a hand on her shoulder.

Charles turned on his heel and stormed out of the room. Quinn could hear the clacking of his polished boots echoing all the way down the marble stairs.

For what felt like a very long time, the only sounds in the room came from the crackling, popping fires.

And then William cleared his throat. "Would you mind very much if I examined you, milady?"

"Would you mind closing the door first, Your Majesty?" Her voice sounded rough and made a whistling sound on the last syllable, as if it was difficult for her to even speak.

"Of course."

Once the door was securely closed, and the three of them were alone in the bedroom, Sophia looked at Quinn again. "You stood up to him. To Charles."

Her body couldn't decide if it wanted to be hot or cold. Her chest and cheeks flamed, but even in the warm room, her arms were suddenly icy. "I suppose I did."

"I was hoping you had it in you."

She blinked and stared at her grandmother. William's hands froze over his medical bag. "Excuse me?"

"If there's anything I learned in my tenure as queen of this kingdom, it's that your greatest challenges will come from the people closest to you. It's harder to stand against someone you're close to than a foreign enemy, every time."

"You… You wanted me to say no to allowing you to come to the castle?"

"Sending me here was the first thing you ever did that made me believe you were actually fit to lead this kingdom."

"Almost being assassinated by your son wasn't enough?" William snapped, startling Quinn.

Aside from going into another coughing fit — and this time Quinn was sure there was blood — Sophia seemed unaffected by his unusual outburst. "I'll admit to being relieved when Quinn used her weapon and survived that particular incident. I didn't expect she would, but I was impressed when she did.. But after several decades of living with Hector and Tolliver, I knew that courage against outright enemies wasn't going to be enough."

She wasn't sure she'd ever been so confused — and that was saying something. She stared helplessly at William.

"Um," he cleared his throat and held up his stethoscope. "May I use this device to listen to your heart?"

"You can do whatever makes you feel better," she said. "It's not going to do anything for me. I'm dying."

"We don't know that," he said. "We don't even know what's wrong. I may be able to help."

"No, *you* don't know that, Your Majesty. I know. You can either choose to not believe me and waste the next day or three using all your tricks and supplies on an old woman, or you can just believe me now and take all of your magic and mystery and use it on someone who might still be alive this time next week if you help them." As if to emphasize her point, she dissolved into a spectacular coughing fit that made Quinn honestly wonder if she wasn't going to die right now, in front of them.

William ran to put the tea kettle over the fire. "I have some tea that should calm your cough. Even if… We can still make you as comfortable as possible right now."

"You can say it. You can make me comfortable until I die. That's what's happening."

The vise around Quinn's stomach tightened down several more notches, and now she was cold everywhere. Enough that she shivered.

"Have a seat, child. It's not comfortable for you to stand for so long."

"I…" Quinn looked around. The nearest chair was over by the fireplace.

"There's enough bed for another ten people to sit comfortably here. You don't actually have to get close to me if you'd like to use some of it."

Apparently one didn't actually have to cross over a bridge to enter an alternate universe, Quinn thought, sitting down on the end of the bed.

"That's better. Take your shoes off, if you'd like. I'm not going anywhere, and the two of you and your guards might as well enjoy dinner after coming all this way. My cook is indulging me just a little these days, though I can't eat most of it."

Quinn took a deep breath. There didn't seem much point in holding anything back now. "So… You didn't pressure Charles to ask me to bring you back to the castle?"

"I'm not saying I've never tried it, but this particular time, no. That was him."

"But you're glad he did *and* you're glad I said no?"

"*Glad* is a strange word to describe any of this, Your Majesty."

Quinn raised an eyebrow, because it was about all she was capable of.

Sophia was silent for a moment because William was looking in the back of her throat using a little mirror Nathaniel had developed that reflected light from the room. Whatever he saw there made his shoulders cave forward.

When Sophia's voice came again, it was unexpected. "Quinn, I know you think I've been a terrible grandmother. I'm sure I have. I haven't stood up and supported you. I…" She had to stop because she was coughing again. This time William helped her, holding the handkerchief while she coughed, and then lowering her backwards into the pillows.

Quinn didn't know how he did it. He was so gentle, so seemingly unaffected by the whole thing except for his unending, caring presence and attention. Once Sophia was settled again, he went to retrieve the kettle and began preparing a pot of his special tea.

When she looked over at her grandmother again, she was startled to see that Sophia was watching William with the same kind of admiration she felt.

"I was a different person once," Sophia said quietly as she turned her attention back to Quinn. "A long, long time ago, when I was married to your grandfather. I was even the mother I meant to be back then, though only your father would have been old enough to remember."

William carried over the teapot and set it carefully on the bedside table. "It'll be just another minute or two."

Sophia nodded. "If things hadn't changed the way they did, I might have even become the grandmother you wish you had."

"I don't…"

"You don't know what kind of grandmother you wish you had — although it would probably have been one who didn't just sit idly by and watch while her son attempted to assassinate you and take over your kingdom?"

Now Quinn was the one who was coughing.

"Oh, go ahead and laugh. It's dark, but it's at least a little funny."

William recovered first. "Well, if we're discussing minimum requirements…"

"And yet, I couldn't reach even those. I'm well aware. You don't have to tiptoe around it. I knew what I was doing at the time."

"Then why? Why would you do that to Quinn?" William spluttered, even as he poured tea into a cup without spilling a drop.

"You wouldn't understand it, William. I could try explaining myself for a million cycles, and you'd never even catch a glimpse of why. Not with the parents you have and the family you were raised in. And I hope that's always the case. That neither of you ever understand why I did it.

Quinn thought she was going to start coughing again, but after a brief moment of struggling, Sophia only cleared her throat — or tried to.

William added a bit of cool water to the teacup and then held it toward Sophia. "Here. It's not so hot now. It should help with your throat and your cough."

Sophia took a sip and then, when William had taken the cup from her again, sat herself up straighter in the pillows and looked right at Quinn. "It wasn't about you," she said. "None of it, Tolliver, the takeover of the castle, my staying at the castle. It was never about you."

"What was it about then?"

The last couple of times Sophia had tried to inhale deeply, it had resulted in a terrible coughing fit, but this time she stayed upright and okay. "I married your grandfather when I was very young. I didn't know much, especially not about being a queen and helping to rule over a kingdom." She glanced between them. "Much like the two of you, I suppose."

William came over to where Quinn was and sat down next to her, scooting so she could lean against him.

"Your grandfather was a good man. Kind, loving. A good husband and father. In time, I think we might have had something like what the two of you already do. I was the challenge to that, I think. I wasn't raised in a family anything like that. But he tried."

William slipped an arm behind her back and she knew they were both thinking the same thing. How quickly and easily even a happy marriage could come to an end the way Sophia's had.

"I didn't know what to do when Jonathan died. I already knew I hadn't been the wife I should have been to him. I was determined to protect the one thing he had left in my care — his kingdom. So I married a man who I thought would be able to help me hold on to it, who would protect us from Dovelnia, to help me not lose that last piece of him."

Quinn had never felt quite so sorry for Sophia over how that choice had turned out. The person she had trusted had been the one trying to take her kingdom from her. The one who had taken her husband, and would eventually take her son.

"I know I made mistakes in that. And I fought for so many cycles to hold onto it. When you came along, I just didn't know if you could do it. It was yours, of course it was — your grandfather's crown. But all I could think was that after all this time, your inexperience, your alliance with Stephen, your *marriage* to a prince from another kingdom. I thought that was going to be it. The kingdom would fall at last. And so I chose to protect the crown over you. To see if my son could take it for the final time and actually keep it."

Quinn sighed. "At least you're honest now."

To her surprise, her grandmother smiled. "I'm on my deathbed, child. A lie isn't going to help me where I'm going. It's funny — in a truly horrible way — that it took me until now to realize that the true gift Jonathan left me to protect wasn't his kingdom."

William pulled her just a little closer.

"I'm sorry I didn't understand that. I'm sorry I didn't protect you. I know I've disappointed him. But you, child? You, he'd be proud of. His legacy and his kingdom, all in the hands of a girl with a tender heart and a strong mind, just like him. Don't ever compromise either one."

It wasn't easy to speak around the sudden heaviness in her throat, but she nodded. "I'll try not to."

"Start by continuing to hold your ground against the biggest threat — those close to you who would attempt to undermine your authority. I'm afraid I can't vouch for the type of children I raised. I'm glad to know my great-grandson is in more capable hands. William, would you hand me the tea again, please? I need to rest now."

REPARATIONS

"IT'S SUPPOSED TO BE me buying you a treat when we go out to spend time together," Zander's mother said when he carried over her cup of chai tea and a raspberry-cream-cheese pastry she hadn't asked for, but he knew she'd like. "Let me pay."

"No, Mom. You did that for long enough, and I loved every minute of it. I want to treat you now."

She eyed the giant cup he set down on his side of the table. "Cappuccino? At this hour?"

"Coffee is a rare treat in…these days. It probably won't keep me up anyway after today, but if it does, it will still be worth it." He took a long sip of the foamy drink. "Yep. Totally worth it."

She watched him for a long moment as she drank her tea. "This is getting a bit elaborate to just be a story about where you've been for the past two months." It was an admission, not an accusation.

He swallowed his coffee and thought for a moment before answering. He was trying desperately to put himself in her place. He knew how ridiculous it all sounded, how impossible it had to be. "How about, just for a little while, just while we're sitting here together eating, you just try and *pretend* that what I'm saying might be true? You can pick up all your doubts and questions and mistrust right back over there by the door when we leave, but just for right now, believe me. Do you think you could do that?"

She pressed her lips together, and then he saw it happen. He saw her expression transform from skeptical and confused to one that was so familiar and understanding he almost wanted to crawl under the table and up into her lap — the way he had when he was little and she'd "believed" all the crazy stories he would tell. "Okay," she said. "Tell me about this world, about you."

And so he did. Time and the world disappeared around them as he told her about arriving in a strange world, about discovering that not only was his ex-girlfriend married, but had somehow become a mother in the short time since he'd seen her.

She laughed when he told her how terrible he'd been at horseback riding when he'd first arrived, how he'd never realized just how painful it could be to sit in a saddle all day when you weren't used to it.

He told her about the rabies outbreak. About how Owen had saved countless lives when he'd brought the lifesaving medicine back through the gate. Going for understanding over order, he told her how they were facing another such emergency in Philotheum right now and how this trip might change the history of things over there for the better.

"So, this is a place you can travel back and forth from?"

He hadn't meant to let that piece of it slip. But she was taking a leap and trusting him, so he decided to offer her the same courtesy. "It was, Mom. Until it got too dangerous." And that was when he told her about Ben. How he'd made the decision, in a fraction of an instant, to give up his entire world, his life, his chance to ever see his parents or his sisters again, in the hope of saving Ben. And how, instead, it had cost them both everything.

"I never had a friend like that — never knew anyone like him at all," he said, as his mom dabbed at her eyes with brown paper napkins. "I only knew him for ten days, but...there was a lifetime in there somehow. There I was, this ridiculous stranger who couldn't even ride a horse or get a sword off the ground. I was disrespectful, even rude, to the queen he was sworn to protect. He could have run me through with his weapon, but he didn't. Instead, he took me under his wing, treated me like the man I never thought I was going to be. And what did I do to repay him? I watched him die because he came to watch over me when I tried to leave."

"Oh, Zander, I'm sure he knows what you did. What you sacrificed to try to save him."

"I know he does, Mom. He told me so himself, before he died. When he asked me to look after his wife for him."

"And that's the girl who's here with you?"

He nodded. "Linnea. She was pregnant that night."

"She's *pregnant*?"

"No. This is what I've been telling you. I know that part is the hardest to understand. She was pregnant for the full nine moons — months — and then the babies were born, almost three moons ago now."

"Babies? Twins?"

"A little boy and a little girl. Benjamin and Adeline. They're really amazing. Beautiful and perfect, both of them. Addie looks just like her mother, though her hair's a bit lighter. Benjamin looks like him."

"Where are they? Back at the hotel?"

"No. Linnea didn't mean to come here. This was supposed to be just me and Nathaniel. We found another gate and — it was stupid. We really should have just closed it. It's too dangerous. If it hadn't been for me wanting so much to come back and talk to you, and of course, the medicine here. Anyway, it's complicated, and it's another reason we have to close the gate and never open it again, but Linnea ended up coming along by accident. The babies are still over there."

"And you miss them."

"More than I ever imagined I could miss something, yes."

"You want to go back."

He nodded. "I don't want to leave you. I don't want to never see Ashley and Sophia again. But…"

"That's your home now."

"I don't know how that happened. I never thought I'd say anything like that. Back when I first got there, and especially when I got stuck, I'd have ripped a gate between the worlds with my bare hands if I could have. But now…I just want to kiss the warm, comfortable hotel room goodbye and go back to my drafty cold one in the castle."

"A castle?"

"Yes. I realize that mentioning it is going to put another kink in your ability to suspend disbelief right now, but I'm going for complete honesty, so… Yes, I live in a castle. It's enormous and beautiful, and also drafty. We don't have electricity."

"So…there's what? Some king over there and he invited you to live in his castle after you just appeared in his world uninvited."

"Well…sort of. Yes. There are two kings there, at least that I know personally. There are more, I'm sure, in other kingdoms. The castle where I live now — there's a king, but he's not actually the ruler. He's the king because he's married to the queen…who happens to be Quinn."

His mother took such a long drink of her tea that he was fairly sure she was actually just tipping an empty cup to her mouth. When she finally put it down, she was remarkably calm. "I guess if I'm going to believe any of it, that's not even close to the worst part.."

He laughed. "No, I suppose it isn't."

"And you're, what? A prince or something?"

"No. William Rose is, though — or was, before he married Quinn and became the king. I'm not sure how that affects his title in the kingdom he came from. He might still be a prince there. This was something Quinn was born into. Her biological father was the heir to the throne of Philotheum before he died."

"And Megan knew all of this?"

"She knew about the other world, but not the rest of it. It's all very… It's a lot. It involves murders and intrigue and politics. We, uh… We might have just finished winning a war for Quinn's throne over there."

"We?"

He bowed his head. "Sir Zander Cunningham, Order of the White Rose, personal guard to Queen Quinn Katriel Rose of the Kingdom of Philotheum, at your service."

She sat silent for a long moment, contemplating this. "So, you and Quinn have forgiven each other."

"Like I said, it was a long time ago. I didn't take it so well when I got there and discovered she was married to William Rose."

"I can imagine not."

He smiled. "But now… We've been through a lot together. It turns out we make much better friends that we would have ever been together. William and her… I never believed there was such a thing as soul mates until I really watched the two of them together. She'd never have been happy with me the way she is with him. And I wouldn't have been, either."

"You know; this is the part of the conversation that's making me wonder if you're not really telling me the truth. I thought you would never quite get over her. I gave up hope, actually that you'd ever talk to her again."

"But we do talk. She's another reason I want to go back, actually, Mom. She's my friend. I don't think she actually depends on my advice as much as she tells me she does, but I like to think that I have something to do with the good direction things have taken in the kingdom these days."

"Because you're a knight."

"Well, not just because of that, but I am a knight, yes."

"Telling me you ran off to be a roadie for a band and you've taken up smoking pot would have been a lot easier to handle."

"But this is still better than shooting heroin, right?"

It worked; she laughed.

"Anyway, roadies only get to haul speakers and instruments in and out of trailers. I get to carry a sword and ride a horse — his name is Ember, and he's really kind of awesome."

"Hey now, roadies get to meet girls, too."

"I think I might have one of those, Mom. I'm kind of hoping I do."

By the time they finally left the café, Zander was surprised that dawn hadn't yet begun to break along the horizon. Neither one of them was tired, though. His mom had switched to coffee hours ago, too.

"You can go back to not believing me now," he said as the bells on the door jingled behind them.

"I don't want to. If you're really going to leave me forever, I want to be able to picture everything you just told me. Your horse and your bird. Those babies. Quinn as a queen. You, saving the lives of children with the medicine you bring back from here."

"Dad will never buy it."

"No. Certainly not today."

"What was his plan? Why did you guys come all this way with the girls and everything if he didn't want to talk to me?"

"He wanted to talk to you, Zander. Just not in a hotel in New York where you could just slip away and leave again. He didn't think you'd put up a huge fight in front of the girls."

He froze and spun to face her, his mouth agape. "You were going to *kidnap* me?"

"I don't think he thought about it that way. In his mind, it was just stopping you from running away again."

"Stop me how? What was he going to do? Put me in handcuffs? Lock me in the basement?"

"He thought it would all work itself out when he dropped you off in a fully paid dorm room next month."

A lot of things almost came out of his mouth right then. He almost asked where and why and what his father was thinking. Fortunately, he managed to bite his tongue before any of it came out. It didn't matter. None of it mattered. Whatever his dad wanted to feel, or how he wanted to handle the tragedy of losing his son to another world, Zander didn't need to interfere. People had their own ways of dealing with things.

And that was when he knew. Somehow, in the middle of all of this, of jumping worlds and losing friends and fighting battles and delivering babies and kissing a girl, he'd grown up.

He wasn't being stupid and leaving behind his world because he had a crush on a girl. He was just doing what people did. The best they could with what they had at any given time.

And that was all his dad was doing, too.

"It might have worked," he admitted. "If the truth was that I'd just run off somewhere for a few weeks trying to track down my ex-girlfriend."

"He was kind of counting on your being broke and heartbroken. Maybe open to having some of that solved."

It was awful, but it wasn't unloving. So he sighed, and he put his arm around his mother's shoulders. "Can you try talking to him?"

"I can, Zander. But I can't make any promises that he'll listen. This other world thing — he's not ready for that."

"I know. But if there's any way we could all spend one last day together, I would really like that. And I'd love to introduce you to Linnea."

"If he won't Zander, the girls and I will."

"You think he'd let them?"

"I think that if he doesn't, he's going to find divorce papers waiting for him when we get home — but I don't think we'll get to that point," she added quickly when Zander stopped walking and stared at her. "It's just that this is my choice, the one I'm prepared to live with. He's going to have to decide on his for himself."

Linnea stirred and sat up in bed when Zander entered the room, despite the fact that he really had seen a thin sliver of pink light in the eastern sky just before he and his mother had climbed the stairs.

"Sorry," he whispered. "I didn't mean to wake you. I thought Nathaniel was sleeping in here, actually." He glanced at the numbers on the door again before closing and locking it. He had come in the wrong room. "My mistake. I'm so sorry."

"Don't be sorry. I was waiting for you anyway." She glanced toward the adjoining doors, which both stood wide open.

"Linnea! You needed sleep! You were exhausted."

"Oh, I slept." She grinned, pushing long strands of hair back and out of her face. "It's just that little noises wake me up easily these days. How are you?"

"I'm all right." He slipped out of his shoes and then walked over to sit on the edge of her bed.

"How did things go with your parents?"

"It was only my mom, but… It was way better than anything I could ever have imagined. I'm so grateful there was another gate and I could come here."

"So you're staying." She smiled, but only one side of her mouth actually rose in a forced gesture.

"No. I'm not. This was wonderful, and I want to spend more time with my mom tomorrow, and my dad, if he'll decide to accept my decision. But then I'm going home. With you."

This time, she initiated the kiss, pulling him toward her until he could no longer tell where he ended and she began. And it didn't matter, because this was where he was supposed to be. They were two people, both thrown into unfamiliar worlds by Ben's death, both forced to make their way in unexpected territory, to build a life out of the shattered pieces of what they'd thought things were going to be like. And somehow they'd found each other.

"I love you," he whispered when she finally pulled away to breathe.

"I love you, too."

And then their lips found each other again.

The sleep was brief, but the best he'd had in a long time, lying there next to Linnea. It had been more a weight on him than he'd realized, living with the knowledge that his mother was worried, and his own worry that she might never understand, would never forgive him.

They woke up in time to go down to breakfast together, him, Nathaniel and Linnea. Before they even got inside, he saw them. Ashley and Sophia, each with a huge, chocolate-frosted doughnut.

"Zander!" Sophia shrieked as they reached the door. She came barreling toward him and leaped into his arms, getting chocolate *everywhere*. He didn't mind. He hugged on her and drank her in until he was sure he'd be finding smudges of chocolate in his hair and behind his ears for the next week.

His mother was there, too. Looking even more exhausted than he felt, but she smiled and stood to greet them.

"Hello, Doctor Rose," she said while Zander was setting down Sophia and picking up Ashley.

"It's Nathaniel," he said, holding out a hand. "Would it be all right if I called you Maggie?"

"Sure." She gave him a tentative smile.

"It's good to see you again," he told her. "I'm sorry it's under such, um...*odd* and challenging circumstances."

"I suppose it's all still actually true this morning?"

"Yes. I must apologize for the part I played in it. I never intended to involve your family or be responsible for creating such a difficult situation. Nobody should have to make such choices."

She put her hand on Zander's shoulder as she answered. "I'm not sure it's all such a terrible thing. It was hard to hear, and it's even harder to think that he might never…" she cast a glance at the little girl in his arms. "Anyway, I've never seen Zander so happy or full of such purpose. Despite what it means for me, I think this might have been the best thing that could have happened to him."

He had to set Ashley down then, because his arms had gone weak, though his heart had never quite been so full.

He didn't want to ruin the moment by asking where his father was.

"And you must be Linnea?" his mother asked.

"Yes, Mrs. Cunningham," she dropped the tiniest of curtsies and extended her own hand. "It's truly an honor to meet you and your beautiful daughters. You don't know how long I've been wishing I could."

"It's all right if you call me Maggie, too."

Linnea's face brightened so noticeably that on someone else, Zander would have thought it was fake, but he knew Linnea. She never pretended for anyone. "Thank you," she said. "And can I just say that I love that blouse? That fabric is incredible, and it looks so lovely on you."

Within minutes, Linnea had won his mother over completely. He should have guessed.

"What do you girls want to do today?" Linnea asked, when they'd finally all gotten some food and sat back down at one of the tables. "That swimming pool looked like so much fun last night. Would you believe I've never been in one before?'

His sisters were shocked and appalled at the admission, though her promise that she would allow them to teach her what to do if they all went swimming together had both of them in her fan club before breakfast was over, too.

It was a beautiful day, the perfect last memory to hold on to before leaving them all for the last time.

They didn't tell his sisters anything, except that he wasn't coming home to Bristlecone right now, because he had some new grown-up work he had to do. They'd forget most of it. Someday, Sophia especially, might not even remember him. There was no reason to make it traumatic. Especially not now.

It all ended perfectly, too, with hugging his mother tightly and telling her how much he loved her, and then returning to the hotel room with Linnea's hand linked inside his.

That day would be the last day he'd hold on to, a picture-perfect memory he'd keep in a special frame in his mind.

He didn't expect to see his father again. Not after that. He'd resigned himself to it and knew he'd have to find a way to make peace with it someday.

So when there was a knock on the door of their room the next morning, his heart didn't even leap.

Until after Nathaniel opened it.

"Hello Mr. Cunningham."

"Doctor Rose. Is my son here?"

Zander's eyes darted to Linnea first, which made her knit her eyebrows and shake her head. "Go," she mouthed.

His father was standing on the other side of the threshold as if there was a force field keeping him out there, so Zander grabbed the key card and his cell phone and went outside.

When his father started walking, he followed. Down the hall, then down the stairs and into the parking lot. For a second, he wondered if he should be worried that his father was actually going to kidnap him. Then he realized that would be impossible. Physically, his father was no longer any kind of match for him. Wouldn't have been, even if there wasn't a dagger in a sheath on his leg.

Then he realized that this was possibly the least productive line of thinking *ever*, so he shut it down and tried not to think about anything except the fact that his father was so close to him right now that he could reach out and touch him.

And so that's what he did.

His father spun around immediately, as if he'd been burned or something, and then Zander really didn't know how to feel. "I'm sorry," he said.

Those words did something, changed something about the expression on his father's face. *Softened it, maybe? Or was he just confused now?*

"You're sorry for touching me?"

"Yes…no…for startling you, maybe?"

"Is this all my fault, Zander?"

He'd had this conversation before. Sort of. Not in reality, but in his dreams. What was the right thing to say? "No, Dad. None of this is your fault, at all. I know I was angry at the same time as I left, but it isn't why."

"You don't expect me to believe this ridiculous story you've sold your mother, do you?"

"No." He didn't. It was too much to ask of anyone, and sometimes you just had to tell someone the truth and let them decide what to do with it. "Did you ever… I gave Owen my backpack. Did he give it to you?"

"That backpack? Full of your clothes and money? I saw it. I looked inside of it. I knew why you sent it."

"You did?" He'd "sent" it because it contained all of his things and enough money to fund college for himself. He'd "sent" it because he'd been planning on reaching the other side himself and having those things. But it had contained a note to his father, asking for forgiveness and some understanding of what he'd been going through before the gate ever happened.

"I know. You wanted to prove to me that you could take on the world by yourself, that you didn't need anything from me. I got the message, Zander. I thought I'd give you some time to cool off. If you want your things back, though I suggest you find Owen. I made him keep it, in case you needed them before you were ready to come and face me."

He threw his head back and studied the bright blue sky, trying to stay calm and reasonable. His father had never even seen the note. Never even noticed how much money was in that backpack. He'd never bothered to even go through it. Well, hopefully Owen would find a use for it.

He could have said a lot of things right then. There were a lot of things he *wanted* to say. But none of them would have changed anything. And he didn't want to leave this in a place where he was fighting with his father. Not more than this.

He couldn't change the fact that it was a situation he'd regret. He didn't have to put out words that would haunt him, too.

So he stuck with what was true and right. "I love you, Dad."

For a second, his father looked surprised, but then he recovered. "I love you, too, Zander. I wish…"

"I know what you wish," Zander interrupted quickly. "And I'm sorry that I can't give it to you. I'm sorry that you're hurt by all this. I'm sorry that I won't be around to give you time to figure this out on your own terms. Just please remember that I love you and I'm sorry. And that I'm all right."

"If you ever do give up this…whatever it is you're doing…and need a safe place, Zander."

It was the best he was going to get. It hurt; he couldn't deny that. But it was the best his father had, and he could be gracious about it. "Then you'll be the first person I call, Dad."

The hug was awkward, too short and too long all at the same time. "Take care, son," was all his father said before letting him go. And then they went their separate ways.

DENOUEMENT

THE DAY OF SOPHIA'S funeral dawned clear and bright, the first sunny day in a long series of chilly and snowy ones.

The crowd was much too small for honoring a woman who'd been queen of her kingdom for over four decades. Only Charles and Ellen and some of the most loyal guards had even been told. The risk of too many people breaking the quarantines was too great.

Even in death, Quinn hadn't been able to bring her grandmother back to the castle once William confirmed that her illness was the same one now ravaging the kingdom.

Quinn's speech was short and sweet, though far more grateful than she would have believed only a moon ago.

And then, there she was, at seventeen cycles old, the only living person to have worn the crown of Philotheum.

But she wasn't alone.

After the brief ceremony, in which Alvin spoke, but then disappeared again before anyone could talk to him, and a nice luncheon in the cottage, Charles finally dared to approach her.

"I'm sorry, Your Majesty, for the way I spoke to you back at the castle. I didn't mean it."

She inhaled deeply and pressed her hands against her sides so they wouldn't shake. "Yes, you did. You wouldn't have said it if you didn't mean it."

"I was just worried about her. I just wanted her to be comfortable."

Quinn looked around at the elegant surroundings of Sophia's estate. "No. You wanted to see how far you could push me and get the control you wanted."

He took a step back and cleared his throat. "Maybe we should discuss this back at the castle, at a time when emotions aren't running so high."

She raised an eyebrow, well aware that the "emotions" he was referring to were hers, not his.

Now her hands balled into fists, and her stomach turned somersaults. "If you have something to discuss, Charles, please feel free to send me a bird. When you do, you can let me know whether you've chosen to go back to living at your old estate, or this one is available to you now as well."

She was sort of going to miss this, Linnea thought, as they checked out of their hotel at lunchtime, and went for one last lunch at a nice restaurant. But more than anything, she was ready to get back home and see her babies again. To see Quinn and William and Thomas, to send a bird to her parents, letting them know everything was all right.

Now that they were a little more used to the offerings, each of them ordered several plates of things that would be hard to come by in Deusterros, although Linnea had picked up several ideas she planned to discuss with the cooks at the castle. Between them, she and Zander ordered five different flavors of "fireworks" that they kept passing between them, enjoying the last sweet, sparkling sips.

Zander was unusually quiet during the meal.

Yesterday, they'd had a wonderful time, spending the whole day with his mother and his sisters. All three of them were just as precious as Linnea had pegged. They'd played in the swimming pool for hours, eaten at three different restaurants — including the fun pizza place again, and Zander had taken the little girls to a whole entire huge store that was filled with nothing but toys.

The purchases he'd made there were so plentiful they were going to have to be shipped home rather than taken on the plane with them. (Linnea didn't know what any of this meant, exactly, but it was what Zander and his mother had joked about in the restaurant last night.)

He hadn't seen his father at all until this morning, when it was time to say good-bye.

Linnea hadn't witnessed this exchange, and Zander hadn't talked about it, but whatever had happened, today was hard.

She wanted to fix it for him, to say the right thing, to cheer him up.

But love wasn't always about that. She knew. Sometimes it was about just sitting close and waiting, about holding his hand and letting him be quiet, or avoid the topic with jokes.

He'd show her the thorns soon enough, and they could deal with them then. Together.

After lunch, they returned the rental car and Nathaniel hired someone to drive them and all of their backpacks to the edge of the state park, and then it was time to hike.

Nathaniel carried something else with him this time, too. A metal detector.

Zander carried two daggers and a length of rope. If Leah was going to show up again, today would be the day.

It was a long hike in the hot sun, but they still made it to the spot by the river where the gate had opened with a few hours to spare.

Which was a good thing.

"Looks like someone's already been here," Zander said, pulling out his dagger before stepping into the clearing.

The backpacks full of supplies that they'd left over the past two days — Nathaniel had made the trek back by himself yesterday — were not buried in the shrubbery where they'd left them.

Instead, everything was scattered everywhere. Boxes and vials littered the ground, mixed in with the rocks, leaves and pine needles.

But the person who had created the mess was nowhere to be found.

"Do you think it was Leah?" Linnea asked.

"I think it's very likely," Nathaniel said, beginning to sort through the debris. "But we won't know for sure unless she shows up and confesses."

"The medicine…" Linnea said helplessly.

"It looks like most of it's here. The really important stuff is in the backpacks we brought today. We'll just have to scavenge the rest and hope nothing's too damaged."

So that was what Linnea and Zander did. For hours, they combed the riverbank, exclaiming at every glint that might be glass, re-boxing vials, trying to get the backpacks as tightly loaded as they had been before.

Nathaniel spent the entire time operating the strange metal-detecting device, hoping to find the magnet buried in the ground that allowed the gate to open. The magical piece that, when removed, would close the gate forever.

Zander and Linnea's efforts paid off. By the time the sun began dipping below the western horizon, every backpack was zipped, every bit of medicine tucked inside. There were more bags than she remembered hauling in, all laid out in a neat row so they could push them through the gate as quickly as possible. A long row of hope for their world.

Nathaniel's efforts were fruitless. Although the device had beeped so often it had gotten annoying, when the vague shimmer appeared between the trees, they had no magnet.

Now, Nathaniel and Zander anxiously scanned the trees, waiting for the battle they knew was coming, while Linnea picked up the first bag and tossed it, gently, toward the shimmer. It disappeared. She picked up the next one. And then the next. Her arms were getting tired, but she kept going, moving as quickly as she could.

And then, suddenly, there were no more bags.

"Okay, Linnea, go quickly. Get to the other side." Zander didn't turn from his post, didn't come over to give her a quick kiss before she slipped through.

It was a silly thing to be bothered by, because she knew he'd be right behind her, but still, it gave her an uneasy feeling in the pit of her stomach.

"Go now!"

His voice cut off as she stepped through.

The first thing she noticed on the other side was the cold. The other world had been so warm that she wasn't at all dressed for cool weather. Goosebumps appeared on the bare parts of her arms and legs almost immediately.

Also, she was alone. Nobody was waiting for her on this side, at least not this close to the gate. She let out a low whistle, hoping that her bird, Zylia, was in the trees somewhere nearby.

Then she began searching for the bag that contained her warmer clothes.

She tried to stay calm. She told herself that things took longer on this side of the gate. What felt like five minutes here was only a second or two on the other side.

But when she was fully dressed in long pants, her cloak, and her boots and she was still standing there alone on the riverbank, panic began to set in.

That it was growing darker and colder by the minute didn't help anything.

And then, there was a noise behind her, and she turned to see Nathaniel coming through the gate.

"Leah?" she asked.

He shook his head. "Never saw a sign of her. Zander insisted on coming through last; he said if anyone was going to be stuck accidentally it should be him. But he *should* be right behind me."

Linnea stared at the gate with wide eyes.

"Sometimes it takes a few minutes on this side." He looked around. "Nobody's here?"

"No."

Nathaniel whistled. Less than thirty seconds later, Aidel, Nathaniel's bird, came swooping out of the trees.

"Little brat," Linnea whispered, though, of course, if Zylia could hear her, there wouldn't have been a reason to say it.

Nathaniel knelt down and wrote a quick note, then shoved it into Aidel's canister. "Take it to whoever is closest," he said, and then the bird was gone again.

"Here," he said to Linnea, handing her the metal detector. "Start running this over the ground while I get some warmer clothes on."

It wasn't difficult; she'd watched Nathaniel do this all afternoon. She turned on the battery pack and then held the end of the device a few inches above the ground, moving in slow, methodic circles right near the gate. It felt good to have something to focus on while they waited.

"What if Leah doesn't show up?" she asked, trying not to betray just how anxious she was that the girl *would* appear while Zander was there to face her alone.

"I don't know. I don't know who she is or what she wants. I just know we need to get this gate closed, and if that means trapping her on the other side, so be it."

When the device in her hands suddenly started beeping shrilly, she nearly dropped it and had to catch herself before she fell into the water on top of it. Fortunately, she saved them both.

And then she realized that wasn't the only noise.

Someone was approaching the clearing. Two someones, at least. And they were on horseback.

She shot a panicked look at Nathaniel. There was nowhere to hide — and they couldn't have if they'd tried, anyway. Whoever it was would have heard the metal detector.

Immediately, she crouched to grab the dagger she'd just hidden in her boot.

And then, the two horses entered the clearing.

"Thomas!" she shrieked, and forgetting everything, she ran to meet him.

He was even faster at dismounting than she was at running, and by the time she reached him, he was ready with his arms outstretched. He held her so tightly she almost couldn't breathe, but she still wouldn't have minded tighter. "Thank the Maker!" he said, over and over again. "You're all right."

When he finally set her down, he looked around the clearing, pausing on Nathaniel and the bags and the vague shimmer still barely hanging in the air. "So it was Zander's world, then?"

"*Yes, but…*" How could he still not be here? He had to be coming! Something must have happened!

"This is it! You found it Nay," Nathaniel called. "The magnet is right here."

It should have been an exciting moment, if a little bittersweet, but all Linnea was feeling was a cold panic as she walked over and looked into the shallow hole Nathaniel had dug.

The magnet wasn't as big as she'd expected. It was just a small silvery-gray rock that could have fit in both her hands. Nathaniel kept digging to expose both sides of it, and the sky kept growing dimmer.

"Don't!" She shouted, when Nathaniel stuck his hand in the hole and began prying up the edges of the rock with his fingers.

"Nay…" Thomas's voice was somber as they both looked over at the gate. The shimmer was only barely visible now. Any second, it would disappear altogether. "We have to close the gate. It's too dangerous."

"But he's coming! He was with us."

"Zander's coming back?" Thomas looked doubtfully at the fading gate. "Are you sure he didn't just tell you that, to make it easier?"

She wanted to smack him. "You think this would be easier than just telling me? No, Thomas. Something is wrong." She stood and took a step toward the gate.

A firm hand grabbed on to her shoulder. "No, sweetheart. Not again. You can't."

If it hadn't been for her twin's arms around her, and the fact that her babies were here, she didn't think she could have resisted. She would have done it, just stepped through. But instead, she watched as the whole thing began to thin around the edges, as the sides began to shrink toward each other.

And as Zander stepped through, she actually screamed.

"Nay? What's wrong? What's going on?" Zander's dagger was in his hand as he ran toward her.

"What took you so long? Where were you?" She couldn't control either her voice or the tears that ran down her cheeks in an unending stream.

"What are you talking about? I went right after Nathaniel. Nothing happened." But despite his words, he pulled her into his arms and held her there, letting her feel the warm weight of him against her. His words echoed in his chest, calming her as she laid her head against him. "Leah never even showed up. You didn't see her on this side, did you?" His eyes swept the clearing, pausing for a second on both Thomas and Marcus.

"No," Linnea said. "I was here the whole time. There was nothing. Just Nathaniel, and then… The gate was almost closed before you stepped through. I was watching it get smaller and smaller, and…" There were the tears again.

"Hey, shhh," he said, pulling her even tighter. "I'm here, okay? Right here? I took one last look around, and then I stepped through, right behind Nathaniel. It must just take longer on this side. I'm so sorry if I scared you."

"Well, you did."

"I know." He kissed her forehead. "I'll make it up to you later, okay?"

Thomas was eyeing them much more approvingly than he'd ever quite looked at Zander before. "Come on, sweetheart. We've got a wagon not far from here. Let's get all of you loaded and get you home. We can ride through the night, and you'll be back with your babies by noon."

As they were loading the supplies on their backs and on the two horses as best they could, Marcus came over and gave her an enormous, all-encompassing hug of his own. "I'm so glad you've returned to us. All of you," he added, glancing over at Zander who was trying to attach a backpack to the saddlebag straps.

"You know," she said. She'd never known how she was going to handle this conversation with Ben's father.

"Yes. And I'm glad. Ben would be pleased to see you find happiness again, Linnea. And Zander is a good man. He's a good choice to help you raise my grandchildren."

"Slow down," she said. "We're not engaged or anything yet."

"I know. I know the two of you will probably take your time, and that's okay. Whatever you decide, it's okay. I just want you to know that I love you three, and if you want to make Zander your fourth — you still have me, too. Always."

She tried to hide brushing away a tear by pulling a strand of hair back from her face.

"Have you seen them since I've been gone?"

"No, actually." Marcus made his voice louder so their conversation was no longer private. "I won't be returning to the castle with all of you, even now. There's a quarantine almost everywhere within a day's ride of the castle. The outbreak has spread nearly to the city. The quarantine has stopped it from getting to the castle, but only because it's so strictly enforced. You four will be the only ones allowed through."

"They left you stranded out here?" Linnea asked, aghast.

"No, of course not. They tried to get us to return, both of us before the quarantine. William has sent at least a hundred messages warning how dangerous it is for me to be out here, but…these people need help. And I wasn't going to leave the gate unattended, either. Not when there was a chance she would come through with you, or that you would be harmed."

"And of course, I wasn't going to let that happen, either. It's just that I'm not risking dying by doing so." Thomas said.

"You've been away from Mia all this time?" Linnea asked. *How much had she missed?*

"She's fine. She's safe in the castle with the babies, keeping everyone and everything away from them. Apparently, she burns my notes and takes a bath before she goes anywhere near them."

"That might be a little over the top," Linnea said, although mostly she just felt grateful. Her babies were safe, and in the best possible hands.

Nathaniel stood nearby, still holding the magnet he'd pried out of the ground by the river. "How bad is it, Marcus? How many?"

"Fifteen children so far and three adults."

"Sixteen children," Thomas said quietly. "We just returned from burying another child in Yellowtree this evening. The second one. That's why we were delayed in getting here. It's slowing, though. There haven't been any new cases in the last few days. People are actually listening, and staying away from the sick. A lot of families are separated right now, though."

"And I'm sorry to inform you, Nathaniel," Marcus said. "But Lady Sophia was among the first of the casualties. Shortly after you left."

Nathaniel closed his eyes while the rest of them looked at each other in sadness and shock. Linnea couldn't believe it. Not that she would especially miss Lady Sophia, but still… She *was* Nathaniel's mother and Quinn's grandmother. *It was still sad,* she thought.

No, actually, she had no idea how one was supposed to feel about the death of someone who'd mostly made one's life miserable while they were alive? Sad didn't seem honest. But glad wasn't right, either.

"Well, we'll have to sort that out later. Right now, Marcus, let me take care of you. I have medicine here that can keep you from getting sick. You might still not be able to enter the castle tomorrow, but once you have this and we keep an eye on you for the few days, you'll be exempt from the quarantine, too. It sounds like William handled it just right in my absence."

"Our children aren't children anymore," Marcus said, shrugging out of his cloak.

"Indeed."

Linnea slept only fitfully in the wagon, drifting off for a few minutes at a time through the night, curled up under a blanket and nestled against Zander's chest. He didn't sleep at all, though, so he couldn't criticize.

Mostly, they talked. Nathaniel wanted to ride instead of sit, so Thomas gave up his horse and sat in the wagon with them.

Zander suspected that what Nathaniel really wanted was for Thomas and Linnea to be together. He liked it better that way, too.

"So, how was the other world, Nay?" Thomas asked. "As exciting as you'd imagined?"

"It was…a lot *more* than I expected. I had fun for some of it, but right now, all I can really think about is how glad I am to be home."

Zander rubbed her shoulders reassuringly. It *was* too much to process right now. Too many things to think about, especially when there were other, more important things on their minds.

"Well, it looks like you two might have done a bit more than just sightseeing over there," Thomas said pointedly, his eyes on Zander's hands.

There was a time that would have made him uncomfortable, made him wonder if he was getting too close to Thomas's sister, if he should back off. Tonight, though, he held her a bit tighter, and she snuggled in closer. "A little," he admitted.

"And that makes both of you happy?"

Their "yesses" came at the same time, making all three of them laugh.

"Then it makes me happy, too."

Zander couldn't help it, he bent down and kissed the top of Linnea's head, and then reveled in the miraculous feeling of her squeezing his hand. The night might have been cold, but under this blanket, he was the warmest he'd ever been.

"Were you ever able to find out anything else about Leah?" he asked Thomas a few minutes later.

"There wasn't a lot of time, but Marcus and I found a few leads that never went much of anywhere. People know of her. We followed one lead to a place that was rumored to be her home, but there wasn't much of anything there. From what we can tell, it seems she's lived a lot of places, moved around a lot. What happened with her over there? Why did she drag you through?"

"We don't know that, either," Linnea said, and proceeded to tell him about their encounters with her in the other world.

"So she's looking for some kind of stone? Do you think she means the magnet?"

"That's the best guess we have, although what she wants with it, I have no idea. Can you use it to make another gate or something?"

Thomas only shrugged. "That's going to take some more research, I think."

"Well, for now, she's stuck in the other world, so unless she shows up again..."

"Not much we can do about it," Linnea concluded.

Other than what was necessary to rest and water the horses, they didn't stop traveling all through the night. They ate breakfast out of the meager provisions in the wagon — Marcus and Thomas had been running low on supplies. Still, dried meat and fruit had never tasted as good to Zander as it did now.

A hot meal in the castle later would be something to celebrate.

He had a hard time not leaping down from the moving wagon when the castle finally came into view, and he knew it was a million times worse for Linnea. She couldn't sit still and kept bouncing up and down to peer over the edge of the wagon.

Thomas wasn't any better. When William's bird came flying toward them, he snatched for her canister before she'd even quite landed, and then had to feed all the rest of their dried meat to her by way of apology.

Neither Larya or Zylia had consented to landing and greeting them yet, though he'd seen them both circling in the sky in the morning light. He supposed it was going to take a while before he and Linnea were forgiven for disappearing out of reach for almost an entire moon.

"The guards at the gate have been notified of our arrival so we'll be let through," Thomas said after reading the note. "Marcus is being asked to go directly to his own quarters and remain there until William has had a chance to examine and clear him to come into the castle. The rest of us, straight inside to the empty guest quarters. We have to scrub completely and change into fresh clothes before being allowed in the family wing."

Linnea slumped back heavily against Zander.

"It's for them," he told her. "It's to protect the babies."

"I know," she said. "And I'll do anything…" He knew she would. Already, last night, she'd let Nathaniel draw blood to send back to William, just to make absolutely sure she carried no sign of the illness. Her vaccination was too recent to be sure about.

Zander, too, had asked to be tested. The babies were just too important. "It's just so hard to wait."

At least everyone back at the castle seemed to understand the urgency of getting them in quickly. Though no servants were anywhere to be found as they entered, four guest rooms upstairs stood with doors open, hot baths waiting inside. The new clothes were already laid out for them. Zander took off the clothes he was wearing and, as instructed, tossed one article at a time into the roaring fire, watching his discount-store socks turn into ashes.

He made it back to the hallway, scrubbed clean, so fast he thought he would be the first, but Nathaniel was already standing there. "Can you give these to William for me?" he asked, handing him a large box. "Don't shake it. There's glass."

Zander nodded. Glass and precious. The medicine that would keep them safe, protect them from the death that had threatened the kingdom.

Only seconds after Nathaniel had disappeared to go and begin tending to the guards and servants, Linnea appeared in the hallway, too. She looked so different than yesterday, dressed again now in a simple blouse and skirt from this world. Her hair was still damp, hastily pulled back into a braid, probably to save time.

She was beautiful.

"Do you want me to wait for a bit?" he asked. "I could wait here, and let you have some time alone with them."

"No." She shook her head. "It's time I really let you in, I think. Unless you don't want to."

"I want to." Oh, how he wanted to.

"Well, I'm coming," Thomas said from behind them. "Although I may just come and say hello to the babies in a bit, if that doesn't make me a terrible uncle. I'm ready to see Mia."

It only sort of worked out that way, though. Quinn was waiting in the hallway outside Linnea's room, and for a long moment, the two girls had eyes only for each other as Linnea went flying into her sister's arms.

"Mia's inside," were the only words Quinn managed to get out.

Well, that worked out nicely, Thomas thought. He gave Quinn's arm a quick squeeze while she was hugging Linnea, and then he ducked into his sister's room.

"Thomas!" Mia's arms were full of baby, but she quickly passed the infant to William and then ran to him. He swept her into his arms and off the ground, spinning her around and kissing her all at the same time. "Are you all right?" she asked breathlessly when he set her down.

"You mean since I sent you a message this morning?"

"Yes."

"I'm fine. How are the babies?"

"Perfect. Ready to see their mother."

"I'll bet." He glanced over to where William was setting down Adeline next to her brother. "They've grown so much!"

"Don't say that to Linnea, please," Mia said, raising an eyebrow toward the doorway. Linnea was standing there.

"How about you two come with me?" William said. "And let them have some time alone."

They followed him into the hallway where Quinn still was, and she hugged Thomas tightly, too. "I want you to tell me everything," she said. "But later, when you've had some time."

He grinned. "I'll try to fill you in on any details I left out of my notes."

"You'd better."

"Quinn, do you think you could go and ask Elisa to meet us in Mia's room?" William asked, as he accepted a box from Zander. "I'll be back to you and Samuel as soon as possible.

Thomas took Mia's hand and held it tightly. At the moment, he didn't even want her heading off to another room by herself. "We're moving up the wedding," he whispered in her ear.

She only smiled.

Linnea felt like she was frozen in the doorway of her room. There they were, lying on the neatly made bad, snuggled next to each other. They'd grown, but not nearly as much as she'd been terrified they would. Adeline was still bigger than her brother, though his happy kicks and squirms were more vigorous than hers. She was babbling at the ceiling. Immediately, Linnea's chest ached and swelled.

"Come on," Zander whispered, fitting his hand into the small of her back and leading her inside the room.

She didn't know where to start. She wanted to pick both of them up at the same time, but she couldn't quite, so she just knelt in front of the bed, eye-level with both of them.

Adeline noticed her first and let out a delighted squeal that made tears begin pouring, unbidden, down Linnea's cheeks.

"See, they didn't forget you. Sit down."

He'd seen her dilemma, apparently, because as soon as she sat, he scooped up Adeline and laid the baby in her arms, and then he picked up Benjamin and helped her settle them both together.

For the next several minutes, she just sat there, kissing and hugging on both of them, letting her tears fall everywhere, but they didn't seem to mind.

"They're so perfect," Zander breathed. "I can't believe how much I missed them." Once she was calm again, she was okay when he picked up Adeline and cuddled her, walking over to the window and whispering stories about what he'd done while they were apart and how hard he and Linnea had worked to get back to them.

"We have presents for you, too. But you'll have to wait until you've had your medicine and we can get them out of quarantine."

Before Zander could get a turn with both of them, though, Benjamin began rooting very decisively against her, searching for milk. It was like she'd never left.

Linnea laughed. "All right, little one. Let me get settled."

"Wait on that for a minute." William's voice came from near the door, but he walked right in as he was talking and set his medical bag down on the be next to them. "That will be an excellent way to soothe them after I've made them very mad here in a few seconds."

Linnea made a face, but set the baby down so she could go and hug her brother.

"Oh, it's so good to see you," he said, squeezing her tight. "I missed you so much."

"Thank you for taking such good care of them," she said. "And for keeping them safe. I know they're fine because of you."

He kissed her forehead. "Don't ever thank me for that," he said, though his voice was as gentle as possible. "They're my niece and nephew. I love them as much as I love Samuel, sweetheart. We were just taking care of them *with* you. It wasn't a favor, okay?"

She nodded and let go of him so he could greet Zander, too.

"I never thought I would be this happy to see you in my kingdom, Zander."

"Funny how life works out in really unexpected ways, isn't it?" Zander was still holding Adeline, but he accepted a sideways half-hug from William.

"Turns out that unexpected is sometimes a synonym for *wonderful.* But..." He leaned in close, and pretended to whisper, though Linnea was clearly intended to overhear. "If you ever hurt my sister, you'll discover that I really have learned how to be a king."

Zander only laughed. "I wouldn't have it any other way."

Quinn looked up anxiously when the doorknob rattled. The last three times she'd done that, it had only been a draft, but this time, the door actually opened.

"How are they?" she asked before William even managed to close the door behind himself.

"Resting now." He set his medical bag down on the table. "Or trying to. Zander is staying with Linnea to help calm the babies. I think he missed them, too."

"I'm sure he did. I'm glad he came back."

"Me, too. It was good to see him. It's nice to see Linnea happy with someone, too."

"Mia and Elisa will be glad she's back, too. I never intended to be the sort of boss who would ask someone to work for an entire moon without a day off."

"Yes, I know. We owe much to both of them. I've spoken to them. They've both had their shots now, so soon they'll be able to leave the castle and have some freedom again." For the last couple of weeks, only Quinn, William, Mia, and Elisa had been allowed even in the same hallway as the babies — and Mia and Elisa hadn't been able to leave at all, to prevent any possibility of them being exposed and then coming back in. "I did tell Mia she could take the next few days off to spend with Thomas after their separation."

"Good."

"And Elisa deserves a nice break, too. So I think you and Linnea and I are on our own with three slightly cranky babies for the next couple of days. Although Zander will probably help a bit, too."

She grimaced. "Did they cry?"

"Uh, yeah, love." He glanced over at Samuel who was happily playing with his toys on the floor. "This is going to be even worse than the first time I stuck you with a needle."

She made a face. "I had no idea that it was even harder to be the parent for this than the kid. I think I might cry harder than he does."

"If you don't, I will."

"I almost believe that. Do we have to?"

"You'd rather risk him *dying*? Another child in Yellowtree died yesterday, because we didn't have this medicine. There's still not enough. It will take us more time than we have to make enough to protect everyone."

"Hey, Sam. Come here, buddy."

It wasn't as bad as she expected. William was quick and gentle. Samuel was surprised by the poke, and not exactly pleased, but, as in many other things, he outshined his parents in this sort of bravery, too. If the stakes hadn't been so high, and Quinn hadn't been so grateful for the medicine, she might actually have cried more than he did.

After it was over, and they'd all survived, she nursed Samuel to sleep on the couch while William made tea and came to sit down next to them. He rubbed the baby's tiny feet through his socks before covering both of them up with a blanket. "He's okay now. We all are."

"Do you think everything else will be okay?"

"Well, we have enough medicine right now to at least help. And Nathaniel knows how to make more. This one isn't as hard. I'm sure we can do it. We'll get through this."

"Until the next crisis."

He kissed her temple. "Until the next crisis. Happily ever after only exists in storybooks, my love. Real life will keep throwing more things at us. Just when we get used to the last one, something new will happen. At some point, for example, we're going to have to address the fact that we never found Leah. But I'd prefer if we didn't do that today. We just have to enjoy the few perfect moments we get."

"Well, this is one of them."

He leaned in closer and kissed her on the lips this time, lingering. She savored the sweet taste of his kiss, of his love for her.

"This is one of them."

OTHER BOOKS BY BREEANA PUTTROFF

The Dusk Gate Chronicles
The continued adventures of the Rose family in
Eirentheos and Philotheum

Rumpelstiltskin's Daughter
A new take on an old fairy tale

COMING SOON
The Gatekeepers
An all-new adventure featuring some familiar characters

Visit www.BreeanaPuttroff.net to find out more!